TURBULENT INTENTIONS

TURBULENT INTENTIONS

A Billionaire Aviator Novel

MELODY ANNE

 Montlake
Romance

This is a work of fiction. Names, characters, organizations, places, events, and incidents are either products of the author's imagination or are used fictitiously.

Published by Montlake Romance, Seattle

www.apub.com

Amazon, the Amazon logo, and Montlake Romance are trademarks of Amazon.com, Inc., or its affiliates.

ISBN-13: 9781503936683
ISBN-10: 1503936686

Cover photography by Regina Wamba of MaeIDesign.com

Printed in the United States of America

This book is dedicated to Drew Fish, who I have adored for a very long time and who makes one heck of a sexy pilot for me to use as inspiration. Love you, Drew, and your beautiful wife. So glad to have you as a part of my life.

PROLOGUE

Tires squealed as a sleek, silver Jaguar shot out onto the highway. An unsuspecting car cruising along slammed on its brakes just in time to avoid a wreck with the Jag. The four brothers sitting in the Jaguar didn't give a damn about the commotion they were causing.

This wasn't unusual.

They continued speeding along, trying to outrun the demons chasing them as they flew down the highway, hitting over a hundred miles an hour and continuing on, faster and faster.

It wasn't quick enough. They kept on going until they hit the edge of town in Bay Harbor, Washington, where they found a dilapidated bar with a blinking neon sign that had some of the letters burned out.

Cooper, who was driving, jerked the steering wheel and came to an abrupt halt outside the run-down building. "Good enough," he said. His fists clenched with the urge to hit something, or better yet, someone.

"Yep," his brother replied from the backseat.

Getting out of the car, they made their way to the entrance, an undeniable swagger in their gait—a swagger that made people turn and watch them wherever they went. Though young, the Armstrong brothers already had a reputation in their small community for stirring up trouble.

When they entered a room, patrons would turn away, glancing back at them with a wary eye. The brothers were the first in for a fight and the last ones standing.

They were wealthy, and not above flashing their fat wallets, Rolex watches, and extravagant cars. They were also arrogant and hot-tempered, a foursome to both be leery of and look at with awe. Cooper was the oldest at twenty-four, each of his brothers one year, almost to the date, behind him: Nick at twenty-three, Maverick at twenty-two, and Ace, the baby, at twenty-one.

On this night, though, they were looking for more than just the usual trouble. They were out for blood, but the demon chasing them was relentless, and no matter how fast they moved, this was something they couldn't outrun.

Their father was dying.

Maybe it was the feeling of helplessness or maybe, for once, it was not being the strongest ones in a room. Whatever it was, Cooper, Nick, Maverick, and Ace were scared, and because they wouldn't admit that, they were trouble to anyone in their path.

This band of brothers had always been revered as much as they'd been feared. They were tall, lean, and had distinct green eyes that hid their innermost thoughts but shone with a sparkle that most couldn't resist.

Walking indoors, Cooper sighed in anticipation. Smoke filled the air as loud music echoed off the walls. A few heads turned in their direction, and Cooper scoped them out, looking for a potential boxing partner.

The nervous energy rising off him in waves needed an outlet, so the first person that gave him the slightest reason would feel the wrath of his heartbreak, denial, and feeling of helplessness.

As if the patrons knew this group was up to no good, they cast their eyes downward, particularly annoying Cooper in their weakness to accept the challenge radiating off his entire body.

The boys ordered beers, then leaned against the bar, facing out as they scanned the crowd. None of them spoke for several moments, each lost in thought.

Cooper was thinking they might just have to give up on this place and find a new location when his gaze captured the angry look of a man shooting pool. Cooper smirked at the guy and practically saw steam rise from the man's ears. The stranger began making his way toward them. Cooper's fists clenched with the need to punch.

"You're the Armstrong boys, right?"

The man was swaying as he stepped closer to them, his glazed-over eyes narrowed. Cooper stood at full attention. This just might be the huckleberry he'd been in search of.

"Yep," Coop said, not altering his stance at all.

"I hear your daddy's on his deathbed." The man said the cold words with glee.

Maybe the man was too drunk to know exactly what he was doing, but instantly the four brothers stepped a bit closer to one another, their knuckles cracking, their collective breath hissing out.

"Maybe you shouldn't listen to gossip," Maverick said in a low growl.

"Oh, I don't think it's gossip. You see, your daddy has run over many real workingmen to get to the top of that mountain he's built for himself. And now he's getting the early death he deserves."

Nick instantly stepped away from the bar, but Cooper shot his hand out and stopped him. "He was looking at me, Nick," he said, his tone deathly low.

His brothers shot him a look, but then they stepped back, letting Cooper deal with his demons, and the drunken bastard before them, at the same time.

"Dave, come on. You've had too much to drink," a woman said, placing her hand on his arm.

"Get the hell off of me. I know what I'm doing," Dave snarled at the woman, pushing her away.

Cooper's fingers twitched in anticipation. He wanted to deck this asshole even more now. It was okay to fight with a man, but to push a lady around was never acceptable.

"Maybe you should lay off the lady," Maverick said. He wanted to push forward and take Cooper's place. Cooper looked at him and Maverick stepped back, though it was costing him to do so.

"Maybe you should keep your damn mouth shut," Dave said to Mav.

"This is Cooper's fight," Nick reminded Maverick when he began to shake with the need to hit this piece of scum.

Dave turned away from Maverick, his beady eyes focused again on Cooper. "Are you just like your daddy, boy? Do you like living off the men busting their asses for your family in those crap factories?"

"At least our daddy provides trash like you a job," Cooper said.

"Not that you would know. You haven't worked a damn day in your life," Dave snapped.

"Nope. And I have a hell of a lot more than you, don't I?" Cooper taunted him, making sure the man could see the gold Rolex he was sporting.

The man spit as he tried to get words out. He was furious. When Cooper pulled out his wallet and slapped a hundred-dollar bill on the bar and told the waitress to take care of the man's tab since he probably couldn't, Dave's face turned beet-red with fury and embarrassment.

"I don't need the likes of you taking care of anything for me," he finally managed to sputter.

Finishing his beer in a long swallow, Cooper took his time before putting the glass down on the counter. The bar was strangely quiet as the patrons watched this scene unfold before them.

"So you're one of those guys who blames his lot in life on the big man in the top office instead of doing a day's hard work, huh?" Cooper said, a taunting smile on his lips.

"I like my damn life. I don't need some rich kid who doesn't know what work is telling me he's better than me," the man blustered.

"I *am* better than you," Coop told him with a wink he was sure would enrage the man. Just to add fuel to the fire, he pulled out a wad of cash and threw it at the man's feet. "Here's some spending money for you. Obviously you need the cash more than I do since I have a mountain of it back home."

"I'm going to enjoy kicking your ass, boy," Dave said, tossing his beer bottle behind him in his rage. Though he did look down at the cash longingly. Cooper would have laughed, if he had been capable of it at that moment.

His brothers didn't even flinch at the hundreds lying on the filthy floor, money that would be swallowed up the second the boys stepped away.

"I'd like to see you try," Cooper said with just enough of a mocking glow to his eyes to really infuriate the man. "Follow me."

His muscles were coiled and he was more than ready. He headed toward the door. He could do it in the bar or flatten this guy outside. Either way was good with him.

"You gonna leave the convoy behind, or do you need your brothers to save your ass?" the man taunted.

The fact that this piece of garbage was questioning his honor infuriated Cooper even more. He took a second before answering, not even turning around to face the drunkard.

"You obviously don't know me at all if you think I need any help kicking your flabby ass," Cooper told him. "Chicken ass," he then mumbled, knowing it would push this piece of trash over the limit.

The air stirred against his ears, alerting Cooper of the attack coming toward him. They'd barely made it out the front doors before the man swung, thinking that because Cooper was ahead of him he would get a cheap shot from behind.

He wasn't counting on Cooper's rage, or his soberness.

Spinning around, Coop threw all his weight behind a punishing blow that made brutal contact with the drunk's face. The resounding crack of Coop's knuckles breaking the man's nose echoed across the parking lot.

The man spit blood as he tried to get up before falling back to the ground. Cooper didn't give him a chance. In half a heartbeat, he was on the ground, slugging the man again and again.

"Should we stop this?" Maverick asked, leaning against the outside wall of the bar as patrons poured out to watch the fistfight.

"Not a chance. Hell, I'm hoping someone else mouths off so I can get a punch or two thrown in," Nick mumbled, looking around.

"It's my turn next," Ace grumbled.

Maverick held his brother back. "You'll get your turn," Maverick promised him.

No one was paying the least attention to the other brothers as the fight in front of them continued on the ground and Dave got in a good punch to Cooper's face.

Within a couple minutes, though, the fight was over. Dave was knocked out on the ground, and with the show over, the patrons of the bar lost interest and went back inside to their cold beer and stale peanuts. The brothers watched as Cooper slowly stood while spitting out a stream of saliva and touching his swollen lip.

A couple of men picked up Dave and quietly hauled him away. The brothers didn't even bother watching them go.

"Should we go back in?" Maverick asked.

"Yeah. I'm done with this trash. Maybe there's another idiot inside looking for a reason to get a nose job," Cooper said.

Before Nick or Ace could respond, Nick's phone rang. He looked at the caller ID and sighed. It rang twice more before he answered.

He was silent for a moment as the caller spoke. Then he nodded, though the person couldn't see him. "Yes, Mom. We'll be there."

He hung up. "We have to go back home," Nick told them. Even without the call, Nick was always the voice of reason.

"I'm not ready to go back there," Ace said, his eyes downcast.

"I can't," Cooper admitted. He couldn't allow the adrenaline high to stop, because then . . . then, he might actually *feel* real pain instead of anger.

"It's time," Nick said again.

They didn't want to listen, but they knew their brother was right.

It was like a parade down the green mile as they moved back to the car and piled in. They drove much more slowly toward home than they'd driven away from it, taking their time, none of them speaking.

When they pulled up in front of the large mansion they'd grown up in, they remained in the Jag, none of them wanting to be the first to open their car door. Finally, though, Nick got out, and the others followed. Their passage into the mansion was quiet, their shoulders hunched.

"Where have you been?"

They stopped in the foyer as their uncle Sherman busted down the stairs glaring at them. The urgency in his voice had them terrified. They knew time was running out.

"We had to blow off some steam," Maverick said, his hands tucked into his pockets as he rocked back and forth on his heels.

"Your father's been asking for you," Sherman scolded. "And there isn't much time left. Your mother will need all of you."

"We're sorry," Cooper said. The others seemed incapable of speech and just nodded their apologies.

Sherman sighed, not one to stay angry for long.

They followed their uncle up the stairs. None of them wanted to walk through that bedroom door. But they did it. Their father, who had once been so strong, was frail and weak now, the cancer taking everything from him, leaving him a shadow of the man he'd always been.

"Come here," he said, his voice barely a whisper.

Slowly, the four boys surrounded the bed, facing the man they would soon lose.

"Time is running out so I can't mince words," their father started.

"Dad . . ." Cooper tried to interrupt, but his mother put her hand on his arm.

"Let him speak, son."

Her voice was so sad that the boys turned to look at her for a moment, their shoulders stiffening before they turned back to their father and waited.

"I've done wrong by all of you," he told them, disappointment on his face. He looked extra long at the blood on Cooper's eye and sadly shook his head. "All of you."

"No you haven't, Dad," Maverick insisted.

"Yes, I have. You're men now, but you have no plans for the future. I wanted to give you the world, but you've only learned how to take because you haven't learned how to earn anything. I know you'll grow into fine men. I have no doubt about it. But please don't hate me when I'm gone," he said before he began coughing.

"We would never hate you, Dad," Nick quickly said.

"You might for a while," their father told them. "But someday you will thank me. I'm doing what I've done because I love you."

"What are you saying?" Ace asked.

"You'll know soon, son," their father said.

"Dad . . ." Maverick began, but their father shut his eyes.

Cooper willed himself to say something, anything to break this awful silence. But he just stood there, anger, sadness, fear flowing through him.

And then it was too late.

Not a sound could be heard in the room when their father stopped breathing. For the last time in each of their lives, the boys shed a tear as they looked down at their deceased father.

Then Cooper turned and walked out. He didn't stop at the front door. He didn't stop at the end of the driveway. He kept moving, faster and faster until he was in a full-blown sprint with his gut and sides burning. He tried to outrun the fact that he was a disappointment, that he'd failed his father. What if the man was right? What if he never became half the man his father was? He ran faster.

Still, he wasn't able to outrun his father's last words of disappointment . . .

◆　◆　◆

". . . And for my boys, I leave each of you, Cooper, Nick, Maverick, and Ace, a quarter of my assets, but there is a stipulation . . ."

It had only been a day since the funeral, and none of the boys wanted to be sitting in this uptight lawyer's office while he read a stupid will. It wasn't as if they didn't know what it was going to say anyway.

Their father, of course, had left his fortune to them; that is, what he hadn't already given them in their enormous trust funds, and to their mother and his brother, Uncle Sherman. They were the only living relatives—well, the only ones they knew about, at least. So this was a waste of all their time.

"Can you get on with this? I have things to do," Cooper snapped.

"You will learn some respect by the end of this," Sherman warned Coop.

"Yeah, I get it," Coop said. "Can I go now? I don't want to hear the rest."

"I think you do," their mother said.

Her sweet voice instantly calmed the boys. They did love their mother, had a great deal of respect for her, and listened when she spoke.

But they had hardened through the years, taking for granted what had been given to them.

That was about to change.

"You won't receive a dime of your inheritance until you've proven that you will actually better not only your lives, but the lives of others."

Cooper spoke first. "What in the hell is that supposed to mean?" He was up on his feet, his chair flying backward with the momentum. His brothers were right behind him.

The world was suddenly spinning and none of them knew how to deal with this latest news.

"If you will shut up and listen, then you will hear the rest," Sherman told them.

The four young men were obviously upset, but slowly they resumed their seats, all of them except for Cooper, who stood there with his arms crossed, daggers coming from his eyes.

"You have ten years to turn your lives around. At the end of that ten years, if you haven't proven yourselves self-sufficient, by working hard, being respectful to your mother and your uncle, and bringing something to the society that you live in, then your inheritance will be donated to charity."

The attorney paused as if he were reluctant to read whatever else was coming next.

"Get on with it," Ace growled.

"Your mother and I shared a wonderful, beautiful, exciting life together. A man isn't meant to be alone. He's meant to love, to share, to grow with a woman who will help guide him through the hardest parts of his life," the attorney began.

"What in the world are you speaking about?" Maverick snapped.

"Son, this is in your father's own words, so I would pay attention," Uncle Sherman said, his tone sad.

Maverick leaned forward, but he didn't seem to be hearing anything that was being spoken at that moment.

"Shall I continue?" the attorney asked.

"Yeah, yeah," Cooper said with a wave of his hand.

"You will receive your full inheritance once you marry."

Dead silence greeted those words as the boys looked at one another, and then at their mother, who had a serene smile on her face.

Finally, Cooper was the one to speak again. "Mom? What in the hell is going on?"

She gave her son a sad smile. "Your father and I have watched the four of you lose your way these past several years. He knew he was dying and he'd run out of time to guide you, shape you. He didn't want to lose you forever, as I don't. So he changed the will."

The boys waited for her to go on, but she sat there silently.

"We're rich without his money," Nick pointed out.

She was quiet for several moments. "Yes, Nick, you are," she finally said.

"Are you going to take away what we already have?" Maverick asked.

"No, I'm not," Evelyn Armstrong told them all. "You don't have to get your inheritance, though it makes your trust funds look like pennies, as you know. But getting the money isn't the point," she said with a sigh.

"What is the point?" Cooper asked, trying desperately not to yell, but only because his mother was in the room.

"The point is to grow up. You need to grow up," Evelyn said as she looked each of the boys in the eyes before turning to Sherman.

"Your father wants you to be good men. He's asking you to show your mother that you are," Sherman added.

"So, even in death, Father wants us to jump through hoops?" Ace snapped.

"No, son, even in death your father wants you to grow into the men you are meant to be," Evelyn told them.

"I don't need his stupid money. I have plenty of it that he's already given me and besides that I have my own plans. If he thinks I'm such a screwup, then he can keep it all," Cooper thundered.

"Agreed," Nick snapped.

"I'm not doing anything because someone is trying to force it upon me," Maverick said, joining his brothers.

"If he thinks we're such screwups, he can go to hell," Ace said, pushing it a bit too far.

"Ace . . ." Coop whispered.

"Save it, Cooper. You're always trying to be the leader, but this is crap. Yeah, I'm the baby of the family, but that just means that I've had to try to make up for every mistake that you guys have already made. I'm done with it," Ace bellowed.

"Calm down, son," Sherman said, rising and resting a hand on Ace's shoulder.

"No!"

Ace yanked away from Sherman and then moved toward the door.

"I love you all no matter what you choose, but I hope you'll listen to your father's last words and know he does this because he loves you," Evelyn said quietly, stopping Ace for a moment. Then his eyes hardened.

"I'm out of here."

Ace was the first to leave. He rushed from the attorney's office, fury heating the very air around him.

Cooper stood there dumfounded. What was happening? They'd not only lost their father, but they'd all just found out that they had never been good enough in his eyes.

"To hell with Dad—and to hell with this place."

Cooper followed his brother, though Ace was already long gone. It didn't matter. Cooper would prove himself, but he'd do it because he wanted to. He would never be someone's puppet—not even his father's.

CHAPTER ONE

What in the world was he doing at the lavish Anderson wedding of Crew Storm and his bride, Haley?

He didn't want to be there, didn't want to be around anyone, actually, but he feared his friends were going to call in the National Guard at any minute if he didn't come out and at least pretend he was still somewhat normal.

It had only been six months since his father's passing. There'd been zero word from Ace, and though he talked to his other two brothers, the conversations were short. All of them were dealing with their demons and the final words of their father.

He hadn't spoken more than a few words to his mother, which he knew was terrible, but he couldn't see her while he was like this.

"It's really good to see you out, Coop."

Mark Anderson stood next to him as they scanned the merry crowd celebrating all around them. Cooper couldn't even try to smile. His lips just weren't turning up.

"I haven't felt much like celebrating lately," Cooper admitted to his friend.

"I understand that. I don't know how I would survive it if my dad died. The man's meddling and always in my face, but I love him. I think the old guy is too damn ornery to let go anyway. He's gonna outlive us all," Mark said with a chuckle.

"Yes, I agree with you. Joseph is a force to be reckoned with," Cooper said, his lips twitching the slightest bit. It was almost a smile.

"Are you enjoying your new job?" Mark asked.

Cooper paused as he thought about the question. He was doing exactly what his father had wanted, even if he was doing it in spite of his dad. He was working for a small airline, using the skill that had been nothing but a hobby for him up until recently.

"I don't know about enjoying the actual job and the paperwork that comes with it, but yes, flying is what I love. I can't seem to get enough of it. Who knew that playing with planes my whole life would turn into a career," Cooper said.

"Even without your inheritance, you're a very wealthy man, Cooper. It isn't as if you have to work. But before you say something, I know it isn't about a paycheck. I don't have to work myself. But choosing to work despite my fortune is a matter of pride," Mark told him.

"I didn't have much pride," Cooper said with a shrug. "Or at least I didn't think I did. Not until that reading of my father's will. I guess he was right in the sense that we have all sort of skated through life. But he raised us that way. I don't know what he expected."

"I think when people know their time is coming to a close, they start to get scared," Mark said. "Not that I would know from personal experience, but now that I'm a father, I get scared. I want my kids to grow into fine men and women. They work on the ranch, and they even go into the Anderson offices and are learning there."

"Aren't your kids really young?" Cooper asked.

"Yeah, but I was a bit spoiled myself. I don't want that for my kids," Mark told him.

"Well, I don't know what earning only a couple grand a month proves, but my father seemed to think that would make me a man, so now instead of flying for fun, I fly for an airline. It's not so bad. It just all pisses me off a little," Cooper said.

"The anger will eventually drain," Mark told him.

"I don't know . . ."

Cooper stopped talking as he scanned the crowd. Coming to the party had been a very bad idea. Maybe it was time for him to take his leave. He wasn't fit company to be around at the moment.

Just as his scan was almost finished, something caught his eye. He stopped and zeroed in on a woman in the corner, sitting by herself.

Mark continued to speak, but Cooper didn't hear what his friend was saying. He was too focused on the blonde woman in the tight red dress who was holding her drink close to her like it was a lifeline.

She nervously glanced around the room, not meeting his gaze, before she looked back down again. Cooper was shocked at the stirring he felt.

It had been a long time since he'd felt any emotion other than anger.

"Who is that?" he asked Mark, interrupting his friend mid-sentence.

Mark followed his gaze and looked at the woman for several moments.

"I have no idea. Haven't seen her before," Mark said. Then he smiled. "But I have a feeling you're about to find out."

"Don't overanalyze this, Mark. I'm just curious who she is," Cooper snapped.

"No judgments here," Mark assured him with a pat on the shoulder.

"I might like to screw the ladies, but I won't give my father the pleasure of marrying one," he said with a little growl.

"What does that mean?" Mark asked, looking a little lost.

"My father seemed to think a man's life isn't complete without a wife. I think all women search for a man with the deepest pockets," he said.

Mark gave him a sad look and shook his head. "Not all women are like that. I married a good one."

"Then you got the last," Cooper said with conviction. Then he walked away.

He didn't know why, but he had to meet this woman who was trying to hide away.

It was sex—that was all. And sex was worth throwing down a few dollars for, he thought with a cynical smile.

CHAPTER TWO

Stormy Halifax would have given anything for the ability to fade into the background. She tried in vain to squeeze herself back even farther into the corner as she watched the designer-clad couples swirling around on the dance floor, all of them laughing and completely at home surrounded by the glamour and glitz of the night.

Only American royalty like the Andersons could afford to pull off a wedding like this one. Stormy would bet her entire bank account, which actually wasn't that much, that she couldn't have afforded even a single flower among the many placed so elegantly in the hundreds of exquisitely designed centerpieces.

She eyed the door longingly. Just a few more hours . . . How had she ever let Lindsey convince her it was a good idea to crash the society wedding of the century? If Stormy made it through the evening undetected, she swore she would never listen to her best friend again.

Of course, how many times in her life had she had that same thought? Too many times to count.

At least she sort of looked like she fit in with the crowd—or somewhat fit in. That meant she looked *nothing* like herself on this beautiful summer night in Seattle.

Lindsey had insisted she wear the ridiculously tight red dress she currently felt plastered to her skin, and her friend had layered on so much makeup that Stormy felt like a clown. With the dyed blonde hair taking the place of her naturally brown hair, she barely recognized herself. When she had gotten a look at herself in one of the gilded mirrors hanging on the walls of the banquet hall, Stormy could hardly believe she was staring at her own reflection. The girl in the mirror almost looked like she belonged at the lavish wedding. Almost.

At least she looked old enough to drink. Even if she wouldn't be for a few more weeks. She reached up and clasped the chain around her neck, feeling more secure, if only slightly. She never left home without the simple piece of jewelry she'd designed herself.

Stormy scanned the room for Lindsey. Only the flies on the wall would know what excitement her friend was off having. Lindsey certainly wasn't hiding in a corner somewhere.

Enough was enough. With or without Lindsey, Stormy needed an exit strategy. She gathered up her glittering clutch, slipped her feet back into the ridiculously high stiletto heels she had borrowed from Lindsey, and then covertly tried to make her way to the door.

She was mere inches from freedom when she felt a solid, masculine hand touch her bare shoulder. Her breath caught in her throat and she froze. Busted. *Okay, play it cool, Stormy. Just smile, pretend like you belong here for five more seconds, and then make a run for it.*

"Are you lost?"

The deep baritone of the voice sent a shiver down her spine. She really wanted to turn and look at him, but at the same time she didn't. Cowardice wasn't normally one of her traits, but she was in uncharted territory and she was trying to flee.

"No. But thank you." She took another step.

"Are you refusing to have a conversation with me?"

Now she seemed rude. His voice didn't change, but she could swear there was a challenge in it. Dammit! Stormy couldn't resist a challenge.

Stormy finally turned, and when she looked up, she found herself gazing into a set of sea-green eyes with the longest eyelashes she'd ever witnessed on a man before. She found herself speechless.

"Let's dance," he said, holding out a hand, not concerned by her lack of vocal abilities.

This wasn't a good idea.

"I don't think so. I really need to go," she told him. But he didn't remove his outstretched hand, and she didn't want to pull away and call attention to them having this conversation.

What if the people standing around realized she was crashing this wedding? She was going to murder her best friend if she ever found her again.

"One dance won't take long." The deep timbre of his voice made her stomach stir. *Uh-oh.*

His dark hair was rumpled, and his stark white shirt, unbuttoned at the top, showed a nice view of his tanned chest. And those shoulders—oh, those shoulders—looked as if they could carry a roof trestle on them. There was a bit of youthfulness in his face, but he had to be a few years older than she was.

What was one dance going to hurt? The racing of her blood proved she wouldn't dislike it. Heck, even if she were caught, it might just be worth it to have this man's arms around her for a few minutes.

He said nothing else as he waited, confident she would cave. He was right. She watched a smile lift the corners of his mouth as he moved a little closer, and she knew she was a goner. His smell was wafting over her, a mixture of spice and leather. She almost giggled as the verse *Sugar and spice and everything nice* flitted through her frazzled brain cells. Wait! That was for girls, not for drool-worthy men.

"I guess one dance wouldn't hurt," she finally said.

The shiver that rushed through her had nothing to do with the warm evening air. She *wished* she could say it was chilly out.

Without saying anything more, the stranger leaned down and took her hand in his slightly work-roughened fingers. He pulled her toward him, casually wrapping his arm around her waist, his hand resting on her now trembling rib cage as he led her toward the overflowing dance floor. Without hesitation, he turned her, pulled her tightly against his hard body, and began swaying to the music.

She couldn't even concentrate on the song that was playing, he was holding her so close. Her heart was beating out of control. Wasn't this something she'd fantasized about many times on those lonely nights that she lay in bed after putting aside her favorite romance book?

She'd close her eyes and picture a handsome man finding her sitting alone somewhere. He'd have a smile that could light up a darkened room, but his gleaming eyes would look no farther than her.

As she began to relax and enjoy the moment, a woman's laughter made her tense all over again. Panic flooded her. What if this really was a dream—the dream she wanted to come true so bad? Maybe someone had even spiked that second glass of champagne she knew she should have turned down? This was too unbelievable to be real. After all, men like this man didn't dance with wallflowers like her.

As her arms rested around the back of his neck, she reached for her own hand and gave it a quick pinch. She knew she looked ridiculous, but she had to be sure this was real. The little jolt of pain drew a quiet squeak from her lips. Oh yes, she was awake. She didn't know whether to be elated or terrified by that fact.

"Is everything all right?" he asked, leaning back, those green eyes gazing into hers, just as she'd always imagined.

"Yes." The word was barely a whisper. Her cheeks flamed as he looked at her, a knowing gleam in his eyes. She was busted and she knew it, but there was nothing else she could do, so she continued to sway in his arms.

"I've been watching you for the past ten minutes. I couldn't keep my eyes off you," he told her.

Oh my! This man was either incredibly smooth, or she really had conjured up her dream man. Either way, she decided to enjoy this moment to its fullest. She found herself gazing at his lips as he spoke. He had beautiful lips—strong, firm, masculine, and turned up in the most appealing way.

"Thank you," she told him, feeling like a fool as she uttered the words.

"Are you here for the bride or the groom?" he asked.

The dreaded question should have panicked her, but she was almost in a trance now and couldn't help but answer honestly. "Neither. I snuck in with my friend. I can't find her now."

His eyes crinkled, though still, there was something restless about him that she couldn't quite interpret. Something was wrong, but before she could analyze that, the feel of him pressing against her wiped anything other than desire away from her thoughts. Stormy didn't have a clue who in the world she was right now. She certainly wasn't *this* woman dancing with *this* man.

She'd had sex once before, two years prior with her high school sweetheart. That had been a disaster and she'd never tried it again.

Dancing with this man was making her think maybe another try wouldn't be so bad. Did that make her an awful person? She didn't know.

When he stopped moving, she felt her throat close. She wasn't ready for him to release her. But he pulled back anyway, and where she'd felt his warmth down her entire front, she now felt cold. Then she noticed the music had stopped.

Maybe it was midnight and time for Cinderella to go home.

"Let's take a walk."

He began leading her away from the dance floor before she responded. His confidence was overwhelming her, but it didn't matter.

There was no hesitation on her part as joy filled her. Later, she might ask herself why that was, but for now, she was in her dream world.

The sounds of the party began fading as they moved away from the tents and lights and then down a trail.

As he slowly walked next to her, with trees on either side of them and the moonlight barely filtering through, Stormy wondered if she should be afraid. As his hand caressed her lower back, though, all she felt was an overwhelming sense of desire and . . . *rightness*. Not knowing why it felt right didn't matter.

She soon found herself on a sandy beach, her shoes dangling from her fingers as she looked out at Puget Sound, the waves splashing gently against the shore. There was very little breeze and the full moon gave everything a soft light.

"This is incredible. I can't imagine being so lucky as to live here," she told the man. That's when she realized she didn't even know his name. Should she ask him? Or would that break their moment together? She sort of liked the mystery of it all.

"I think Joseph's place is a little too close to the hustle and bustle of Seattle. But I do love the Sound. It's a great waterway."

"Are you here very often?" Was she being nosy now?

"Yes. I don't live too far away." He stopped walking and she stood next to him, enjoying the clasp of his fingers in hers. "Sit with me."

He again didn't wait for a response, simply led her to a log and then sat down, pulling her to his side as they gazed out at the water. He put an arm around her and the feel of his hard muscles enveloping her gave her both a sense of peace and panic at the same time.

She tried to remember a time she'd ever felt so much agitation at just the mere touch of a man, but she couldn't think of a single moment. Only this man—only right now.

"I don't live far away either," she finally said, the silence too intimate. Should they exchange information? Was that what she wanted? Or what he wanted?

When he was silent for several moments, her brain spun. She began wondering if she was being a fool. This could be simply a case of a man trying to hook up at a wedding. It happened all the time, didn't it? Did she really want to be that girl the guys laughed about in the morning?

She realized she didn't actually care what gossip might spur from this.

Maybe she should be more worried. But how often in her life had she done something reckless? Not very often at all. What this man was stirring up inside of her she couldn't understand and didn't want to stop feeling.

"Where exactly are you from?" he asked.

The question helped slow her racing heart. "I've lived all over the world—in my youth, mostly third world kind of accommodations."

That had the man silent for a moment. Then he raised an eyebrow in curiosity.

"You can't just leave me like that. Go on," he told her.

"My mom and dad were missionaries until I was about ten, then they worked modest jobs after that," she began. "I was born in Portland, Oregon, but I lived abroad with my parents for half of my life, then in the Portland area after that. After I turned eighteen, I decided to move to Seattle."

"Now you have me curious of all the places you've been."

"Gosh, let me think," she said. "Africa, South America, Asia for a short time, and a few more places." Noticing she had his undivided attention bolstered her confidence and made her want to keep sharing. It was sort of nice.

"Of all the places you've lived, which one was your favorite?" His fingers were playing with her hair, making little flutters in her stomach.

"I can honestly say I've loved every place I've lived, save maybe a few apartments I've had in the city. But of all the places . . ." Stormy looked up at the starry sky to recall the fondness of a distant place in her memory. "I'd have to say it was Kosovo."

"Kosovo? Where exactly is that? In the Mediterranean somewhere, right?"

"No, it's not exactly in the Mediterranean, as it's landlocked on all sides, but it's right next door to Serbia, Montenegro, and Albania. It's a fantastic place. Incredibly dangerous at the time, but it was cool," she began. "I mean, one minute you'd be drinking Turkish coffee at a café and hear a car driving by playing Euro dance pop on the stereo, while the next car to pass would be blasting dance music in Arabic. The country was a collision of Western and Eastern European culture, with distinct flavors from Turkey and the Middle East. Being a Westerner, of course, gave me instant celebrity status, which as a preteen, I didn't mind so much."

"That's always nice for a teen," he said as he pulled her even closer. The thing was, for Stormy, it felt right. Somehow she was connecting more with this stranger than any other person she'd ever been with before. "What do you do, Cinderella?"

She smiled at the name. Hadn't she been thinking about how this all felt like a dream, like she was going to disappear when the clock struck twelve? His words fit how she was feeling.

"My job isn't interesting," she hedged, and then she found herself playing with the locket hanging around her neck. "But I love to design jewelry," she admitted while her cheeks flamed the tiniest bit. Why had she told him that?

His fingers clasped the locket she'd been clutching as he moved to study it. "This is beautiful," he told her. "Did you make it?"

"Yes," she shyly admitted.

"You have a real talent," he told her, making her more nervous. Why did this man's opinion matter at all? It shouldn't. But somehow it did.

"It's just a silly dream of mine. It can't lead anywhere," she told him with a laugh.

He let go of the locket and gripped her chin, forcing her to look at him. She was voiceless as his gaze held hers captive.

"Dreams are meant to become reality. Don't ever think you can't do something just because it's difficult."

She knew there was a story behind his words. She desperately wanted to know what that story was. "I think it's time for you to share something about yourself." she said, very aware of how close his lips were to hers.

"No. I think we've talked enough for now," he said with a slow smile that melted her from the inside out.

Then she was moving. Effortlessly, he lifted her and sat her across his lap as he gazed down into her eyes. She was lost as his head slowly lowered, the moonlight glinting in his sparkling eyes.

"I'm going to kiss you," he said, waiting only a moment to give her a chance to say no.

Maybe she should refuse. After all, she didn't even know the guy's name. But she didn't want to refuse him or deny herself. She wanted to see if his kiss was going to be even better than his touch.

His head descended and then those exquisite lips of his were on hers, and she couldn't think anymore. The kiss was better than she could have ever expected. Her mouth opened to his, and he was caressing her in a way no one had ever done before. She felt the gentle touch of his tongue trace the edges of her lips before surging forward and commanding her mouth.

Shivers traveled through her frame as she rubbed her body against this man, trying to relieve the ache she didn't quite understand. When he pulled away, she leaned against him, not wanting the connection to end.

"My boat is right over there against the dock. Say the word and we can go and have . . . a drink or . . . something more."

His fingers were lightly trailing up and down her back and his eyes shone down at her clearly, the full moon making it seem more like dusk instead of closer to midnight.

This is where she should tell him *thank you, but no thank you.* Instead she felt herself nodding as she looked up at him. "I'd like . . . a drink," she said.

He hesitated a moment longer, and Stormy couldn't read the look in his eyes. But right then, she knew that she didn't want him to change his mind. Because if he continued walking her to the boat, she was going to do the first seriously reckless thing of her life—she was going to sleep with a stranger.

Then he smiled.

"Right this way." He stood with her still in his arms, and then he let her go so that her feet touched the sand. She hadn't realized she'd risen to her toes in an effort to taste even more of his kiss.

Excitement and a feeling of trepidation warred within her. But as her fingers remained tightly bound with his, the excitement won out. They made their way down a dock lined with several beautiful watercrafts. Her sexy mystery man led her to one of the boats and she stood before it and gasped.

"This is what you call a boat?" she asked, hesitating before stepping to the plank that led onto it.

"Yes." He seemed confused.

She suddenly giggled. Who in the world was this man?

"This is bigger than my place," she told him. If her night ended because he realized she wasn't one of the rich and famous, then so be it. She could only fake so much about herself and being impressed with the giant yacht in front of her was out of her control.

"Yeah, I got this several years ago. I guess it's a bit extreme," he said with a shrug as he shifted on his feet.

He wasn't running away from her yet. That was good.

The sleek yacht spanned at least a hundred feet, and it wasn't even the biggest at the massive docks. That's what was scary about this world of wealth she'd stumbled upon. But the part above the water appeared to have two floors. She didn't know what was below the water's line.

Finally, she allowed him to lead her on board, where she looked at the red hardwood floors and lush furniture. Once inside the cabin she couldn't even tell they were on a boat anymore, unless she concentrated on the gentle rocking motion she could barely feel.

"I didn't know boats had such large rooms," she said nervously as he led her to a living area.

He guided her to a comfortable chair and then stepped over to a big walnut bar with a giant mirror and shelves behind it.

"I don't like to feel closed in," he said before chuckling.

She had to wonder what he found so funny. But she wasn't going to ask.

"I noticed you with champagne earlier. I'll get you another," he told her.

In only moments, Green Eyes was sitting next to her, handing her a beautiful crystal champagne flute. She clutched its long stem and immediately took a swallow. She'd had a few glasses at the wedding reception, but the effects were wearing off, and she didn't want to chicken out on this once-in-a-lifetime adventure.

They sat together and she sipped her champagne, enjoying the quiet of the boat. Her eyes to roamed the yacht's opulent cabin and occasionally stole a glance at the man who'd brought her there. When she'd emptied her glass, he refilled it. She leaned back and smiled at him. She wasn't sure what to do next, so her lips were probably twitching a little.

"Maybe it's time we exchanged names," he said after the long silence.

She was feeling a nice buzz now and decided to play it bold. "I don't think so," she told him.

He turned his head to the side and his brow wrinkled. "Why not?"

"Because I'm enjoying the mystery of all this. I've never done anything like it before." She clutched her hands in her lap and twisted her fingers, but then forced herself to stop. She didn't want him to see how unsophisticated she truly was.

"Done what before?" he asked.

"Gone off with a man I've just met."

"There's nothing wrong with taking a walk or having a drink together." He scooted closer to her, his fingers rubbing along her bare knee. She was grateful she wasn't wearing stockings. She wanted nothing between his touch and her flesh.

"Ah, but that's not all we're going to do—is it, Green Eyes?" she said. *Damn.* Her cheeks instantly flushed after she threw those saucy words at him.

She was playing with fire, and she hoped to get burned.

"I hope not," he said after a moment's silence. And then he was smiling wider than the Cheshire Cat.

Stormy sensed the atmosphere change in the room, and she felt a little lightheaded as the sexual tension swirled around her. Green Eyes set down his glass, took the empty one from her fingers, and then stood up, pulling her straight into his arms.

This time he didn't hesitate when he kissed her—this time, it was fast and hard, and her knees gave out on her, but he was right there to catch her.

And she knew she'd made the right decision.

CHAPTER THREE

As the yacht slowly rocked on the water, Cooper Armstrong looked over at the beautiful woman sleeping naked beside him—perfection on his bed. Just an hour before, they'd had the best sex of his entire life. That was certainly saying something since he hadn't exactly been a saint in his days.

His Cinderella had tried to insist on leaving right after, but it had already been four in the morning. He'd promised to get her a taxi at dawn. Yet, he was reconsidering her leaving so soon. He was even harder now than he'd been an hour ago and he wanted her again. He wasn't even sure one more time would be enough.

From the moment he'd spotted this woman at the wedding, he'd been feeling all sorts of emotions other than rage from his father's passing and the reading of the will. He wasn't quite ready to have her depart and let the good feeling end. Who was this woman? And more importantly, what was she doing to him?

From that very first glance into her somewhat terrified deep brown eyes and at the moue of her sensual pink lips, he'd had to walk over to her, had to see how she'd feel in his arms. Maybe the two of them would make love one more time, and then he'd be able to let her go. He didn't have time for a relationship, and he sure as hell didn't want one. Women couldn't be trusted—not when he had a bank account that made him more attractive in their eyes.

He knew he was a catch. It wasn't arrogance, it was fact. When a person had his looks, his wallet, and his ambition, it made him the perfect target. But the women of the world didn't know that he wasn't taking the bait. His goal was always to get what he wanted from a woman, give her the pleasure of his masterful bedroom skills, and then quickly slip away before the hook could slide into his flesh and snare him.

Even as he had this thought, he began running his hand lightly down his mystery woman's sleek body, the span of his fingers almost covering the width of her back.

She began to stir, but didn't quite wake, not even when he turned her so her luscious breasts were fully available to his touch. Running his finger over each one in turn, he smiled as they instantly hardened for him. She shifted, and he knew the best way to rouse her from her sleep.

He bent down and licked one nipple before sucking it into his mouth and gently clamping his teeth over it. She groaned, making his erection pulse painfully. As Cooper kissed his way back up to her neck, she reached for him, and he took her red lips with his. He could worship this woman's body night and day and still never have enough of her.

That was a sobering thought. And he didn't want to sober up—not yet.

When she trailed her hand down his abs and cupped his manhood, he lurched upward into a sitting position. He was so close to releasing right then and there. How had that happened?

"It's almost morning," he mumbled.

"Um . . . morning," she replied somewhat shyly.

"I know I promised you a taxi when you woke up, but I had another idea first," he told her, his fingers whispering along her skin.

She moaned again, and he was hopeful she would agree.

"I need a few minutes," she told him, and he nearly panicked as she sat up. He wasn't ready for this to end yet.

"Okay," he told her, and he was the one wanting to whimper when she climbed from his bed and walked into his bathroom.

He lay back on the bed and reached down to squeeze his erection, trying to lessen the infernal pulsing. It didn't help. When he heard the shower come on, he sat back up. Should he follow her or not?

When he couldn't stand it anymore, he jumped up from the bed, opened the bathroom door, and grinned as steam hit him full in the face. She obviously enjoyed very hot showers. But he could make it even hotter.

The mirror had already fogged up, and when he drew the curtain aside, the sight of this woman, with water glistening off her body, had him dripping in excitement. He just stood there for a moment as she rubbed her slim fingers down her breasts, across the flat plane of her stomach, and dipped into the folds of her womanhood while cleaning herself.

Enough of this watching!

Cooper stepped inside the shower with her, and when she opened those dark eyes of hers, which were already filled with wanton delight, he nearly fell to his knees.

"You are so damn sexy," he groaned, pushing her back against the coolness of the tile wall and making her gasp.

"Only with you," she admitted.

That knowledge was the most intense aphrodisiac ever. He moved his hands oh so slowly from her hips, up her sides, and around the edges of her breasts. His magic fingers came close to her swollen nipples, but not close enough. She groaned her displeasure at the way he was teasing her.

After looking into her expressive eyes, he finally let his thumbs glance over those hard peaks before sliding his hands to her stomach and circling them behind her to squeeze the cheeks of her firm ass.

"Kiss me," she said, and she reached behind his head and pulled him to her.

He was more than happy to oblige.

Running his tongue over her lips, he quickly parted them and thrust inside, in just the way he wanted to thrust into her heat. She drew him more tightly to her and returned his kiss with the same intense passion.

A cry of pleasure escaped her beautiful lips when he slid a hand back around and rubbed his fingers against her wet heat, and then pinched her little bundle of nerves, making her shake.

"I need to taste you," he said, after ripping his mouth away from her lips. He licked his way down her chest and dropped to his knees.

Gripping her thighs, he pushed them apart and looked up at her smooth perfection, her sweet folds gleaming with water and pleasure. He ran his hand up and didn't stop until he'd buried two fingers deep within her.

Only then did he lean forward to suck the most sensitive part of her into his mouth, flicking his tongue repeatedly against it as his fingers found a perfect rhythm of pumping in and out of her.

His midnight woman clutched his head tightly, and her cries told him she was coming closer and closer to release. Yes, he wanted to give her pleasure—over and over and over again.

So he didn't stop pleasing her with his fingers and tongue until she screamed and almost crumpled right there in front of him.

Cooper stood up quickly, more than ready to be inside this woman. Bracing his foot on the tiled shower bench, he lifted one of her legs and draped it over his so his hardness was poised at her entrance, her thighs spread wide. He gripped himself and rubbed his arousal along the open seam of her pink core.

"Ohh, that's so good. Please . . . more," she moaned, leaning her head against the shower wall.

Moving his manhood up and down over her swollen nub a few times more, he waited until he was coated in her juices, then he poised himself for entry.

"Open your eyes," he commanded her.

She opened them just a little, and, after pulling her up, he slid all the way inside her tight heat.

Her mouth opened in a gasp and he took the opportunity to thrust his tongue inside in perfect rhythm with the way he was plunging into her body, all while gripping her delectable derrière.

The sound of their wet bodies slapping against each other was driving Cooper wild. He sped up and almost poured his seed into her when she tightened around him again. She gave another long and impassioned cry.

He stopped thrusting and held her as she shuddered in ecstasy, and he gently caressed her mouth and squeezed her buttocks. When she slumped against him again, he pulled from her. An act of amazing willpower.

"I'm so worn out," she said, leaning her head against his shoulder.

"It's not over, beautiful, not yet," he whispered into her ear.

"I can't do any more," she told him.

"Oh, yes, yes, you can," he assured her.

Her eyes flew up, and he smiled at her before he turned her around and pressed his arousal against the exquisite cushion of her ass.

"Grip the edge of the bench," he told her as he pushed against her upper back.

She leaned down, leaving her derrière up in the air. Dropping to his knees, he bit each of those cheeks in turn before soothing the red spots with his tongue, and then he stood again and rested his pulsing erection in the valley she was presenting to him, enjoying how perfect the deep red looked against her light skin.

With his foot, he pushed her legs apart—wider—wider—even wider. When she was fully opened up to him, he reached around and found her still-swollen nub, which he stroked a few times, making her twitch against him.

With his other hand he guided himself down the middle of her ass until he reached her core, and then he thrust back inside her. Now it was time for them both to feel pleasure.

She groaned as he moved his hand between her folds, up her belly to her tender nipples, and then back again. He continued caressing her with one hand while gripping her hip with the other, thrusting and thrusting.

"Come for me one more time, baby," he told her as he felt his release drawing nearer.

He flicked his fingers against her bud and she screamed as she convulsed around him so intensely that he almost reached orgasm without any movement at all. But he *had* to move. Pushing deep inside her, he released a hot stream of pleasure, pulsing over and over again until he was entirely drained.

When he could finally take a step back, Cooper felt lost pulling away from her heat. And she nearly collapsed before him, but he was able to catch her.

"That was . . . it was . . . I don't even know how . . ." She was clearly at a loss for words.

"It was perfect," he told her as he lifted her in his arms and then stepped from the shower. He grabbed a couple of towels before carrying her back to his room.

He dried her off before laying her down gently on the bed, and he quickly dried himself. Then he joined her, pulling her back into his arms. He wasn't willing to let her go just yet. Or anytime soon, for that matter.

He'd be careful, he assured himself. This was only sex—just really, *really* good sex. The thought didn't appease him like it should have as he finally closed his eyes and fell into an exhausted slumber.

CHAPTER FOUR

Never before had Stormy had to do the walk of shame, but as she grabbed her tiny handbag and slowly crept away from Green Eyes' bedroom, she glanced back over her shoulder and took in a deep breath.

Dang, the man was good-looking—beyond good-looking, actually, especially now, with stubble on his strong jawline and his muscled arm thrown up above his head, the blankets resting very low on his beautiful hips. Just a few more inches . . .

No, she didn't need to entertain that thought. This was a man she would never see again. Their only connection was the Anderson wedding—a wedding she'd crashed. Her one night of debauchery couldn't cause any repercussions.

When she was on the upper deck of his boat, she peeked out to see whether anyone was around. How paranoid was that? It was about eight in the morning and the wedding reception had gone on long into the night. Everyone was most likely asleep and cruising for a champagne bruising.

Still, she was going to have to trek back up the trail they'd come down the night before, sneak out to the front gate—which had seemed to be a mile from the Anderson castle—and then pray that it was open. The last thing she wanted to do was trudge back to the house and beg someone to let her out.

They'd know exactly what she'd been doing. And even though they had no idea who she was and she would never see them again, her embarrassment would be incalculable. She knew it shouldn't matter, but she cared about what people thought of her.

Stormy made it to the top of the trail and then peered out at the house, surprised to see activity in the backyard. Trucks were there hauling things away and the yard was almost back to normal, or what she assumed was normal, after that enormous party. Wow! These Anderson people moved really fast.

Putting her head down, she walked as quickly as her body-hugging little red dress would allow. She made no eye contact with anyone as she hurried along.

"Hello there!"

The boisterous voice startled her so much, she dropped her purse and jumped into the air. As she came back down, off balance, the heel on her shoe snapped, and after wobbling for a moment, she landed hard on her rear end.

"I'm so sorry, darling," the man said—a freaking giant.

He approached quickly, moving far faster than she would think a man his age could. Bending down, he reached for her hand and easily tugged her back to her feet, where she teetered on the broken shoe.

She had no doubt that this was the famous Joseph Anderson, and she fully understood his reputation as a man to whom no one could ever say no.

"Don't worry about it. I was in my own world," she said, looking *way* up at his concerned expression. He had to be many, *many* inches over six feet. She only stood five feet six—in heels, and she was now short one of those. His silver hair only made him more distinguished in her opinion, and the twinkle in his surprisingly sharp blue eyes made her instantly inclined to trust him.

"Come on inside and we'll get you fixed up," he insisted as he pulled her toward the house. She stumbled behind him.

Uh-oh, maybe she could imagine telling him no after all. She wasn't going into his house. Not a chance. She had to get away before Green Eyes awoke.

"Oh, no. I was just getting ready to leave," she said, trying without success to tug against the beast of a man.

"I can't send you off without making sure you're all right, not after causing you to fall," Joseph said.

"I promise you, I'm okay. I really just want to get going now," she said as she continued to stumble along after him.

He stopped and looked at her, and Stormy's cheeks flushed at what he must be thinking. He had to know she'd just walked away from someone's bed. He must be wondering which guy it had been. Maybe he was worried about it being one of his kin. For all she knew, Green Eyes was related to Joseph. The man had sported a really nice boat that was docked on the Anderson pier.

"I'm Joseph Anderson, by the way," he said, releasing his protective grip on her hand. It seemed as though he expected her to now introduce herself. Something she absolutely didn't want to do.

"It's very nice to meet you, Mr. Anderson. As I said, I'm doing just fine, so I'll be on my way," she said as she retreated. The first thing she did was remove her shoes and grip them tightly in one hand.

"Where's your car parked, Miss . . . ?" He trailed off, obviously waiting for her to give her name again.

"I rode here with a friend. I've called a cab, and it's picking me up at the gate, so I'd best hurry," she said. She hadn't yet called the damned cab, but she was planning to as soon as she escaped from the intimidating Anderson patriarch.

"Then I'll walk you to the gate," Joseph said.

This walk of shame just kept on getting worse and worse. Now the man was going to catch her in a lie. Her humiliation was complete.

"Well, I haven't actually *called* the cab yet. I was just getting ready to when I ran into you. So I had best get going and do that. By the time I get to the gate, the cab will be waiting for me," she said with a sheepish laugh.

"Nonsense, young lady. If you were a guest at the party, I insist on having my driver give you a ride home," Joseph said, once again tugging on her arm.

Stormy gasped. "I couldn't have you do that."

"I won't take no for an answer."

And that was why the man always got his way, she decided.

Within a minute, a black car pulled up; a man emerged from the driver's side and opened the back door for her. Stormy found herself practically pushed into the car, and the only relief she felt was when the car pulled away from the Anderson mansion.

She didn't look back to see Joseph reach down and pick up the locket that had dropped from her neck, or the smile he wore as he held it.

All fairy tales must come to an end, and when she got home and walked inside, she was cruelly thrust back into the real world—her carriage was now a pumpkin again, and her glass slipper left behind . . .

CHAPTER FIVE

Six Years Later

Sitting on the deck of his favorite café in the old neighborhood, Sherman Armstrong leaned back as another roar of thunder sounded high in the sky. He knew he was the very image of the old grandfather resting in his favorite chair while children ran by wondering about him.

He liked that mystery about himself.

He was a stout man, though his body was a bit older and weaker now, and he was forced to use a cane while walking. He had a square jaw, bit too big of a nose, and had sometimes been called Dumbo because of the size of his ears. Yet one thing that was fully working, and sharp as ever, were his bright blue eyes, which showed an inextinguishable youthfulness and a lot of hard-learned wisdom. Life had taught him things that no one and nothing could ever take away.

Though Sherman was an incredibly wealthy man, he didn't have a large wardrobe. He sat on the café's deck wearing his favorite blue cardigan. Tomorrow he'd most likely wear the brown one. Those were the only colors he ever selected for his warm, wool sweaters. Of course, he did have a variety of plaid shirts that he mixed with the cardigans. Today he was wearing a green-and-blue one under his sweater.

He'd lived in the house across the street, where apartments now stood, when he was a young buck right out of the military in the sixties. This neighborhood was worn down and sometimes unsafe, but it was where he'd made a life for himself and for his beautiful bride, Betty Sue.

It was the place where he'd raised his family, and it was the place he would continue to visit until he took his last breath. His family had told him it was time to move on, but it never would be—not in his opinion.

"Do you think this storm will hang around for a while?" Sherman asked Joseph. He and Joseph Anderson had been friends since they were in grade school . . . and Sherman valued that friendship more than all the money in his bank account.

"I sure hope so," Joseph told him.

"Then maybe I will accept your offer for brunch after we finish our coffee. You have a hell of a view from your place," Sherman said with a laugh.

"That is very true, my friend. Say the word, and my driver will get us out of here," Joseph told him. Katherine wasn't allowing him to drive in bad weather anymore, not with his need for speed, and the accident that had almost cost him his life.

Looking across the street, he caught a glimpse of Stormy Halifax as she struggled to push open the doors to the apartment complex she lived in—the wind fighting her each step of the way. He had begun to stand to assist her when she managed to push through to the sidewalk.

She didn't pause, looking to be in a hurry as she splashed her nice clean work clothes while rushing through the puddles of water to get to her waiting taxi.

Sitting back down, Sherman smiled and lifted his hand. A frown marred his forehead when she didn't look over. He watched her bend to open the car door, but suddenly she popped back up and then smiled and waved.

It was a tradition. She'd been living across the street for three years, and if she came down early enough before she had to rush off to work, she would dash over and chat with him for a few minutes. But even if she couldn't do that, she always left him with a wave and a smile.

Sherman had grown very fond of the young woman. As she pulled away, a sad smile flitted across his lips. The young girl was trying to make it on her own, but sometimes a person was stronger not weaker for asking for a helping hand in times of need. She was a stubborn one, though, and wouldn't allow him to help her.

Well, he thought, as her cab drove down the street on her way to a job that wouldn't take her anywhere, he *was* going to help her—one way or another. His spreading smile took years away from his wrinkled face. It was a good thing Joseph was with him to brainstorm.

"She's such a fine young woman. I've been trying to help her for quite some time, but she's determined to do everything on her own. That girl isn't someone who even cares to utter the word defeat," Sherman told Joseph.

"She looks familiar," Joseph said as he stared after her, searching his memory. "What's her story?"

"Her parents were missionaries for a lot of years and then working-class folk, didn't have a whole lot. Her father died when she was twenty, and it was real hard on her. Her mom was sick so she dropped out of school to take care of her, and then her mother passed last year. She hasn't managed to get back on her feet quite yet. But she will. She was taught young not to complain in life, and she lives by that motto," Sherman said.

"There's nothing wrong with asking for help once in a while," Joseph said as the two of them watched the cab disappear. "But I've always admired a woman with a strong backbone. That's the kind of girl who won't be led easily astray."

"Yes, I agree with you there," Sherman said. "I was sort of hoping to set her up with one of my nephews, but I can't seem to get them in the same room with her. She's always so busy . . ."

"Well, my dear friend, you should have come to me sooner," Joseph boomed with a laugh, making Sherman, who was used to his boisterous friend, jump.

"Why is that, Joseph?"

"Because if there's one thing I know about, it's matchmaking," Joseph said as he sat back. He pulled out two deliciously scented cigars. "We'll need these. This will take a while."

"I sure won't turn one down," Sherman said, accepting the fragrant tobacco.

The two men lit up and then leaned back as the thunder moved further north but still gave them a good show to behold.

"Tell me more about this girl," Joseph said.

"Stormy is kind. I visit my old friend Penny in those apartments quite often, and if Stormy sees that I'm carrying anything, she'll insist on helping me. And on days like this, when the weather takes a turn for the worse, I guarantee you, she'll swing by after work to make sure everything is okay with Penny, who isn't remembering things so easily these days. Stormy's become like a granddaughter to me and a few other people in that old apartment building, and I just adore her beautiful heart and her sweet words. I miss her when a few days pass that I don't get to chat," Sherman said.

"It sounds like she's made of the good stuff," Joseph said, disappointed he didn't have any sons left to set her up with. Of course, he loved Sherman's nephews like his own, so he'd be happy to see this Stormy with one of Sherman's boys.

"Yep, she is. I hate seeing her living all alone. She should be settled down, having a nice young lad to help carry some of her burden. The forty years I spent with my beautiful wife before the Lord decided she needed to be elsewhere were the best years of my life," Sherman said.

"I can't imagine what would happen to me if I lost my Katherine," Joseph said.

"I still miss Betty every single moment of each day. Now, I find joy with other people, but it's never going to be the same. She was my soul mate and there's no replacement for her. Everyone should have that at least once in their lifetime."

"I agree, Sherman. I fully agree," Joseph told his friend.

The storm began to clear and the two men heard a jet fly over them. Sherman looked up at the sky with a bit of envy.

"You still miss it, don't you?" Joseph asked, completely understanding.

"Oh, I miss it each morning I wake up," Sherman assured his friend.

What felt like many years before, Sherman had been a pilot for the military, and then privately, crop dusting fields and eventually flying jetliners. He'd soared high above the clouds, leaving all his cares on the ground as he sat behind the controls of a powerful jet engine.

There were days he'd give just about anything to be up there again, trying to beat the morning sun as he rushed down a runway at one hundred plus miles per hour.

Pulling a keychain out of his pocket, he handed the faded blue ring to his friend. The scratched letters of Pan American were still printed on the face.

"I remember this," Joseph said with a laugh.

"I spent a lot of years with them. It's the keepsake I refuse to let go of," Sherman said.

"We all need to have keepsakes from the good old days. But Sherman, when your nephews are married and bringing more family home to you, then you won't look so much at the past anymore. I love my present and I look forward to the future," Joseph assured him.

"I think you are absolutely right, Joseph," Sherman said. He put the keychain away and smiled. And then he grabbed a pen and paper and smiled even more broadly.

Let the matchmaking begin.

CHAPTER SIX

Stormy was startled from her short slumber by what sounded like someone trying to break down her apartment door. She had finally fallen asleep around two in the morning after getting home late from work.

Laying there a few more moments, she was furious when the pounding continued. Who would be so rude at such an early hour? It was only seven o'clock. Finally, when the noise continued on for what seemed to be forever, she threw off her covers with a frustrated sigh and stood up.

Glancing again at the vintage alarm clock, which was sitting on two upside-down milk crates covered with a piece of blue fabric, she realized only a minute had passed.

Throwing herself back down on the bed, she refused to answer her door, though she was now wide awake. She wouldn't reward the person's rude behavior by acknowledging his or her presence.

When five minutes passed and the intruder still refused to leave, she finally got up and pulled her pink terry cloth robe around her to stomp across her cold, worn wooden floors. She passed through her sparsely furnished, small living room and stood in front of her door.

"Whoever is out there can get the hell away from here before I cock the shotgun I'm currently holding," she said, hoping her voice sounded a lot braver than she felt.

Silence greeted her statement.

"I'm not kidding. I grew up on an army base and I know how to use this thing," she lied as she looked down at her sweaty palms. She didn't even own a gun, but the person on the other side of the door didn't know that.

Her neighborhood wasn't the worst in town, but it most certainly wasn't the best.

Several seconds passed—they seemed like freaking eons—and Stormy put her ear to the door. Only silence greeted her now. Great! The jerk had woken her up and now was running scared.

Maybe she should make a recording of her small speech and keep it at the ready for anyone stepping in front of her door before the hour of ten a.m.

Her hands still a bit shaky, Stormy made sure her security chain was tightly locked in place. Finally, she cracked her door a couple of inches. She peered down the hallway as far as she could see and found no one out there.

Had she scared the person off? That thought pleased her immensely. She was one tough girl. Yay for her.

Still, she really wanted to know what all the pounding had been about. "Is anyone out there?" she called out. Not a whisper could be heard in return.

A little bucked up, she slowly removed the chain and opened her door wide enough to look out to the other side of the hallway. The sound of the door creaking open gave her goose bumps, but when she looked down both sides of the hall, there wasn't a soul in sight.

Her eyes narrowed, and she immediately suspected that the creepy college dropout who lived a few units down might have been playing a prank on her. He never had a shortage of cheesy pickup lines or dirty jokes to share with anyone of the female gender. Perhaps he had just hammered on the door before heading out, thinking that he was being amusing.

Just as she began to turn and close the door, a flat white object on her mat caught her eye. Holding her robe closed with one hand, she reached down with the other and picked up the envelope.

Once safely back inside, with her lock securely in place, she noticed that the return address was the rental office of her building. She walked back to her bedroom, which was little more than an alcove with no wall or door.

Wondering what the management could be sending her, she tore open the letter. She sat on the edge of her bed and hesitantly pulled the piece of paper out. Oh, how she hoped it was simply an announcement about sink repairs. No such luck.

Dear Ms. Halifax:
Remodel to begin in four days. This is your final warning.
You must be out in seventy-two hours.

Stormy's heart sank in her chest as she crumpled the paper in agitation. She had known this was coming, but still, she'd hoped beyond hope she could get an extension. Finding an affordable place in Seattle wasn't easy.

But the new management was trying to spruce up the image of the building for some big investors who were coming in. Dammit! When it rained, it poured. Since everything was going wrong anyway, she decided she would just let it all go and try to forget about it—for at least a solid ten minutes.

It was time to get ready for work. Suddenly a loud clap of thunder erupted close by. She could hear a slight tapping on her window that was increasing in tempo. Fall was quickly approaching in Seattle, and the rainy weather was steadily increasing.

Stormy was always invigorated by big storms, not fearful like so many other people. They actually helped to cheer her up, most likely because they were her namesake. She'd been born the night of a great thunderstorm and her parents had thought her name was literally coming to them from the skies. She had to admit, though, she'd rather watch a storm from a warm, safe place and not go out into the middle of it.

She reminded herself again that it was a work day. Maybe it was good the management had woken her. With a sigh, she walked across the cold, broken tile of her bathroom. The bathroom was small and quaint, complete—*har, har*—with a toilet, a single shower stall, and a vanity that barely managed to hold her hairbrush and a few basic beauty products. It was a good thing she wasn't into a lot of cosmetics and skin lotions.

She turned the faucet on, then pulled the lever, bouncing on her toes as she waited for what seemed like forever for the small tank to send anything above freezing through the rusty pipes. When the water reached lukewarm, she jumped in, and then sighed when it finally matched her body temperature.

It didn't take long to get ready, and then she was off. The sooner she faced the wet, cold morning, the sooner she'd be out of it. There was a bright side.

She arrived in the lobby just as the rain picked up to a sheeting downpour outside the old building.

"Are you going out in that, darling?" one of her neighbors asked as she waited for the morning paper to arrive. The widow, Penny, whom Stormy had a soft spot for, had the same routine every single day.

"Yes, I have no other choice," Stormy replied.

"You know, missy, if you don't learn how to slow down just a little bit, one day you're going to find that you've let life just up and pass you by."

Stormy could feel pressure behind her eyes at the words. "I know that. But sometimes you don't have much of a choice but to keep on running," she said sadly.

"There's always a choice, dear."

Reaching up to grip the pendant from her lost necklace, her hand fluttered away when she came up with empty skin. It had been six years and she still reached for it. The night she'd lost it, more of her dreams of becoming a jeweler had washed away. Sadness filled her at her neighbor's words, more so than she cared to admit.

"Sometimes, there's really not a choice," she finally said, her voice barely above a whisper. "Thanks for being there for me, Penny. Now, stay inside and keep warm."

She would actually do well to heed the woman's advice. But she knew she wouldn't.

CHAPTER SEVEN

The sun's rays pierced through the overcast sky as the rain began to subside, and the now warming pavement of Seattle's well-traveled roadways produced puffs of steam that were whirled around by the cars rushing along.

The light at a busy Broadway intersection turned red as a sexy Porsche 911 came to a stop just shy of the crosswalk. Drumming his hands impatiently on the steering wheel was the less than humble airline pilot Cooper Armstrong on his way to Sea-Tac Airport.

Cooper was once again in a mad dash to get to work early. Of course the airplane needed his special attention, and there'd be no flight for the day without his presence. Sure, there were other pilots, but none as good as he was, he thought with a cocky smile.

Within seconds, a car pulled alongside him to his left. Giving little thought to the vehicle, he calmly glanced over and saw the passenger window gliding down.

Cooper waited to see how hot the woman was who was about to offer her phone number. But instead of a sexy brunette or smoldering redhead, Cooper saw his fellow pilot and good friend Wolf Young.

Had he not been so distracted, he would have recognized the dark blue BMW M3 immediately.

Wolf could be a little hotheaded, and he had a touch of arrogance. Hell, it was why the two of them got along so damn famously. But one thing they didn't have in common was their idea of punctuality. Wolf certainly liked to push the envelope when it came to getting anywhere on time.

"Are you still driving that grandma's car, old man?" Wolf shouted over the sound of his revving engine.

Cooper refused to take the bait—all of it, anyway. He wasn't about to be late to work because Wolf had goaded him into a race.

"I was about to ask you the same thing," Cooper said with a mocking smile.

"Ha. My car will kick your car's ass any day of the week." Wolf revved the engine again for good measure.

"Are you ever going to grow up, Wolf?" Cooper asked, though he could feel the adrenaline racing through his veins at his friend's obvious challenge. Damn . . .

"I sure as hell hope not," Wolf shouted. "I'm racing. Let's see if you can keep up." And his window began to go up, though only partway.

To his great frustration, Cooper felt his ego taking over his decision-making processes. Just as his friend knew would happen. And though Cooper hated that his reactions were so predictable, he couldn't seem to stop his next words.

"Fine, you want to find out what this *grandma's* car can do, Wolf? You'd better prepare yourself for defeat." Cooper shut his window. He could picture the excitement on Wolf's face, and heard Wolf gun the motor in anticipation of starting.

The two men watched as the traffic on both sides of the street began to slow, indicating their light was about to change. Both cars surged forward, only held back by their feet on the brakes, as they prepared for the first sign of a green light. Time seemed to stand still, then the light finally changed.

In an almost simultaneous motion, Cooper and Wolf dumped their clutches and stomped on the gas pedals. With a roar, their cars leapt from the white line. The sound of squealing tires and the smell of smoke filled the air as both cars sped off.

Cooper glanced at his speedometer, which was climbing quickly to 65 miles per hour as they barreled down the city streets. Their cars darted in and out of midmorning traffic, getting everything from the middle finger to honking horns. Cooper knew in the back of his mind that he'd seen police officers on this road, but his boyish arrogance would never allow him to slow down.

Wolf made a sudden attempt at a pass, while Cooper responded with a sharp maneuver to block him. The sound of Wolf's engine down-shifting could be heard as Cooper watched him in the rearview mirror. His lead grew as he pushed his Porsche even harder.

Cooper knew that Wolf would do anything to win. He'd raced the guy before and had learned a few of Wolf's tricks and strategies. *Come on, Wolf, make your next move,* Cooper silently taunted as they approached the on-ramp to the freeway.

Although the traffic was somewhat heavy, the open expanse of the freeway was a golden opportunity. *This is your chance, Coop. Give it all she's got.* He quickly shifted into third gear as he turned onto the ramp, looking back to see Wolf only inches away.

The cars surged up the ramp, both engines growling as they were pushed to their limits. As Cooper crested the top of the ramp, he refused to be fazed by all the sounds of disapproval. In fact, he accelerated past 100 miles per hour.

Cooper's confidence about his upcoming victory was quickly squashed by the sight of Wolf's shiny grille in his rearview mirror. Deciding it was time for some dirty tactics, Cooper cracked an evil smile as he noticed a large truck with its turn signal on that was moving into his lane.

Without hesitation or fear, Cooper shifted into fourth gear and hammered down on the pedal. The sound of gravel could be heard under his car as he swerved around the merging truck and slightly onto the shoulder.

Try that on for size! Cooper could see Wolf and his blue car swerving from side to side while attempting to find a hole. He sped off, taking full advantage. After a couple of minutes he figured he'd won, free and clear.

Glancing in his mirror, Cooper could no longer see any sign of Wolf. *Looks like you gave up too easily, my frie—what the . . .*

Cooper could see a BMW fast approaching from his right side, like a bullet fired from a gun. Cooper knew there'd be glee on Wolf's face, taunting Cooper as he drove. His heart pounding, Cooper pressed his engine as hard as it would go.

His focus turned back to the road in front of him in time to notice the distinct sky-blue nose of a Crown Victoria protruding from the vegetation lining the median. It wouldn't be the first time he'd had a run-in with the local police department, and he was only too familiar with those cars.

To prevent a catastrophic ticket, another bad mark on his driving record, he quickly downshifted and applied the brakes. With a slight chirp of the tires, he slowed to just five miles per hour over the speed limit in the knick of time.

He looked back at his rival and friend as the gap between them began to close at a quick rate. Cooper noticed Wolf wasn't slowing as he moved to the left lane to make his victory pass.

Knowing Wolf didn't need any more stressors in his life, Cooper did all he could to point out the police cruiser. He soon realized his warnings were going unseen as Wolf kept on speeding, his focus too narrow to care.

You fool; you couldn't say I didn't warn you, Cooper thought as he watched Wolf's brake lights glow and his tires smoke in what looked like a panicked deceleration.

Yes, the police cruiser lit up with flashing red and blue lights and pulled out, maneuvering behind Wolf's car, signaling him to move to the shoulder. Cooper, now safe, took the next exit to the airport.

He glanced at his large aviator watch as he pulled into the airport employee parking lot. He was on time, since his street-racing session had ended with little cost to his normal commute. He pulled into his usual spot and stepped from the car looking absolutely impeccable in his hand-tailored uniform.

Catching the first employee shuttle bus he could find, he sat quietly with his flight bag and suitcase positioned neatly beside him. Since he'd been flying out of the Seattle airport for the better part of six years, he had his daily routine down to a science. Even if he had been off for the past month on vacation.

Still, it was almost choreographed. He showed his identification, passed through the screening checkpoint, and headed for the coffee shop.

He'd deal with his friend soon enough. For now, it was back to work. Still, he had to admit that the race had been a good rush, taking away some of the boredom of the drive he knew so dang well that he could do it while asleep.

Now it was back to the real world.

CHAPTER EIGHT

The taxi pulled up in front of the Sea-Tac terminal after a nauseating ride, swerving in and out of traffic and around single-minded travelers. Stormy Halifax tossed the driver his money, two hours worth of work gone in twenty minutes of wasted time on the commute, and leapt from the cab, running straight for the front entrance of the airport.

She was all set to begin her average day with its monotonous routine. She was one of the baristas at a small latte shop, Republic Coffee, located in the Seattle-Tacoma International Airport. The small and quaint café was nestled in between the food court and a local gift shop.

Stormy had been at her job for only a month, but it was such a hassle to get there that she wasn't sure she even wanted the job to last anymore. If only she didn't need the money so desperately.

The airport was a bustling madhouse with an endless sea of people on what seemed to be a busy travel day. Republic Coffee stayed fairly busy throughout the day because it was near the top of the escalators and the main entranceway to a majority of the airline gates after security.

As Stormy stepped off the escalator, she was immediately assailed by oblivious passengers, the smell of coffee, and the sound of a gate agent getting reamed by an unhappy customer.

Yes, it would obviously be another long day of coffee drudgery, pushy passengers, and egotistical pilots. She could handle most of it, but the pilots were the absolute worst.

When she first started working here, she'd found them fascinating—a great number of them were sexy, confident, and downright charming. It didn't hurt that they were well paid, flashing bulging wallets at the coffeehouse and flaunting expensive watches and sunglasses.

By her third week, though, she'd discovered that most of the pilots made no secret about wanting one thing only. A lot of them had a different girlfriend in each city on their routes.

She absolutely wanted no part of that. She'd rather be single than be some arrogant man's plaything. After she'd turned down several "kind" offers, they'd finally taken the hint and stopped asking her for dates—or one-night stands, if she was being honest. Yes, she'd had one of those, but that was in the past.

Stormy had just signed into her register when a man in a clean, pressed button-up shirt, impeccably tailored even to the most stringent of military standards, walked into her field of vision.

His gleaming gold pilot's wings adorned the left side of his broad chest, and above his right chest pocket he wore a bright name badge with the words "Captain Armstrong, Trans Pacific Airlines."

This pilot stood about six feet four, with piercing green eyes. He wore a captain's hat embroidered with a gold leaf and it had his airline insignia centered above the visor. Peering out from the underside of the visor and on the visible side of his temple was nearly black hair, well trimmed and styled. His skin tone was slightly dark, perhaps a hint of a Mediterranean heritage. His face was clean shaven, showcasing his incredibly sensual lips.

His physique was a sight to behold, with broad shoulders, a muscular, well-defined chest, and deltoids, biceps, and triceps filling out his dress shirt. Stormy's eyes followed the natural progression of his impressive physique, dropping to the black belt fitted perfectly at his hips.

Why did he look familiar?

It wasn't until he was right in front of her that the connection clicked.

Flashes of a moonlit beach—a hot, steamy shower, and even hotter kisses—large, strong hands tracing her body . . .

Reaching for the missing necklace again, she fought the dizziness she suddenly felt. She knew this man, though he was someone she'd never thought she'd see again. And now she knew his name, or at least his last name. Her body trembled as she faced him. It had been years, six years to be exact, and he'd changed, but the instant ache between her thighs was a quick reminder that her body hadn't forgotten him.

Closing her eyes for a moment, she allowed herself to remember that night, remember every moment of it with him expertly caressing every inch of her, making her cry out over and over again. She'd done things with this man she'd never done before, and certainly hadn't done since.

How did one follow up with another man after being with someone like Green Eyes? He'd been incredible, and she hadn't once felt the same reaction with another man.

Her cheeks flaming, Stormy looked at Green Eyes and waited for recognition to light his eyes. But there was nothing there except a slight tilt to his head and definite interest in his expression.

He had no clue who she was.

Damn! She hadn't thought she was quite that forgettable, even if it had been six years earlier and she'd grown more curves and lost that youthful glow only a twenty-year-old could have. Well, her hair was now its naturally dark brown color again, too . . .

Still, her ego took a nosedive.

But did she really want him to know who she was? Would he expect a repeat performance? Would that be so bad? Questions with no answers flooded her mind as she stood there unable to speak.

"Did you hear me?" Green Eyes asked.

"What? No. I'm sorry," Stormy replied. He must have placed an order with her, and she hadn't processed a single thing that had come out of his mouth.

"I want an Americano, four shots with room for cream."

Her brain was still muddled and she just stared at him blankly. Dammit. With all the blood rushing through her brain, she couldn't quite grasp what he was asking.

"I want an Americano with four shots and room for cream," he repeated, very slowly now. "I've been gone a while, but I would hope the servers here could still actually *serve* coffee."

"Yes, sorry, I'll get that right away."

She turned and knocked down the container of half-and-half, cream spilling all over her leg and the floor. Silence echoed off the walls for several moments until he spoke again.

"Have a rough night?" he asked with a laugh.

She shuddered. She was really thrown off her game right now, and though it frustrated her, she was fighting tears. "Excuse me?"

"Come on, doll. I know women, and obviously you're having a rough day, maybe not getting enough sleep. Maybe you should dump the man who's giving you those circles under your eyes and let a real man make sure you're resting like a baby," he boldly told her, then added insult to injury when he winked.

She was mortified to know she'd slept with this man. Even more mortified to realize she still couldn't regret it, even if he was acting like a typical alpha pilot who thought panties were automatically supposed to drop when he entered the room. Taking a deep breath, she decided she wasn't going to keep acting like an A-class klutz and she was certainly going to stand up for herself, which wasn't something easy for her to do.

"I can't figure out if you're hitting on me or insulting me, but either way, your behavior is unacceptable." There. That was good, she convinced herself.

Her anger partly stemmed from him not remembering her and partly because his attitude toward her was now ruining her one Cinderella moment in time. No, she hadn't escaped at the stroke of midnight, but she had run away, though he'd never come calling for her. Not that she wanted him to, she told herself. But still, she sort of liked living with the fantasy of a lover lost.

He was no longer lost, dammit!

"I would never insult a beautiful woman," he told her as he leaned a little closer across the counter. "However, I could give you a good night's rest."

Stormy didn't know what to be more offended about, but she most certainly was horrified he would speak to her this way. Seriously, how could he not have even the smallest inkling of recognition?

Best sex in his life? Apparently not.

Her pride was wounded, and she was hurt, which made her words sharper than she normally ever spoke.

"You will never give me *anything*, especially not at night. I don't go for coarse, primitive men like you," she said, a bit too loudly in her attempt at being stern, making several heads turn in their direction. "I have standards."

But right after snapping at him, her cheeks flushed as she looked around the rapidly filling coffeehouse. This was hardly the place for private discussions. People were going to assume she was crazy and a man-hater. She just might be a little bit of both.

He didn't seem offended. "Well then," he drawled.

"I'm sorry," she mumbled. She was going to get into serious trouble if her boss came out from his office in the back.

"Don't worry about it, doll. But while you're standing there, maybe I could get my coffee." He was still leaning in way too close for her comfort, and her body was still reacting to his.

With trembling fingers, she picked up the coffee cup and turned away before speaking just loudly enough for him to hear.

"Obviously another pilot with an ego big enough to make up for a small package." Of course it was anything but small, but he didn't know that *she* knew that.

"Stormy!"

Stormy's shoulders hunched. Dang it, of course her boss would chose the exact moment she lost her cool to come and check on her. Now the wretched man would bust her for being less than her absolute best with a customer.

But Green Eyes had deserved her wrath. If only her boss were a woman, this would be so much easier to explain. However, Henry hadn't liked her from day one, and now she was practically handing him a solid reason to fire her.

The man had a high-pitched, nasal voice that was like nails on a chalkboard. Henry was known as Mr. Customer Service and took any opportunity he could to insult the girls in front of the clientele. It was his petty form of vengeance, or so the theory went, for being turned down left and right by the opposite sex.

"Henry, I'm—"

Before Stormy could even finish, Henry interrupted. "Captain Armstrong, I'm sorry about the delay and about Ms. Halifax's behavior. This one is on us."

"No, no, everything is fine," Captain Armstrong said with a smile. "Ms. Halifax is clearly having a rough morning, and maybe she just wasn't getting my sense of humor." As the man spoke to Henry, his eyes never left Stormy, as if to apologize for the entire scene he'd helped create.

It didn't matter. Despite his clear remorse, she was still seething.

"Nevertheless, your coffee's on us," Henry said before turning to Stormy. "Finish with the captain, and then immediately join me in my office."

Stormy's heart sank to her stomach. Her day had just gone from bad to worse. She had zero doubt that she was about to get canned—and on the same day she'd received an eviction notice. What was next, getting struck by a rare strike of Seattle lightning?

As she began to come to terms with the gravity of her situation, images of living on the streets or staying at a homeless shelter began to circle in her mind. Jobs, even service jobs, didn't come easy, especially if you'd been fired from your last one.

"Hey. You okay?" It took a moment to realize that the captain was speaking to her.

But when she did, she gave the man a withering glare before deciding she'd best make this coffee a great one, since it was most likely her last one.

"Right! One quad shot Americano coming right up!" Stormy made quick work of making the coffee and handing it over the counter. "I apologize for my behavior," she told him through gritted teeth.

The pilot took a sip of his hot coffee before smiling. "Thanks for the apology. You don't need to worry about it, though. I can take it as good as I give it. Hope your day goes a little better than the way it's been so far." He tossed down a hundred-dollar bill as if it were petty cash and then strode off to his gate.

Stormy stood there motionless as she watched the incredible backside of Captain Armstrong as he walked away. Damn, she wished he were short, fat, and ugly. Why was it that if a man was good-looking, it made you think he was actually a decent human being? It had to be the smile. No, it definitely had to be the eyes.

Possibly the backside.

Whatever the hell it was, she wanted to hate him—but she couldn't quite do that. For now, she could just feel anger.

The man had insulted her, most likely gotten her fired, and he couldn't even apologize. He figured throwing out a ridiculous tip would make up for his rude behavior. Either that or he wanted her to know he was rich, thinking he could buy a night with her.

He would be wrong on both fronts.

But there was an upside here. Being fired would mean that she wouldn't have to deal with him or any of the other jackass men who roamed the airport hallways thinking they were God's gift to women.

The one thing that worried her the most, though, was the fact that she was still stupidly attracted to the man. How in the world could she find him attractive? What was wrong with her that she found it acceptable to be attracted to the man who couldn't be bothered to remember they'd slept together?

Stormy had been loved and taken care of by incredible parents. She'd had a few hard knocks in life, but who the hell hadn't? She'd never been neglected or tortured. On the whole, her life had been pretty damn great, actually.

Enough reflection. Hardening her resolve to deal with her slimy boss, she squared her shoulders and forced herself to turn toward the office. Though her feet were dragging, she made her way inside and stood in the doorway.

Henry made her wait while he scribbled for several moments in some notebook behind his pathetically small desk. It was a power move on his part. Not surprising, she thought. How much respect could the man have for himself, working at a crap job with horrible wages despite his law degree from Harvard?

Too bad the man had been caught concealing material evidence in a case and had been disbarred. He had wound up a manager in a small coffee shop. And he took his anger out on everyone.

"Are you trying to get us shut down, Stormy?"

She hadn't expected that. "No," she said.

"Well, if you don't follow the rules, you get fined, and if you get fined enough, you get shut down. So again, what are your intentions while working here?"

"To do my job and collect a paycheck, sir."

"Well, your job is to ensure that customers receive satisfaction. If we piss off the pilots, then we lose their business. Then we lose *all* the airline employees' business and we get shut down." His voice rose the longer he spoke.

"I'm sorry I snapped at Captain Armstrong. But he was being rude as well," she pointed out.

"The customer is *always* right," he thundered. "Deal with that."

"I apologize. I won't be rude again," she said, feeling tears behind her eyes.

She hated that she sometimes cried when she was angry. She wanted to show she was furious, not a weakling, dang it!

"Look, Stormy, Captain Cooper Armstrong visits us many times during the week. You need to be more observant, take the time to actually notice the crew members who stop in frequently, and be extra courteous to them. I know this is a new shift for you, but just look at their name tags so you'll remember them more easily, and be sure to give them that employee discount!

"Follow my lead. I go out of my way to take note of every employee I see. Don't let these thick glasses confuse you into thinking I'm a blind man!" Just as he was finishing what he was saying, he nearly tripped over his own desk.

Stormy reluctantly nodded her head in agreement with her boss— why make things worse? "Is that all, sir?" Using the word *sir* to address this guy tasted sour on her tongue.

"Yes. Now go man the register. The line is growing and Amy can't do it by herself."

Stormy turned to walk out of the office. "Stormy, remember . . ." Stormy stopped, but barely kept herself from groaning, since she knew what he was going to say. ". . . Republic Coffee is happiness in a cup."

Completely disgusted with this company droid, Stormy left the office to return to work, though she did it with a sinking feeling in her heart.

Upon her return to the floor of the coffee shop, she found herself in a daze as she wiped the tables and straightened up the boxes of tea and refilled condiments. So Captain Armstrong's first name was Cooper? She now knew the full name of the man she'd slept with six years ago. So much for him being Green Eyes. She was too frazzled to even think about it right now.

Amy was working behind the counter preparing a passenger's coffee. Amy finished ringing up the passenger, then looked over at Stormy with a defeated look on her face.

"Why did you let that man get to you?" asked Amy when they were alone.

"I'm actually not sure," Stormy answered while playing back the conversation. It wasn't any worse than any other she had on a daily basis. "I guess it's because I'm sick and tired of these pilots thinking they have a right to get into my pants," Stormy said with a wink, attempting to make light of the confrontation.

"Ha! Surprise, surprise, Captain Gorgeous is another full-of-himself womanizer. A Greek god of a man who sounds like a sexist, self-absorbed moron when he speaks, ruining all of that other stuff . . . you know, the hot part. If we could just silence him and tie him to a chair, we'd get a lot more female customers, and then not have to deal with all the guys who come in here expecting a cup of coffee and a quickie on one of the tables." Amy spoke as she began steaming milk for the customer whose order Stormy had just rung up on the register.

"It's not just what Armstrong was spouting. I'm used to all that," she stated as she got back to the conversation. "It's just that I've met him before."

"I hear a story coming," Amy said with glee.

"No, no story. I was just surprised to see him, that's all. It's been a lot of years since the last time."

"I want to know what's going on, but I've learned in our short time together how close-lipped you can be. I'll wait it out," Amy said.

"Good," Stormy said. "This week has all around sucked. I have to move on top of everything else."

"Don't you like your apartment?"

"It's not that. It has new management and they are remodeling. I've known that I'd have to vacate for a while, but time just crept up on me and now I have no time and nowhere to go." Stormy's brown eyes began to well up with tears. Again. She had to get a hold of herself.

"Oh my . . ." Amy gasped, now staring at her with sympathy. "Is there any way they can give you more time?"

"Nope," she said as she carried a basket of dirty dishes into the kitchen. "I've just come to realize that it is what it is."

Amy shook her head. Thankfully, they were busy the rest of the afternoon, so Stormy didn't have much time to stress out over her living situation or her crappy job.

That also meant that Amy didn't get a chance to ask any more questions. The reality was that Stormy had zero clue what she was going to do next, so how could she give any answers?

CHAPTER NINE

Stormy's bus pulled up near her apartment building after her seemingly never-ending day. She dragged herself from it, then walked to her place and made her way into the lobby.

By the end of any day, her feet were trashed from standing for so many hours straight, so she normally took the elevator, but it was inevitable that fate continued working against her on a day as horrible as this. A large sign was taped to the metal doors: Out of Order.

Stormy trudged up the stairs with her giant purse in tow. As she was about to reach her floor, she began digging for her keys. Good coordination skills weren't one of Stormy's strong points—add a tired mind, and in true fashion, the strap slipped from her shoulder. Half the contents of her purse spilled out.

The sound of keys, makeup, and coins could be heard all the way to the bottom of the stairwell. Stormy dropped to her knees and began to sob. She'd had enough, and there was nothing that was going to hold it back.

When she heard a door open, and then someone moving down the stairs toward her, she tried pulling herself together, but she was just too tired. She looked down, hoping whoever it was just passed on by. The last thing she wanted to do was talk about why she was sobbing in the middle of a stairwell.

"What's the matter, darling?" Sherman asked, compassionately stopping next to her.

The sound of his warm voice made her lean back against the wall as she looked at him, trying desperately to still the tears. She opened her mouth to speak, but nothing came out.

"It can't be all that bad," he assured her as he patted her hand.

"I'm sorry," she said with a hiccup.

"Don't apologize, just tell me what's got you so upset," he said with the gentle smile she loved him for.

She'd been blessed to meet this man at one of the worst times in her life—a couple months after she'd lost her father. Sherman had been kind, and reminded her so much of her dad that she'd immediately latched on to him. Over the years, if too much time passed without seeing him, she had to go and seek him out. Then when she had lost her mother, Sherman had been the one to hold her.

"You're here late tonight," she finally said as she began to control her tears.

He was picking up items near where she sat and putting them back in her purse, which made her want to break out into sobs again, but she somehow managed to hold them back.

"I ended up visiting too long with Ms. Penny Little. Then the dang elevators broke again, so I had to talk myself into coming down all these stairs," he said with a chuckle.

"I'm sorry. I'll help you down them," she told him, glad to focus on him and not herself.

He gazed at her fondly for a moment. "This is why I appreciate you so much, young lady. Even though you're obviously having a bad day, you're still willing to help an old man out," he told her before shaking his head. "I know how badly your feet hurt at the end of a day, so I won't be responsible for you walking any extra steps."

Her heart warmed at his words. She wanted to be seen as a good person, as good as her parents had been, and she felt as if she were failing them every single day. She wasn't nearly as giving, as caring, as sacrificing as they'd been, so for a man she admired to tell her she was better than okay made her want to jump across the short distance between them and grab hold of him in a bear hug. She barely managed to refrain from doing just that.

"I like you, Sherman. You make me smile when I feel like crying."

"There shouldn't be anything in life that makes us sit and cry all alone," he told her while patting her shoulder. "Instead of giving up and plopping down in this dingy stairwell, tell me what's wrong and I'm sure we can find a solution."

Stormy struggled with whether or not to share her woes with him. It really was her own fault for allowing things to get so out of control. But as he sat there with an encouraging smile on his lips, she decided she really did need a friend to complain to. When she was done, maybe she wouldn't feel like the world was coming to an end.

"I'm losing my apartment, my boss thinks I'm a horrible employee, and everyone I meet seems to hate me—especially disgustingly attractive pilots who could at least have the courtesy to remember my face."

Sherman sat there quietly for a moment, and Stormy wondered if maybe she'd offered up too much information. Most likely she had, but then again, it wasn't as if he was going to go around blasting her secrets to the world.

"In life there are always trials. We don't necessarily understand why they happen, but eventually we see there's a reason for them. Sometimes everything has to go wrong before it can turn around and start going right," he said before pausing and looking at the contents of her purse still trailing down the stairs. Then he turned back to her and continued speaking.

"It will work out for the best sooner than you think. As clichéd as that might sound, it's true, and all you have to do is pick yourself up. I'll even loan you my cane if you'd like," Sherman said in his most gentle voice.

"You can never find that cane," she replied.

"Because then I'd have to admit I'm getting old."

She smiled. She also realized that he was right. She would get nowhere sitting on the stairs crying. She needed to gather her fallen items, go to her apartment, and start making plans. Her mother had always told her a person chose to feel sorry for him- or herself, and no matter how bad a day she might be having, she could guarantee someone, somewhere else was having a worse day.

"There's always tomorrow," she finally said. "I'm going to miss you, Sherman. You've always been so good to me."

"I really wouldn't worry about tomorrow yet, darling. Things are going to pan out for you—just you wait. But for now, you need to go on inside, have a nice cup of hot tea, and get some needed rest."

"I'm not doing that until I walk you down," she insisted.

"I already told you—" he began but she cut him off.

"I have a purse full of contents to collect anyway, some of which are probably at the bottom of these stairs," she said with a genuine smile.

He gave up the argument and took her arm as they stood and began descending. The amazing thing was that her feet stopped hurting as the two of them trekked back down several stories and toward the front door.

"You will not walk with me outside," Sherman insisted. "Never once in my days alive have I allowed a lady to go back to her home unescorted."

Stormy laughed for the first time that day and then leaned in and kissed his cheek. "Okay, I'll concede to at least that."

Sherman gave her a strong good-night hug and then disappeared through the door. Stormy made her way slowly back up the stairs, walked into her apartment, and closed the door, latching the chain behind her.

She decided to take Sherman's advice and let this horrible day go. Tomorrow had to be better. There was no possible way it could get worse.

Sherman walked inside his house and picked up the phone. Impatiently he stomped his foot as he waited for the call to be answered.

"Hey, Uncle."

"That's not a proper greeting, boy," Sherman told the young man.

"Sorry," Cooper replied, his chuckle clearly coming through the line. "Hello, Cooper Armstrong speaking. How might I help you?" His tone was almost serious.

"I'm too old to play around," Sherman scolded before changing his tone. "Now, the reason for the call . . . I need a favor . . ."

CHAPTER TEN

The commute to work was making her late again. Of course her bus would get stopped behind a traffic accident. And she couldn't afford another bank-account-draining cab ride.

But she wasn't nearly as stressed as the day before. Today, she was feeling a whole lot different about her predicament. After talking with Sherman, she was feeling more optimistic about life in general, and she was determined to face the unknown fate that awaited her—be it good or bad.

Finally, the bus arrived at Sea-Tac and Stormy rushed through security and up to her job, out of breath as she looked around for her boss. His beady eyes were thankfully focused on something in his miniscule office.

"Good morning," Amy said, with far too much joy for any human who wasn't a morning person. "How ya feeling today?"

"Better," Stormy answered while cracking a smile as she clocked in.

The airport was alive with activity, like a frantic ants' nest. People were coming and going from all over the world as they strolled through the terminals. Stormy thought that learning about people and their adventures to and from exotic destinations made working at an airport coffee shop much more interesting. See, she could look at things either positively or negatively. At least by looking at her recent life in a positive light, she was in a much better mood.

As she was making a fresh pot of house coffee, she was interrupted by the small bell on the counter.

"Good morning," Stormy said without turning.

Since she was so accustomed to the sound of the bell, there was no hesitation in her response. When she finally spun, expecting to see another typical passenger, she stopped in her tracks at the reflection of Captain Armstrong in the polished brass of the espresso machine.

Green Eyes.

Her nerve endings instantly began firing all at once as she felt the impeding confrontation. Without thinking, she darted in the direction of the back stockroom. Gosh dang it. All of that pep talk and at the first sight of Captain Armstrong, she'd panicked.

Chicken! She continued to scold herself even as he yelled after her.

"Does this mean you're not going to serve me today?" Cooper called out. She didn't notice him leaning over the counter to get a glimpse of where she'd disappeared to.

"I'll be r-right there," Stormy stuttered as she rounded the corner farther away from him.

What am I doing and why can't I just face this man? He's an ass, but he's no different than many other men. I can face him without panicking, she thought to herself as she wiped the sweat from her palms onto her apron.

Stormy brushed her brown hair behind her ears as she composed herself. Quickly taking several deep breaths, she squared her shoulders and prepared to come back out.

"Come on, I have a plane to catch," Captain Armstrong called while ringing the bell.

With one last deep breath, Stormy turned around and came back to the counter. She spoke as if nothing were wrong. "What can I get you today?" she said, while taking notice that Henry was out of his office chair and walking from his door to watch the transaction.

"I'd like my usual, please, and try not to force yourself to smile too much," Cooper said in a quiet tone with just the tiniest hint of tenderness. As he subtly smiled from the corner of his mouth, the slight impression of a dimple formed in his left cheek.

While wondering if he was actually concerned about her, Stormy almost felt like sharing with the guy. Damn, it had to be the eyes, she guessed. They seemed to tell her to trust him. Though, from personal experience, she knew that wasn't the case.

"I haven't exactly been in the most smiling kind of moods," she said with a false laugh. "Because of our little interaction a couple days ago, I might just lose my job."

He stood there, his smile slowly dropping. For just the briefest of moments, she was shocked to see that he might actually feel the tiniest bit bad. She wasn't sure how that made her feel. It was too much and it messed with her opinion of him.

She didn't like it.

"I don't know what to say. I . . . I'm sorry," he said, looking at a loss.

"Don't try to be sympathetic, Captain Armstrong. It's not your style," she said. Then she squared her shoulders again and got back to business. "I'm sorry, you said you wanted your usual? Was that with four shots?"

"Yes, doll. Glad you remembered."

She gritted her teeth, but she kept on making the drink and then handed it to him.

"Look, Stormy . . ." he began when an announcement came over the intercom.

"Captain Armstrong, please report to Gate A6. Captain Armstrong, A6."

He sighed as he looked at her. He opened his mouth as though he wanted to say something, and then he closed it again before giving her a look she couldn't quite interpret.

"I have to run," he finally said. He grabbed his coffee and took off as if the plane would start itself and leave without him if he didn't get there immediately.

Stormy was left hanging at the coffee counter without the slightest clue of what Captain Armstrong had been about to say. As she shook the confusion away, Stormy's eyes caught Amy's, and it became apparent that Amy had been observing the awkward transaction between the two of them while stealthily peering from the back room.

Stormy just shrugged her shoulders as if to say, *What can I do?*

At least he hadn't been nearly as rude as he'd been during their last interaction. However, it was becoming increasingly insulting that he still had no clue who she was.

CHAPTER ELEVEN

Trans Pacific Flight 232 had just arrived at the gate after a six-hour domestic flight from John F. Kennedy Airport to Sea-Tac. The jetliner happened to be running a bit behind schedule, and Cooper's co-pilot had the gate agent page him.

Captain Armstrong concluded that his life was always moving at Mach 10 as he sprinted through the terminal, having to adjust his hat from time to time to keep it on his head. It was a good thing that Cooper felt an intense need for speed at all times.

It was why he still flew the jets. He didn't have to, was constantly told not to since he was the CEO of the airline. Though his actual role wasn't something that too many people who worked for him knew about.

He'd learned his lesson that night six years before when his father had passed. He didn't want to be the man flashing wads of cash and expensive toys when so many in the world struggled. Besides, by flashing so much money around, he seemed to attract the piranhas, who then only annoyed the hell out of him.

Now, that didn't mean he didn't like his possessions. He liked them plenty. It just meant that he tried to maintain a semblance of normalcy once in a while. And flying gave him both satisfaction and the rush he looked forward to every time he was responsible for a plane full of passengers.

Their lives were in his hands. It didn't get more thrilling than being at thirty-five thousand feet in the sky while going five hundred knots per hour.

Cooper almost plowed over a family pushing a double-wide stroller and decided he needed to get out of his own head before he crushed someone or tripped over a laptop cord. He wouldn't be flying anywhere with broken bones.

He wasn't even late. *Dang copilots and their panic.* Oh well. It was probably wise that he'd left the coffee place when he did.

Although Cooper could pilot some of the world's largest and most sophisticated airliners, he still couldn't comprehend the sometimes unfathomable complexities of a woman's mind. He said what he wanted and that usually tended to be enough.

And in Stormy's case, she seemed so familiar to him. He didn't know what it was, but he was drawn to her. Maybe it was because she was stunning. And it probably had something to do with the fact that she actually had a witty intellect, something most of the attractive women he dated didn't have a clue about. He was getting real bored with airheaded bimbos, not that he'd admit that out loud.

For some unknown reason, Cooper was determined to show Stormy he was a good guy the next time he saw her. She had to be thinking he was a real asshole by this point, which he somewhat deserved.

He'd pushed about every button he could to see her fiery temper come to the forefront. She looked that much more stunning with her cheeks flushed and her eyes flashing fire, so he couldn't seem to help himself.

As he approached his departure gate, he continued pondering Stormy. He just couldn't seem to comprehend how she was so oblivious to his charm. He knew he was a bit arrogant, but when women were constantly falling at his feet, it was a bit tough not to be. He'd never before had to take so much time to work a girl.

Okay, seeing her twice might not seem like a lot of time to the average person, but normally it took him a total of five minutes to entice a lady. He smiled distractedly, stopping a passing traveler in her tracks. He didn't even notice. This was just the typical response he got from the opposite sex.

Cooper figured Stormy had to either be younger than he thought she was or just a prude. It was impossible to *not* like him. The thought was absurd.

He could admit, though, that maybe his sarcasm wasn't charming her. He had, unintentionally of course, almost gotten her fired, then he'd walked away as if he didn't give a damn. That wasn't the best seduction technique he'd ever employed.

He brushed off the last of his negative thoughts. It wasn't too late to rectify the situation. He'd just bombard her with his full arsenal of charm and she'd be a goner within a day—two at most.

One more visit and she'd be panting at his feet. His smile grew as he arrived at his departure gate. He lifted the lanyard from under his suit jacket, displaying his airline ID card to the attending gate agent.

"We've been waiting, sir," The woman stated in a harsh tone as she motioned for Captain Armstrong to proceed down the Jetway.

"Sorry, I'll be quick. Give me three minutes and you can start boarding," he responded as he walked past her and down the tight hallway to begin prepping his aircraft for departure.

Cooper rounded the corner and entered the galley with a new optimism in his step. He flung open the flight deck door and, to his surprise, saw Wolf sitting in the copilot's seat and going over the checklists.

Wolf turned to look at who'd walked in. "Nice of you to join us," he sarcastically greeted Cooper before turning back to what he was doing.

"I was buying coffee since I figured you were busy getting another speeding ticket," Cooper responded to his friend with equal sarcasm, always willing to poke a sleeping bear.

"Yeah, not all that funny . . . that was a three-hundred-dollar car race that I can't afford right now."

Cooper plopped himself in the captain's seat. "Oh, you big baby, I'll pay your ticket. Quit being a sore loser."

"It's not the damn ticket. You know I can pay that without blinking. It's the mark on my record," Wolf grumbled.

"Then be more aware," Cooper told him.

Wolf's annoyance level with Cooper was now even more apparent. But then Wolf's expression turned from annoyance to a smirk. "I did beat you after all, so I suppose it would only be reasonable for you to pay the ticket . . . *and* my car insurance for the next two years!"

Cooper shook his head while flipping a few switches on the overhead control panel as the two shared a laugh.

Cooper wished women could get over petty annoyances as easily as men did. Men didn't hold grudges and carry on for hours, having to talk about their feelings and why something happened. Hell, it was better left unsaid, in his humble opinion.

He sat back and started buckling in, suddenly looking forward to a flight he'd done a thousand times. He was *really* looking forward to his next round of coffee with a certain spunky barista.

The flight began to board and the flight crew focused on their typical preflight checks. A group of attendants was in the main cabin, busily guiding passengers to their proper seat assignments and assisting with carry-on bags.

Meanwhile, on the flight deck the sound of radio traffic and the hum of electronics combined with the chatty flight attendants and boarding passengers was almost deafening. The plane wasn't scheduled to return to New York, but was heading to El Paso, Texas, for a quick turnaround and would be back in Seattle by nine thirty that night.

As Wolf began to read off the checklist, his voice grew fainter as Cooper became entwined in his own thoughts about the coffee woman again, which infuriated him.

"Enough of this!" he blurted out loud, completely out of context with what Wolf had been saying.

The man was in the middle of conducting the first officer's pre-takeoff checklist and Cooper was fully ignoring him. Wolf looked at him with confusion.

"What, thirty-five thousand isn't high enough?" Wolf asked in an alarmed voice.

"No, no . . . thirty-five thousand is fine. Sorry, my mind was wandering."

He reached into his pocket and his fingers rubbed over the worn gold of the locket he carried with him every flight. It had been his good luck token for six years. Odd that he was reaching for it so much more often lately.

"Hey, I'm looking for the flight manual," Wolf continued.

"Oh, that's no problem. I have it right here in my flight bag . . . shit." Cooper paused. "I left my bag at the coffee shop. I have to go get it," he exclaimed as he quickly stumbled from his seat and out of the flight deck.

"What about . . . ?" Wolf stopped mid-sentence as Armstrong had already left.

He never did anything as foolish as losing his flight bag. This was the exact reason for him to quit obsessing about the damn brunette at the coffee shop. Now it was messing with his job.

CHAPTER TWELVE

Putting away a container of milk, Stormy turned and something caught her eye. Right in front of the counter sat a large black leather briefcase with *Captain Armstrong, Trans Pacific Airways* printed in bold letters on the side.

She knew it was important, and if she didn't get it to him the flight could be delayed. She grabbed the bag and began to sprint for Gate A6, the one he'd been directed to over the intercom earlier.

"I'll be right back!" she called to Amy and Henry as she bolted past the counter and out to the main corridor.

Her heart beating madly, she made her way toward the gate. She wasn't sure if it was because she was running, or if it was because she was going to see Cooper again. If it was the latter, she was in more trouble than she'd thought.

While frantically heading toward Captain Armstrong's gate, Stormy's mind wandered as she imagined him thanking her in all sorts of ways for saving his flight.

She moved quickly through the crowd.

Gate A7 . . . Gate A8 . . . There it is!

"Gate A6!" she blurted as she rounded the corner to the Trans Pacific corridor.

Suddenly she found herself in an area of the airport unlike the familiar sight and scent of a Sea-Tac coffee shop. The walls were adorned with Trans Pacific logos, big blue letters embossed with red and gold. The employees were dressed to the nines in their sharp uniforms. She shifted uncomfortably, feeling utterly out of place.

"I'm . . . looking . . . for . . . Captain . . . Armstrong," Stormy wheezed, straining to get the words out with what little breath she had left to speak to the gate agent standing behind the podium.

Before the agent could respond, Stormy heard a deep voice behind her.

"I'll take that off your hands." Stormy turned around to see the man of the hour standing with his coat hanging over his shoulder and a smile on his face.

"I thought this might be one of those 'don't forget' type of things," she responded, still out of breath with her bangs lightly sweeping across her forehead, drawing attention to the tiny beads of sweat forming beneath them.

It was hard for her to hide her sense of accomplishment. She smiled brightly, the gaze of her eyes betraying the secrets of her ridiculous crush on the man who didn't deserve her attention.

"Yes, I would get in just a bit of trouble for leaving it behind," he told her.

Dang it. She really needed to get herself a little more under control. Trying to adjust her breathing, she realized there was no more reason to keep standing there with this man.

"Well, you have your bag," she began as she took a step back. "I better get back to work now . . ." The sentence trailed off.

"Thank you. I'm sorry I pulled you away from the coffee shop," he said. "Is there anything I can do for you in return?"

Well, you can work your magic with that magnificent tongue of yours . . . That wasn't what she said out loud.

"No, of course not. I'm just doing the best I can in my *customer service* job," she said with a hint of sarcasm.

"I do appreciate good customer service," he said with a laugh as he leaned toward her. Like a magnet, she felt herself wanting to touch him. It took a lot of willpower to stop.

His eyes narrowed, and she could feel the waves of pheromones coming off the man. If only she didn't have firsthand knowledge of what it was like when he sank deep inside her body . . . A shudder ripped through her as she moistened her dry lips. The action drew his gaze to her mouth, which made her moisten her lips again. She swore she heard a growl escape his throat, but she wouldn't bet money on it. She had to be mistaken.

It looked as if Cooper was about to speak again, but then a gate agent abruptly interrupted the conversation. "Captain, we need you on board now if we're going to get this flight out on time. We need to close the door."

Just short of shoving, the gate agent ushered Cooper through the Jetway door and slammed it shut behind him. Stormy found herself standing there looking at the empty doorway.

Turn around, she commanded herself. *What the hell?*

Looking down at Stormy over her purple reading glasses while pecking away at her keyboard, the gate agent said, "Sorry, sugar, someone has to keep this airline running like clockwork. My name's Meredith, by the way. Fifteen years I've seen love find its wings in this terminal. Don't worry, he'll be back about nine tonight, Gate A3."

Meredith was an attractive woman, somewhere between the ages of forty and fifty. She had a no-nonsense aura about her, but also projected the nurturing of a mother, in tune to everyone and everything around her.

"Nice to meet you, Meredith. I'm Stormy." She spoke softly and was clearly embarrassed. It was as though Meredith had been reading her thoughts since she arrived at the gate.

She hadn't realized she was that obvious. She really hoped she hadn't come across as desperate. "I'm not looking for love and I'm definitely not taking any flights with the captain," Stormy finished as she smiled and then turned to walk back to the coffee shop.

"*Mmm-hmm*, you watch yourself with those flyboys. If you're looking for something other than rolling around in the hay, it's best you stay clear of this terminal." Meredith giggled and shook her head as she continued to feverishly peck away at her keyboard. Stormy chose to ignore the comment and continued walking away.

As she made her way back to the shop and began her daily duties all over again, her mind was in a fog. She couldn't figure out what exactly had happened. Had her normally sarcastic customer suddenly turned soft? And what did it matter to her anyway?

She was sure he simply felt responsible because of almost getting her fired, but why the sudden turnaround?

"You won't believe what happened," Stormy uttered with excitement the first chance she got to speak to Amy.

"What is it?"

"He was nice today. I mean *really* nice! I'm sure I'm mistaking his intentions, and there's more to the story than I'm willing to share at the moment, but it was sort of an okay feeling to have him act like a normal guy instead of a pompous baboon."

"Yeah, they sometimes get extra nice when they think there's a chance they're about to close the deal," her friend warned.

That took a bit of her happiness away because Stormy realized Amy was probably right. Stormy had been a bit starry-eyed today and the good captain couldn't have missed it. Dang it. It would have been nice to enjoy her five seconds of happiness.

Their conversation got interrupted when customers began appearing. The sound of the espresso machine steaming milk and the sudden rush of patrons effectively put an end to the discussion, and the two women found themselves constantly busy.

The day continued, and it seemed that due to delayed flights, the flow of passengers would never end. Stormy was serving coffee after coffee, mocha after mocha, and it felt like two o'clock couldn't come soon enough.

Just as the last customer in line was being served and Stormy began cleaning up, a familiar voice was heard over the sound of running water.

"Stormy, we're slammed with these delayed flights, we need you to stay until nine." It was Henry.

"I have to go home early. I have an appointment."

Stormy's initial reaction was frustration with the thought of the day's drudgery lasting even longer. No sooner did her heart sink with disappointment, though, than it dawned on her that she might just have a chance to get a glimpse of Cooper again if she were there. Before she could change her mind though, Henry spoke.

"You can leave," he said with a snap. "But then leave your badge and uniform." He turned and walked away, assuming she was going to do what he wanted.

His actions made her want to quit right there on the spot. He didn't have the right to tell her she must work a double or get the heck out of there. Damn, it would be nice when the day came that she could tell this man to shove his job where the sun didn't shine.

The rest of the day really did pass in a blur, though, and she even found herself jotting out a new ring design on a napkin during her lunch break, but even so Stormy was soon dead on her feet. When it was coming close to closing time, a particularly nasty passenger who had missed his flight came into the place.

"Give me a triple shot mocha and make it hot."

"Would you like room for cream?" she asked, barely even able to stand at this point, let alone smile.

"Did I ask for cream?" he snapped.

"No, sir," she responded through gritted teeth.

"Then just do your menial job and make my damn coffee," he said, looking down at his phone and furiously typing something on the screen.

Though it took all of Stormy's final bits of patience, she made the coffee and pushed it across the counter toward the man. He picked it up and then felt the steaming cup for a moment before setting it back down and ripping off the lid.

"Does this feel hot to you?" he yelled, making her jump.

"I'm sorry if it isn't hot enough. I can steam it more," she said, though steam was pouring off the drink.

"Feel it," he demanded and reached for her hand.

That was Stormy's breaking point. Ripping her arm back before the man could touch her, she accidently hit the cup and knocked it on its side, the hot liquid splashing all over her angry customer.

"What the hell!" he screeched, jumping back.

"Seems pretty hot," Stormy muttered before she thought that might not be the best thing to say.

"I want your manager right now," he hollered.

If Stormy had the energy to care, she might have realized the mess she was in. But as Henry came out, profusely apologizing to the man, then stepping in and remaking his drink for free and giving him just about anything he wanted, she simply stood there and waited.

When he was finished, Stormy stood back and began taking off her apron. It didn't matter if the incident wasn't her fault, didn't matter if the customer wasn't always right. Henry wouldn't see it that way.

When the man exited their business she turned and looked at Henry, who was glowering at her.

"I know, I know," she said, too tired to even care. "I'm fired."

Henry seemed a bit disappointed he hadn't been able to say the words. But he didn't stop her from handing over her badge, keys, and apron.

So much for this day being the best one possible.

Refusing to let it get her down too badly, she turned and walked away from the job that hadn't been her best one ever, but hadn't been the worst either. Now, she had to hit the streets all over again.

At least she was too damn tired to care.

When her phone rang as she left the terminal, she considered throwing it beneath one of the many busses passing by, but then a smile lifted her lips when she saw who it was.

"Miracles do happen. The too-busy-to-ever-call-her-best-friend woman is answering her phone," Lindsey grumbled with zero greeting.

Stormy laughed.

"I've been in a funk lately and not fit to socialize with anyone," Stormy said by way of apology.

"I'm not just anyone. I'm your bestie, so no matter how bad the funk, you always, and I mean *always*, talk to me," Lindsey insisted.

"I know. How's the move going?"

"It's heaven," Lindsey said, but Stormy could hear something in her voice.

"What is it?" Stormy demanded.

"Mike's place is tiny. I mean *tiny* with a capital T . . . or should I say small T. I don't know why I agreed to this."

"Because you love him," Stormy pointed out.

"Yes, I guess . . ."

"Okay, we need to get together soon. You're worrying me, Lins," Stormy said.

"I'm good. I promise. Now, let's talk about you," Lindsey insisted.

Stormy chatted with her best friend while she rode the bus home. She didn't tell her she was being kicked from her apartment because that would upset her and she would insist on Stormy coming to her place. There was no way Stormy was going to share a postage-size apartment with the two new lovers.

Besides, Stormy would figure it out. She always did. Even if she had gotten knocked down more times than she cared to admit. The ending result wouldn't be her dream situation, but it would eventually work out and she'd survive.

CHAPTER THIRTEEN

His limbs practically twitching as he walked down the Jetway, Cooper had to stop himself from running as one of the flight attendants chatted away about her plans for the weekend.

He'd been in the plane for the past five hours after a ten-hour day. He was pushing the max time allowed and he was ready to blow off some steam. He sure as hell hoped his brother was up for a round at the gym. Last time they'd boxed, Maverick had gotten in a lucky shot, giving him a bloody nose.

It was payback time.

With flight bags in tow, Cooper walked toward the exit. As he turned a corner, he glanced up and noticed Stormy moving down the concourse ahead of him.

His weariness faded when he realized she was still in the building. Before he was able to try to chase her down, his phone rang for the third time in three minutes. Whoever was trying to get ahold of him was being obscenely insistent.

It must be important. If not the person was going to get chewed.

Stopping, he dug out his phone and answered. "What?"

He wasn't going to try to pretend to be pleasant when the person on the other end was most certainly interrupting him.

"Is that any way to answer your phone, young man? We've talked about this before."

"Sorry, Uncle. I've just had a long day. Can I call you back later?" Cooper asked, looking back down the terminal but having lost sight of Stormy already.

The phone call didn't really matter then, did it? He'd never find her now. But why in the world would he even want to in the first place? It wasn't as if it would be smart for him to try to get involved with her. Especially now, since he'd finally agreed to go out with Wolf's cousin.

"I was just making sure you're home day after tomorrow. We're going to be bringing the family friend to your place," Sherman reminded him.

"I thought we hadn't finished this discussion," Cooper said, instantly irritated.

"Yes, we did yesterday, and you agreed when I asked for the favor," Sherman reminded his nephew.

"You know I don't like strangers at my place," Cooper told him.

"You're hardly even there. It will be good to have a trustworthy person on your property to keep an eye on things," Sherman scolded. "Besides, it's a guesthouse. You won't even know they're around."

"I've heard the speech before," Cooper told his uncle.

"Well then, I won't have to keep on with the lecture," Sherman answered right back.

"This will only be a couple weeks, Sherman," Cooper warned. "I mean it. No stretching it out."

"It's only until your mother finishes with her guesthouse remodeling, then the friend can go there," Sherman assured him.

For some reason Cooper wasn't feeling all that assured.

"I don't want any sob stories at the end of this about how Mom's place isn't ready. If it's not, then one of my siblings can take over having a house pet—I mean guest," Cooper told him.

"Dang, Cooper, you're in a bear of a mood tonight," Sherman said.

"Yes, I am. I've had delays all day, and I need to blow off some steam," Cooper said.

"Then I won't hold you up any longer. Take it easy, kid. It's okay to have some time off, especially when you own the company."

"Would you sit back in an office with your feet on solid ground if you could fly?" Cooper challenged.

"No, of course not," Sherman conceded.

"Well, I can't quit flying either. I do this because I love it, not because I have to," Cooper said for what felt like the hundredth time.

"I know, kiddo. But you could cut back," Sherman said.

"Yeah. I might agree to do that," he said with a chuckle. He could always fly his private jet. She was a beauty.

The two hung up, and even though Cooper knew the chances of seeing Stormy again were pretty low, he still rushed from the building and looked around outside. Hadn't he just told himself it was pointless?

Surprisingly, he did spot her, but it was too late. She was getting on a bus, leaving the airport. The entire walk back to his car, he couldn't shake his disappointment at missing her. He hadn't actually gone on a date yet with Wolf's cousin so he wasn't committed or anything.

Maybe he would just ask Stormy out on a date, take her to bed, and then get over his odd obsession. Maybe this was all because she felt like someone he knew, or should know.

His fingers rubbed once more against the locket in his pocket before digging out his car keys.

One thing Cooper knew about himself was when to fight his feelings and when not to. If the obsession was still running through his brain in a couple of days, he was certainly going to do something about it.

That settled, he sat down, turned his key, and pressed his foot against the gas and smiled as the motor purred.

CHAPTER FOURTEEN

Leaning her head against the window, Stormy decided there were much better things to do in a day than apartment and job hunt. She was exhausted, hungry, and trying desperately to be positive and not feel that her life was going downhill fast with the brakes severed.

The bus stopped a block from her apartment and she slowly stepped off and then threw her bag over her shoulder and began moving toward home. She passed the park, and though it was late, she automatically looked toward the bench Sherman often sat at when he left the café.

When he wasn't there, she felt the smallest bit of disappointment. She was exhausted and really should want nothing more than to get to her apartment, hopefully by elevator, and then go straight to bed. But she was also sad and would love to talk to Sherman, knowing she'd surely feel better. It was late, though, and the chances of him being at the café were low.

"Are you going to just pass on by without a hello?"

Sherman's voice startled her out of her reverie, and she looked over at the corner table, seeing him sitting there in the darkest spot, a cigar in his hand, and a smile on his lips.

"I didn't expect you to be out this late," she told him, moving to the warmth of the outside heater.

"You know I can't go home too early. Then I'd fall asleep and miss my late-night show," he told her. "Come on over here and keep me company while I smoke this cigar my buddy Joseph gave me."

Though Stormy was exhausted, she was more than happy to do what he asked. "I've always loved the smell of a good cigar," she told him.

"Yes, it's one of my last few vices," he said. "And the waitresses leave me alone to smoke them out here as long as no other customers complain. Now, take a load off and let me run inside and get you a soothing cup of tea."

"You don't need to do that," she said, but he had already put down his cigar and was moving toward the front door.

Stormy waited a few minutes, and then Sherman was back with a tray holding a teapot, a cup, and some cream, honey, and sugar. She quickly fixed herself a cup.

"Thank you," she said as she held the warmth between her fingers while taking calming sips of the sweet brew.

"I love the company," he assured her. "How was your day out on the town? It seemed to be a long one," he said.

Stormy sighed. "It hasn't been the best couple of days. I have to be out of my apartment in two more days, still with no prospects, and I was fired from my job yesterday because of a horrible customer. I spent all day searching for a place and a new job and came up with zilch."

"Ah, sweetie, that job was beneath you anyway," Sherman said as he patted her leg.

"I really should have finished school. But then my dad . . ." she trailed off, not wanting to think about that horrible time in her life. Instead, she sat there finishing her cup of tea and quickly refilling it to keep warm while she doodled on the napkin in front of her, effortlessly creating a pattern of star-studded dangly earrings.

"You're young, Stormy. You have plenty of time to figure it all out," he told her before leaning in and checking out her design.

She folded the napkin and put it away, instantly embarrassed.

"What is that you're trying to hide from me?" he questioned.

"Oh, it's nothing. I waste a lot of time doodling when I should be being more productive," she said with a laugh.

"It didn't look like a waste of time. It looked beautiful," Sherman said.

Her cheeks flushed at the praise, but she wanted the subject changed.

"This hasn't been the best week and I am trying to get back on my feet, but it seems every time I start to rise, my feet are getting kicked out from under me again," she told him.

He eyed her for a minute and then thankfully let the matter of her sketching patterns drop.

"There's always a bright side, darling, to everything. Sometimes the journey to get to the light just takes a bit longer than at other times."

"I love that you always look for the rainbow in the middle of the storm," she said. "I'm already feeling like I can stand again."

And unbelievably she *was* feeling better. All it had taken was sitting there and drinking tea with Sherman while he puffed on his cigar. Maybe it was a special herbal blend that was soothing her nerves. Whatever it was, she was grateful he'd been there.

"I think I might have a solution to one of your problems, Stormy," Sherman suddenly said.

"I didn't come here for you to try to fix things, Sherman. Just talking with you has made me feel better," she said as she leaned over and patted his free hand.

"I know you don't like to ask for help, but I have connections, young lady, and it would be a real insult to me if you didn't accept what I'm offering," he said more sternly than she'd ever heard him speak before.

"Well, I guess I can at least hear you out," she told him.

Stormy was sure she wouldn't be accepting whatever it was he planned on offering. She couldn't take advantage of their friendship.

"I know of a great little two-bedroom cottage that's sitting all empty and alone," he said, making her heart thump. This might be something she wouldn't mind accepting if it were affordable.

"I'm listening," she said. What if it were truly great, though, and just outside her budget? That wouldn't end her day on a positive note.

"It's a beautiful place with sweeping views of Puget Sound, all the fog your heart could ever desire. The cottage sits on the property of my relative, and the house is just up the hill so you wouldn't feel as if you were in the middle of nowhere, but you'll also have privacy," he said. "And it's all yours, if you want it."

The idea of living right on the water in a place where no neighbors were pounding against her walls was a dream she'd never imagined coming true. But as all dreams had a tendency of shattering when you opened your eyes, she was leery. There would be no way for her to afford such a wonderful place.

"I guess the big question is how much does the person want for rent? I don't have a terribly large rent budget, Sherman. There's not a lot I can afford." Stormy refused to make eye contact as she told him this.

She hated talking money with people, especially someone like Sherman. No, he didn't flash his money around, but she knew he was far from poor. She didn't know what exactly he had, but she was sure it was enough to never have to want for anything.

"I think this just might be in your price range, Stormy. The person who owns the property is gone a whole lot and has finally figured out that it's better not to leave the grounds unattended," Sherman said. "And with you about to be homeless, it works out best for all parties concerned. As a matter of fact, there's no rent. You would just take care of the house, make sure no one is coming in when the owner is gone, and maybe stock up on some supplies for when they are back."

She looked at him with suspicion.

"This seems a lot like a handout to me, Sherman," she told him.

With innocence shining in his eyes, he held up his hands in surrender. "It's nothing like that, I swear," he promised her.

She still wasn't sure about this. Things that were too good to be true had a tendency to come back and bite her on the ass.

"Who's this home owner?"

"It's my nephew. He really isn't home much at all and you probably won't even see him—which is why he needs someone living in the guest cottage. But at least I can vouch that your landlord is an upstanding citizen." Sherman told her.

"Oh. I don't know why, but I just assumed the owner was a woman," Stormy said, unsure if she wanted to live so close to a man, even a man related to Mr. Sherman.

It wasn't that she was a man-hater or anything, but wouldn't people talk if she moved to his property, make assumptions of who she was and what she was doing there? It mattered to her what people thought about her, though she knew that was stupid. They weren't living in the olden days.

"I assure you my nephew is utterly harmless," Mr. Sherman said with a laugh.

"I wasn't thinking anything other than that," she quickly said. "It's just that people . . ." She trailed off. She knew her reasoning shouldn't be uttered aloud. He didn't comment, but continued to prod her for an answer instead.

"How about it, Stormy? Help ease my conscience and take this one favor. If you hate living there, you can always move when you have a little bit saved up," he told her.

Was this charity? Maybe, but he really *wanted* to do it, so that made it okay, didn't it?

"That's a good point," she said. She wanted to say yes so badly, but still . . .

"You're a kind soul, Stormy, and I wish you'd allow me to do more for you," he told her, again patting her hand.

Stormy was speechless at his generosity. She was torn over what to do. She certainly didn't want to be a charity case, but it sounded like this was legitimate. Besides, it wasn't like she had a whole heck of a lot of options in front of her. She was going to be homeless in less than forty-eight hours if she didn't accept this.

"All right, I'll take the place, but *only* if I'm not going to be a burden, and if your nephew lets me know, with a proper amount of time to move, if our arrangement isn't working for him," she said.

"It's a big piece of land. I really don't see any problems occurring, but if it makes you feel better, we can write something up," Sherman said with a smile, handing her a piece of paper with the address on it. "Here's the key."

"You were pretty sure I was going to do this then," she said as she laughed, holding the address and the key for a moment before putting them in her pocket.

She wanted to laugh and cry at the same time. This man was her guardian angel.

"Do you need help with moving?" Sherman asked, kind enough not to comment about how quickly she had caved.

"No. I already spoke to my coworker, and she has an old, roomy Volvo to help me. There really isn't all that much to move," she told him.

"That's good, but promise to call me if you need help," he insisted.

"I will, Sherman," she said, suddenly choking up. "You have to promise me we aren't going to lose touch because I'm going to really miss you," Stormy said before standing up and then reaching out and giving him a warm embrace.

"Well, my dear, I'll miss you, too, but this change will be good for you. Just be sure and take care of yourself," he said, sounding slightly choked up himself. That had to be her imagination though. "And yes, we will see each other often. Someone has to make sure my nephews behave so I come out there weekly. Now, you have a big day ahead of you tomorrow, and my old bones need some rest."

He looked down and glanced at his watch before his eyes widened. "My golly, it's going to be nearly midnight by the time I get home. I should get going, and so should you, lest you turn into a pumpkin. Or maybe it's the motor coach that turns into the pumpkin. In either case, Cinderella, this old dog needs to get going." Sherman patted Stormy on the back; her arms were still wrapped around him like a child who wouldn't let go.

"Thank you again. Good night, Sherman." With that, the two squeezed each other one last time and then Stormy rushed off toward home while he watched her safely cross the street.

There was now an extra spring in her step as she looked forward to her upcoming move. She was going to have trouble getting to sleep, even though she was exhausted down to her very bones. But she was moving to a real house, and things were now most certainly looking up.

CHAPTER FIFTEEN

The two men stomped through the trimmed grass in their newly purchased black clothes, hoods over their heads, thinking they were being quiet, but their steps and voices could probably be heard two blocks away.

"Quiet down or we're going to get busted," Sherman whispered in anything but a quiet tone.

"I am being quiet. You're the one making all the noise," Joseph responded, excitement clear in his voice.

"I can't believe we're doing this," Sherman said with the tiniest hint of an apology in his words.

"If you're going to be a proper meddler, then you have to do what has to be done," Joseph told his friend as they stopped in front of the quaint cottage.

"Such a shame, though," Sherman said, but his lips were turned up in anticipation.

"Do you have the wrench?"

"Of course I have the wrench, Joseph," Sherman told him with a roll of his eyes.

"Where is Cooper off to this time?" Joseph asked as Sherman took out his key and opened the cottage door.

"I think Atlanta. All I know is he's gone," Sherman assured Joseph.

The two men stepped inside the quaint cabin and went over to the kitchen sink, then slowly sat in front of it after opening the cupboards.

"What do we do now?" Joseph asked as he looked at the pipe and then at Sherman.

"We just undo this bolt right here and turn on the water," Sherman said with glee.

"Well, get on it before someone comes and busts us," Joseph said as he rubbed his hands together. "And make it look like a faulty bolt."

"I know what I'm doing," Sherman grumbled before he slowly bent and began undoing the pipe. "Damn this old body. I used to be able to get up and down so fast." He cursed as his knuckle hit the pipe and instantly bruised. "Got it!"

With triumph, the two men stood, helping each other up as they turned the faucet on, not too high, but enough to flood the floors.

When water began dribbling out of the cupboard, the men high-fived and then quickly made their exit from the cottage.

Safely back in their car, they needed to brag of their deed to someone, so they called their good buddy Martin who was having his own matchmaking delights in Montana. The man, of course, was jealous of their masterminding tactics.

"Tomorrow will be a good day," Sherman told Joseph.

"I only wish we could be there to see Cooper and Stormy together," Joseph pouted.

"Oh, we will, my friend . . . at the wedding," Sherman said with a confident grin.

With a smile, they drove off. Anyone who might say they'd lost their touch in their old age certainly didn't know the men well at all. They were in the primes of their lives as far as they were concerned.

CHAPTER SIXTEEN

As promised, Amy arrived at Stormy's apartment bright and early the next morning. Stormy's spartan lifestyle offered little resistance to the big move.

Her low-income life had ingrained in her the ideals of simple living. She kept possessions to a minimum, not out of some obedience to a pious and minimalist lifestyle, but more out of the necessity of tight spaces. Not only that, but until she'd been ten, her parents had dragged her all around the world, so packing had to be kept to a minimum.

The largest and most difficult of Stormy's items was her futon, which was used exclusively as a bed. In fact, this was Stormy's only piece of furniture, aside from her milk crate nightstand.

"I hate this old thing. It's not the most comfortable, and I'm more than ready to leave it behind," Stormy said with a smile. "I'm moving into a cottage, so even if it isn't furnished, which I forgot to ask Sherman about, I'm sure it has soft, plush carpet."

"Smart thinking, but the rich people like their decorating, so you probably will have one of those Monarch Vispring beds with something like three thousand springs in it."

"I've never heard of that," Stormy said.

"Yeah, cause it's priced at about fifty thousand bucks," Amy told her.

"For fifty thousand bucks, the dang bed better massage me, bathe me, and tuck me in for a good night's rest," Stormy told her.

"No. That's what the master of the house is for," Amy said with a wink.

"I guarantee you there's no way *that's* gonna happen," Stormy said emphatically.

Amy gave her a look that said she didn't believe her, but at least she let the subject drop.

After the last of her items were loaded into Amy's full car, the two women climbed inside and drove off, bound for Gig Harbor.

The drive was typical for Seattle, traffic was bumper to bumper, but they soon found themselves crossing the straits of Puget Sound on the Tacoma Narrows Bridge. *The point of no return*, Stormy thought to herself as she started running over the items she might have left behind. Her mind was eased knowing that she'd taken all that was important to her and anything left wouldn't have mattered anyway.

The bridge ended with the entrance to the quaint neighboring town of Gig Harbor. This once bustling fishing and boat-building community now existed as more of a tourist attraction. People from all parts of the Northwest came to enjoy the small shops and attractive parks that adorned the area.

As she and Amy passed through the small streets, lined with various shops and seafood eateries, Stormy looked upon the busy marina, which was bustling with small sailing ships and some rather nice seagoing yachts.

The drive through town didn't take long as Gig Harbor's population of a little over seven thousand people was only spread over an area of about one hundred square miles.

"What was the address?" Amy asked as they rounded the corner onto Goodman Place.

Stormy didn't respond as she rolled down the window, allowing the crisp sea breeze to blow in. Her eyes were hidden behind a black pair of cheap sunglasses, her brown hair flowing around her face as she inhaled deeply. Her focus and gaze were trained on the surroundings and all the houses lining the streets.

The homes ranged from older two-story Victorians to modern family dwellings, some even passing as mansions, all with immaculately landscaped yards and varying yard art, including some beautiful fountains.

She'd always imagined living in such a place, settling down, and establishing roots. A life of travel had been her parents' dream, not hers, and she could picture herself in a community like this one, getting married and having children.

She could imagine herself strolling down the sidewalk with a toddler at her heels and a baby in a carriage in front of her. Not far behind them would be their puppy, a beautiful golden retriever.

With a jolt to her system, Stormy pulled herself from those thoughts. What was she thinking? She was in no way ready or wanting a family yet. She had to take care of herself first before she could even think about settling down and raising a family.

She didn't even have a boyfriend, let alone any money in her bank account. It wouldn't do her any good to have kids when she couldn't afford to clothe, feed, or diaper them.

"The address!" Amy called as she waved her hand in front of Stormy's face to break the enchanted spell that had her staring. "Hello?"

"Oh right, the address," Stormy responded while she pulled out the piece of paper Sherman had given her. "7200 Goodman Place," Stormy said. "Right over there."

They pulled up to an ornate gate with a keypad next to it.

"Whoa! This guy lives alone?" Amy questioned as she pulled up to the gate. They could see the highest peak of the roof at the end of a tree-lined driveway. "It's really . . . nice—nicer than I was expecting."

Stormy opened the car door and stood in amazement at the sheer size of the property, and she wasn't even inside the gate yet. She didn't have a response to her friend, so she said nothing. She was very intimidated, to tell the truth.

"Do you have the code?" Amy asked.

"I, uh, I don't know. I didn't know there was a gate." Stormy fumbled in her pocket for the piece of paper Sherman had given her. Quickly glancing at it, she found a six-digit code. "Try this."

Amy put in the code and the gates quietly slid open. Both girls just stood there and stared for a while before jumping back in the car and silently making their way down the gorgeous stone driveway.

They pulled in front of the main home. The place was intimidating with its towers rising high into the air and the rockwork stretching endlessly on both sides.

"Where is the cottage?" Amy asked.

"I think we need to keep driving down the road. It curves next to the house," Stormy told her.

This was a very bad idea. A very, very bad idea.

Before they went anywhere, Stormy's phone rang. She looked down and saw it was Sherman calling. Maybe he was going to tell her this wasn't going to work out after all. She wasn't sure she'd be upset about that because whoever owned this place would surely know she was an outcast.

"Hello," she said, her voice barely above a whisper.

"Stormy, darling. I hope I caught you before you arrived at the place," Sherman said, his voice echoing a bit.

"I can't hear you real well," she told him, pushing the phone tighter against her ear.

"I'm driving with the windows down. One minute, darling." He paused and closed them. "There, is that better?"

"Yes, much," she said, her eyes still taking in the sight of the mansion before her.

"Good, good. Did I catch you in time?"

"We just pulled up," she said, her voice shaking slightly. "Sherman, I'm not so sure about this . . ."

"About what, darling?"

"This is so much more than I was thinking. I . . . I can't take care of this place," she said.

"Oh, my nephew has plenty of people taking care of the place. What he needs is a nice girl like you to make sure they're doing it right," Sherman assured her.

Stormy really wanted to run away, but where would she run away to?

"I . . . uh . . . suppose I could stay," she said, still unsure.

"Good. Good. That puts my heart at ease. The reason I'm calling, darling, is because there was a disaster in the guest cottage last night with the water pipes. The entire cottage flooded, ruining the floors. It's going to take about a week for it all to get repaired," he said.

"Oh." Now where was she going to go?

"Don't you fret. The key you have is to the main house anyway. The cottage keys are in the foyer. Just go on inside and you can take the first room you come to on the right at the top of the stairs. It's all been settled."

"Are you really sure about this, Sherman?" she asked.

"Positive. I'll be out in a couple of days to see how you're settling in. I have to run now. Enjoy your evening on the water."

Before she could utter another word, the line went dead and he was gone.

"The cottage had a problem. It looks like I'm staying in the main house for a few days," Stormy said to Amy.

"Lucky you!" the girl replied with a laugh. She was trying to make a joke, but Stormy could feel her friend's jealousy. "Let's go on in. I'm dying to see the place," Amy finished as she handed Stormy the purse she'd left in the car, and then rushed toward the front door.

The path to the entrance from the driveway was made of sparsely placed flagstones, each stone placed on a clean-cut carpet of deep green grass. The beautifully landscaped yard was no less amazing than others they had seen while driving through the small town.

Stormy moved up the walkway, the sound of rippling water filling her ears as her eyes were drawn to a nearby water feature. The fountain was an eight-foot stone ring encircled with concrete fish. Each figure spouted a thin stream of water toward the center, creating a harmonious sound akin to a babbling brook.

She peered through the water's surface, which was littered with broad lily leaves and purple flowers, and noticed a giant orange and black spotted fish darting in the shallows.

Amy walked over to see what had made her friend smile. There were two fish that kept circling Stormy's fingertip as she encouraged them to come closer to her.

"Come on, Stormy, let's go. I want to see the inside of this palace," Amy said. "We can play with the fish later."

"Fine, just so long as you know that you're zero fun right now," Stormy retorted as she grabbed her bag.

The duo made their way up the beautifully set rock stairs to the front porch, and up to the large double-door entrance. Stormy reached out with the key in her hand, but she stopped, thinking the homeowner might be there and prefer she wait for him to answer.

Here we go, she thought as she pressed the illuminated doorbell button. The chimes sounded like church bells as she heard them echoing through the inside of the home. They waited for about a minute, and when there was no sound of movement, Stormy pressed the button once more, then knocked on the door. Stormy stood there feeling slightly awkward on the front porch.

"Don't you have a key?" Amy questioned as she tapped on the door lock.

"Yes I do, but I feel kinda weird about using it," Stormy responded. "Sherman said there were people who worked at the house, so maybe they'll answer."

"Well, I feel awkward standing here," Amy said.

Stormy reluctantly placed the key in the lock when no one came after about five minutes. Amy grabbed Stormy's hand and twisted, unlocking and opening the door.

"There, I saved you from thinking about it," Amy joked as she gave her a pat on the back.

The door swung open and both ladies felt as if they were intruders as they stepped into the home's large three-story foyer. Directly across from the entrance, a great hallway opened up into what looked like two bigger rooms.

The foyer displayed an elegant sweeping staircase that rose from the floor as if it had been carved from a single piece of wood.

Immediately to Stormy's right was an ornate pair of French doors that were closed against a dimly lit office. Another hallway was beyond that, lined with a few mysterious doors, presumably bedrooms, bathrooms, or closets. To the left of the elegant entryway was the great room, its boundary marked by an enormous archway.

Polished hardwood floors with plush dark leather furniture formed a U shape around a beautiful fireplace on the far side of the room. On the crafted mantel stood a framed American flag, a model of a sailing ship, and the portrait of what appeared to be a World War II naval aviator.

As Stormy and Amy pressed forward, they noticed the great room transitioned to a dining room, comfortable yet formal. The dining room and kitchen shared a glass wall that was nothing more than large windows and French doors that opened up to a vast deck overlooking the harbor.

The home was impeccably decorated with aviation and nautical themes, old family photos, and various mementos. Even with all its elegance and charm, there was something undeniably masculine about the house. A bachelor pad—even if the bachelor in question was impeccably stylish, self-possessed, and fabulously wealthy . . . *This place certainly needs a woman's touch. There aren't any flowers or throw pillows. But still, I'm impressed*, Stormy thought as she continued exploring.

This was a house a family could grow in and she had a distinct vision of it someday holding a picture perfect family—complete with children, golden retriever, and minivan in the driveway.

She moved through the foyer, looking at the pictures along the wall that led back to the kitchen and dining room. And that's when she froze in her tracks. Amy was nowhere to be found, but it wouldn't have mattered if she were in the room or not.

She recognized the man in the picture with three other handsome guys. Taking a step closer to the photo, she gazed at the image of Captain Cooper Armstrong and three other men that were so strikingly similar in appearance, she had to assume they were either brothers or cousins. Stormy continued scanning the photos of them participating in flying, fishing, sailing, and a multitude of other outdoor sports.

What kind of prank was destiny playing on her? She couldn't be in the home of the man she had engaged in a one-night stand with, and then who had completely forgotten her. Fate wouldn't be that cruel.

Her heart thundered as she stared at the picture, maybe for a minute, maybe an hour. No, she wouldn't believe that her luck could be so completely horrible. There had to be another explanation. He had to be friends with whoever owned the place. That was certainly it. Didn't all the rich guys hang out together?

Yes, she convinced herself, he must just be a friend. Because who in the heck hung pictures of themselves all over their walls? Her heart slowed down as she smiled. Of course it wasn't Green Eyes' house.

"Okay, girl, I know it's fun looking all over the place, but I found your room and I'm halfway unloaded already," Amy said, making Stormy jump. "So get your butt moving, and help me finish. I have a hair appointment I refuse to miss."

"I . . . uh, don't know if I can stay here," she said. Maybe she wasn't as calm as she'd thought she was.

"Don't be ridiculous. This is a dream-come-true kind of house. You're absolutely not gonna leave," Amy said with an outraged gasp.

"Do you recognize this man?" Stormy said, pointing her finger hard against the glass.

Amy looked and then her eyes widened slightly. "Isn't that the pilot who was such an ass to you at the airport?"

"Yeah, among other things," Stormy mumbled.

"Well, maybe he's really good friends with whoever lives here," Amy said. "Guys don't put pictures of themselves on the walls."

Exactly what Stormy had just been thinking. Okay, she was definitely overreacting here.

"Look, Stormy, you can't give up this place. You literally have nowhere to go," Amy reminded her. "I hate to point that out, but it's the truth."

"I can go to a motel," Stormy said almost desperately.

"And you'd last a week because your money would run out and then you'd be broke *and* homeless," Amy pointed out. "Then what?"

"You don't understand," Stormy tried saying.

"I get it," Amy interrupted. "But sometimes we have to put our feelings aside and do what's best for us, not what we think we need to do."

"It's not his place," Stormy said. She was more and more sure of that. But still she looked around nervously.

"Hello," she called out. There was nothing. "Is anyone home?"

"Um, darling, if no one has appeared yet, then I don't think they're going to," Amy said with a laugh.

The only response that could be heard in the house was the sound of a ticking grandfather clock. Maybe it was an omen.

Amy left Stormy behind, obviously reluctant about doing so. After an hour, she decided to explore more of the home now that her meager possessions were put away.

Maybe she would find out exactly who resided in the house. She was saying prayers at two-minute intervals that it wasn't Cooper Armstrong.

CHAPTER SEVENTEEN

Sweat dripping down his brow, Cooper pushed himself even harder as he ran along the rocky terrain of the Gig Harbor coastline. A breeze ruffled through his hair, and once in a while a mist would come up and cool him down.

Still, he ran faster and harder.

When he stopped at the trail that led back to his property, he pulled off his shirt and wiped his brow. The ten-mile run had been exactly what he'd needed to burn off the excess energy he'd been feeling from being cooped up in small flight decks for the past week.

Man, he loved to fly, but sometimes it was a little claustrophobic.

Walking up the path to his house, he made it to the back patio when he stopped, realizing that something wasn't right.

Carefully he opened his back door and stepped through. There was the noise again. Someone was moving around his upstairs. The staff was off today, so no one was supposed to be in the house.

Moving to the front of the house, he glanced out the window and didn't see anything to set off alarms, but then there was that same noise, sounding like shoes scuffling across his hardwood floors.

Well, if someone was there to rob the place, they'd picked the wrong house. Stealthily, he walked up the stairs, determined to catch the culprit. He was furious when he found his bedroom door open. That was his private space, and no one was allowed to step foot inside.

Taking a menacing step forward, Cooper stopped in his tracks when he saw Stormy move past his bed and then peek into his private bathroom. What in the world was the woman he'd been thinking about far too often doing in his bedroom? Had his imagination suddenly conjured her up? Was he daydreaming?

She crossed his spacious floor and ran her fingers along his mocha-colored walls. The natural light filling the room cast a soft glow on her features, and he felt himself growing hard when her fingers caressed his satin drapes as she pushed them aside to peek out onto his large balcony.

His eyes traveled from her to the centerpiece of his room, his very large and comfortable four-poster California king-size bed. It was made and just asking for him to throw her onto it and mess it up.

A ray of sun hit Stormy, casting an almost ethereal glow about her. In her white lace summer dress, she certainly looked like an angel. The plans he had for this woman, though, didn't come down from heaven.

Never before had Cooper allowed a woman into his bedroom. He took them to hotels or went to their homes, but he didn't like them to invade his personal space. Surprisingly, even though he had no idea how Stormy had gotten into his house, he didn't mind her being exactly where she was.

Shaking his head, he scowled though she couldn't see him. There was a reason he didn't invite them back to his house—he didn't want them after him for his ass . . . ets.

Then it hit him.

Uncle Sherman! His eyes narrowed as he realized what the old coot was up to.

First of all, a so-called *family friend* needed a place to stay. Then *conveniently* right before she was to move into the guest cottage, the pipes had burst, causing him a hell of a headache, not to mention the cost of repairs, and the *family friend* now got to stay inside his house.

He and his uncle were going to have a talk *real* soon.

"I assume you know Sherman Armstrong," Cooper said as he stepped through his doorway and alerted Stormy of his presence.

She jumped as she spun around, the move nearly toppling her over. Dammit! She was far too close to his bed for her to be getting horizontal. His brain had already begun to picture her lying on top of his dark blue comforter.

"Cooper . . ." His name came out breathlessly, and he really had the urge now to lie her down and hear her saying that in the exact same manner as he slid in and out of her body.

"That's what my friends call me," he said with a crooked grin as he leaned back against his wall. "If you really wanted in my bedroom so badly, all you had to do was ask," he added with a wink he knew would infuriate her.

Stormy's cheeks flushed with embarrassment as she moved away from the bed and farther from him.

"This *is* your house." She said the words almost as an accusation. Sherman hadn't told her any more about where she was staying than he'd told Cooper who would be staying with him. *Family friend, my ass*, Cooper thought.

"Yep, it is."

"I . . . uh, didn't know . . . when Sherman said his nephew had a place, I never thought . . ."

She seemed to be getting her equilibrium back as they faced off. Interesting. He actually believed she hadn't known it was his place. What was also interesting was the fact that he wasn't upset about having a guest anymore.

His pride wasn't unaffected when he saw the appreciative light in her eyes as she took in his appearance. He'd had a great run today. Yes, he knew his dark hair needed a good brushing, and he was covered in sweat, but she didn't appear to mind.

The more she looked at him, the tighter his snug shorts felt, and he was *very* aware that there was a bed nearby to alleviate the pain he was feeling. He glanced at his bed, and then back again at her—and he smiled.

Stormy's eyes widened the slightest bit as she looked into his and then looked down, before jerking her head back up and looking more like a mouse cornered by a very hungry cat.

"I'm . . . uh . . . sorry for coming into your room. I was just looking around, trying to get a feel for the layout," she finally muttered. "I really like your chest . . . I mean, uh your house, especially your room," she said before turning scarlet. "I mean that it's very hard . . . I . . . uh . . . I mean comfortable."

She finally lifted her hand and put it over her mouth to stop the flow of words.

Hot damn, he wanted this woman with something that bordered on obsession. Not good! Her sweet scent drifted over to him, bringing an exotic flavor that had never been in his masculine room before.

His mind wandered as he imagined moving across the room and pulling her into his arms, a gasp of approval sliding across her lips right before he claimed her mouth. He would slowly peel her summer dress away, revealing her shoulders and then her sweet perky breasts for him to feast upon. He wouldn't mind nibbling his way down her body, trailing his fingers until he found her center.

His hardness was now a screaming mass of pain that he seriously had to do something about. Moving quickly over to his bathroom, he grabbed a towel and wiped the sweat from his brow before moving it over his naked chest and then holding it in front of him. This woman got under his skin like no woman ever had. Something about her called to him, and even though his mind couldn't for the life of him clear the foggy feeling that he'd met her before, his body decided it didn't care either way.

"My room is open to you anytime," he heard himself say.

And then he enjoyed the gasp from her suddenly puckered lips, but he didn't get to feel her warm breath against his mouth. Dammit!

"I think I should finish unpacking," she stuttered. "I won't be here very long," she added as she took a step toward his bedroom door.

She seemed to think twice about it, though, when she realized she was going to be left with no choice but to come intimately close to him. He decided not to move. He wanted her nearer to him.

"Be my guest," he offered when she stood there for a few more seconds, completely frozen in place.

"Well, okay then," she said and she began to make a wide arc past him. He inhaled while she walked past.

She made it to the door before he spoke again. "We'll talk after I shower, Stormy."

She stopped in his doorway but didn't turn around. She was feeling the sexual tension as much as he was. Cooper really wasn't disappointed about his new housemate.

Screw the shower. He needed to move! After dressing in some swim shorts, he made his way outside.

It took a while, but his arousal finally died down. Still, there was something niggling against his brain—something about her smell— about the gasp from her lips and the widening of her eyes that was so damn familiar.

But how could he ever forget a woman like Stormy if he'd met her before?

He couldn't have. He might be somewhat of a rogue, but he didn't forget his bed partners. Maybe he hadn't bedded her, though; maybe he'd just met her at a party? But why wouldn't she tell him if he had? Cooper flashed through his mind the last couple of years of women, and there was no Stormy.

He would figure it out. She was now his guest. He had plenty of time.

CHAPTER EIGHTEEN

Breathing deeply in and out, Stormy moved down the staircase, not wanting to hear the shower running with Cooper inside the large room—wet . . . naked . . . soapy. Oh, living here was *so* not a good idea.

As she walked, she became engrossed again in the beautiful nautical pictures lining the walls. Whatever else she could say about Cooper, she had to give the man his due. He had good taste.

When she felt it was safe again, she moved back upstairs to her sparsely furnished room. Luckily there was already a mattress and dresser in it, but no extras. Her few possessions didn't take up much space at all.

She was drawn to the large window and the view of the large, well-manicured backyard and the nearby harbor beyond. She hated that the place belonged to Cooper because otherwise, it would be a dream come true to live in such a lavish location.

Beggars couldn't be choosers, though, and she'd just have to make the best of the situation. She was an adult. She could handle this. She needed to handle this. She turned back to the luxurious bed. Even though she wasn't thrilled with her new housemate, the place clearly had its perks. She swiftly rushed over to the ultra-comfortable oasis, flung herself on top of its welcome warmth, and sank down into the soft mattress. She couldn't stop herself from allowing a giggle to escape.

Yes, it was childish, but she hadn't been in this nice of a place, well, ever. The picture of her parents was already set up on her nightstand, and she smiled at the people she loved so deeply. She'd have slept on the cold, hard ground for the rest of her life in exchange for another minute with them both.

She was glad of the values they'd taught her. They wouldn't have approved of her living with a man—especially a man she felt something for, a man she'd already slept with. But they also had always told her to make her own choices—even if those choices weren't the smartest ones.

Her father had always told her that people were shaped by the decisions they made. There was no such thing as a wrong decision, just a path you were meant to travel and grow from. She hoped the path she was now choosing wasn't a bad one.

The sharp sound of a car door slamming grabbed her attention away from the picture and to the open window. Reluctantly, she got up and moved across the room. With one hand, she drew aside the drapes and peered down on the driveway.

The sight of Cooper with a hose in his hand pointed at a sleek silver Jaguar had her mouth watering. He hadn't taken a very long shower. But she knew she was in a bit of trouble as she found herself once again appreciating his incredible physique. Staring at him for who knew how long, Stormy found herself trying to be more confident.

The man wasn't kicking her from his home. Maybe she should try to make a friendly gesture. After all, the two of them hadn't exactly been the best of friends up to this point. Who cared if he didn't remember sleeping with her? She had to get over it.

Matter of fact, it was probably much better for all concerned if he had no idea that they'd been lovers for a night. It had been incredible for her, but it wouldn't be wise to repeat that night, so at least they wouldn't have to deal with the sexual tension from it, right? Right!

But she could say thank you to the man for offering her a place to stay. Her decision to seek him out had nothing at all to do with the fact that he was in his driveway—half naked. Nope. It had nothing at all to do with that, she assured herself.

Moving quickly now, she practically ran down the stairs to the kitchen. Searching around, she located a large container of iced tea, grabbed a couple of glasses, and poured them each some before squaring her shoulders and moving to the side door. She stepped outside.

Looking up at the bright, sunny sky, she felt she could get used to this tree-lined area. The crisp sea breeze blew gently across her cheeks as she carried the drink to Cooper. She thought about rubbing the icy glass against her flushed body. Of course, it was only the heat of the warm day, not the fact that she was feeling anything else as she came closer to the man who could work magic with his hands and mouth.

Only a few feet away from Cooper, she had to admire how good he looked in nothing but a pair of shorts, his firm upper body gleaming with a splash of water and maybe a trickle of sweat. A trail of soapy water was slowly making its way toward the waistband of his wet swim shorts.

She must have made a noise, because suddenly Cooper turned in her direction. She really wished he weren't wearing sunglasses because she had no idea what he was thinking as he set down the hose he'd been holding and then trailed his fingers through his damp hair.

"Settling in okay?" he asked. It took her a moment to process his words.

"Um . . . yes, I am," she finally murmured. "It's hot out, so I thought I'd break the ice and bring you a drink."

Maybe she should have just stayed in the house, dang it.

Giving her a smile that could melt butter, he thanked her and then took the glass. She watched as his throat flexed while he downed half the tea. "I was thirsty," he said, wiping the moisture from his lips.

Her stomach clenched with need unlike anything she'd ever felt before.

"Well then, I guess I'll let you get back to it," she told him, taking a step back and nearly falling on her ass.

He chuckled then reached out. Before Stormy knew what was happening, he was wrapping his arms around her and tugging her against him.

"What in the world are you doing?" she asked, her voice trembling.

The sudden fire that ignited in his eyes was making her far too warm. She couldn't figure out what else to say as he gazed down at her.

"You looked a bit hot. I thought I'd cool you off," he told her.

She'd been warm, but him pulling her against him had instantly overheated her.

"I'm good," she said, tugging from his wet hold.

With a chuckle, he released her. Stormy was fully out of sorts, but looking down, she saw the hose at her feet. Bending, she picked it up, a twinkle in her eyes.

"What are you doing?" he asked. This time, he was the one to step back.

"You look a little hot," she said, repeating his words. Then she unleashed the cold spray right against his chest.

His smoldering eyes weren't so hot anymore as he yelped and lunged backward. When she saw him glance toward the bucket of sudsy water, she decided it was a good time for retreat.

"See ya later," she hollered, dropping the hose and spinning around.

It was too late, though. She didn't make it three steps before icy-cold water launched over her head and soaked her white dress, plastering her clothes to her suddenly freezing body.

She stopped and spun back toward him, glaring at his head, which was lowered to the ground. He was bent over laughing. She moved up to him and tried to push him over, but that backfired on her.

He was far too fast for her, and suddenly she found herself being lifted and then both of them were tumbling on the grass on his perfect front lawn.

Gasping for breath, Stormy was disoriented as the world spun around her. Then, she lost her air when he pinned her beneath him, his solid body on top of hers. She was pretty sure it wasn't the hose pressing against her thigh.

"I've wanted to do this from the moment I saw you in that coffee shop. I feel like I've known you forever and it's haunting me." No more warning than that was given before his head descended and his lips were fastened on hers.

The kiss was exactly what she remembered, and she sighed into his mouth, forgetting for a moment what a bad, bad idea this was. Within a second, she was lost in his embrace.

The kiss ended far too quickly, though, when Cooper pulled back, confusion in his eyes as he gazed down at her.

"I know you," he said, making her heart race.

"Of course you do. I worked at the coffee shop," she said, out of breath.

His finger came up and traced her lips as his eyes narrowed.

"No. I've kissed you before, tasted you."

It wasn't a question. He was certain of it.

Her heart stopped in her chest as she gazed up at him. This would be the time for her to tell him that indeed he did know her. She tried to get her mouth to form the words. Instead, what came out wasn't what should have.

"I don't know what you're talking about. Now get off me," she said, wishing the words would have come out a bit more firmly.

"What are you hiding from me?" he said, still not releasing her.

"Nothing. I just can't breathe with you on top of me," she told him.

With what seemed like reluctance, he rolled off her. That's when Stormy realized they were on his front lawn making out like a couple of teenagers who couldn't care less what the neighbors thought. Sure, she couldn't see his neighbors, but that didn't mean they couldn't see them.

No more words were exchanged as she rose to her feet and walked away, her arms folded across her chest. She couldn't shake the idea that countless onlookers could see through her wet dress. She cast her eyes to the ground, not willing to see if that were true or not.

What Stormy knew for sure was that she couldn't stay in Cooper's house. There was no way. If she did, she was sure she'd end up in the man's bed again. And that was a road she wasn't willing to go down.

Stormy wasn't too far into the house when she heard Cooper following her. Dang it. He could be a man and give her a bit of space, couldn't he? That would be the nice thing to do.

"Stormy, we need to talk," he called. He was too close.

She froze for a second trying to figure out which way to go. She knew for sure that she couldn't face him again right now. No way. So, doing the only thing she could think of, she decided to hide.

Rounding the base of the stairs, she shot into the hallway and opened a door, deciding the bathroom was the best place to duck into. She shut the door too hard behind her, and then sought a light switch.

There wasn't one to be found. After a moment, her eyes adjusted to the bit of light coming in from the bottom of the door. That was when she realized she wasn't in a bathroom at all—she was in a closet.

She could hear Cooper's approaching footsteps on the hardwood floor as her back slid down the wall and her arms tucked her legs up into her chest. Feeling extremely foolish and very trapped, her heart raced as Cooper stopped on the other side of the door.

"Stormy, are you all right?" Cooper asked as he knocked on the door.

Utterly humiliated, Stormy knew she was going to have to answer. "Yeah, everything's fine."

Everything *was* fine except for the fact that she was sitting on the floor in a closet feeling like a total fool. Now her new housemate had to think she was crazy and was wondering how quickly he could evict her.

She wanted to be evicted, though, didn't she? It was better than her reminding him that he was right to think he knew her. That they had slept together and he was only now remembering it.

Stormy wasn't too thrilled to have to remind a man he'd bedded her.

"I was just really cold and thought I would look for a coat," she called out when he said nothing to her last statement.

"You had to shut the door to find a coat—in the dark?" he asked.

"The wind must have blown it closed behind me," Stormy said quickly, impressed with her quick thinking.

"Well, if you need it, there's a light in there hanging from the ceiling," Cooper told her. "I'm going to be a gentleman and give you a break," he said before pausing. "Then we will finish what we started."

Her heart thundered at those words. What did he mean by *finish what we started*? Was he talking about the discussion or the kiss? Oh, she wouldn't mind finishing the kiss. She really wouldn't mind that.

If she had the ability to kick her own ass, she would, because she couldn't sleep with Cooper Armstrong again. At twenty years old, she could write the night off as youthful idiocy, but now at twenty-six, it would just be plain irresponsible.

Stormy was more than grateful to hear his steps retreating. Slowly, she turned the closet doorknob and opened it. After stepping outside, she looked back in and saw how ridiculously small the closet was. There would be no need for her to step inside for a coat—not unless she was hiding.

She was grateful he hadn't called her on her foolishness.

Taking her time, she climbed the stairs and locked herself in her room. It was the best place for her to be after her childish behavior. Lying down on her bed, she closed her eyes.

She'd call Sherman and let him know that she needed to get out of the agreement. Sherman's best intentions were not worth this level of humiliation. No, she'd be out of here in a few days max, she assured herself, because being housemates with Cooper would never work—not without her spilling her guts to him or ripping off his clothes. Either situation would be pretty dang disastrous.

CHAPTER NINETEEN

The gym was hot and muggy, and the boxing ring already had a layer of sweat from previous bouts, but that didn't stop Cooper and Maverick from circling each other with grins on their lips and sparks in their eyes.

"Are you sure you're up for this, boy? You've seemed a little off lately," Maverick taunted him.

"Don't you worry about it, little brother. I can still kick your ass," Cooper told him, his feet dancing as he moved in closer.

"I'm not the one who should be worried."

Before Maverick could mock him more, Cooper threw a left jab and cracked his brother in the jaw, then quickly followed up with a right hook.

"Damn, I guess you have your game back," Maverick said, shaking his head as he bounced back to regain his balance.

"I told you," Cooper warned, feeling much better now that he was sparring with his brother and getting out some of his extra adrenaline.

They went a few rounds, both of them getting in some lucky shots before Cooper's mind wandered to his new housemate again. She'd managed to avoid him for two days straight.

He was going to have a conversation with her if it was the last thing he did. Something was scraping at his brain and until he figured it out, he wasn't going to stop obsessing about it.

Suddenly the breath whooshed from Cooper as Maverick landed a hard thrust into his stomach, then quickly followed up with a double shot to the head, effectively knocking Cooper on his ass.

Maverick danced back and laughed.

"Damn, you really are off your game. You should have countered that, old man."

"It's just this freaking woman who's living with me. I can't figure her out," Cooper said in frustration as he slowly got back to his feet, his ears ringing slightly.

"Okay, this isn't any fun at all. Let's go sit in the sauna and you can cry about your woes," Maverick said as he climbed down from the ring.

"Hey! I want payback," Cooper called to him.

"It isn't happening today. I'll give you a week and then we'll go another round," Maverick said as he pulled off his gloves and began undoing his tape.

"Fine." Cooper followed Maverick and the two of them quickly changed and went to the sauna.

The heat seemed extra suffocating today, though. Pretty much how his life was at the moment.

Luckily no one was in there with them. Cooper leaned back, a picture of Stormy rising up through the steam to appear in thin air and mock him.

"Tell me about the girl, 'cause I have to know. I haven't seen you this obsessed since that one-night stand you had six years ago," Maverick told him.

And then the air left his lungs as the room became even more suffocating.

"Hey! You okay? You aren't having a heart attack on me, are you?" Maverick asked as he stood up and came closer.

"I need out of here." Cooper lunged for the door with Maverick close on his heels.

"What in the hell is going on?" Maverick insisted as Cooper leaned against the wall.

It took a few moments for Cooper to speak, and then he looked up at his brother wondering how much he should share. That really wasn't a question. They shared everything, so of course he would talk.

"Stormy *is* the girl from six years ago," Cooper finally said.

"What? Okay, I'm lost," Maverick said as he moved to the bench and sat down.

"So am I," Cooper said slowly. "Why wouldn't she bring that up? Why is she trying to hide it?"

Maverick was silent for several moments. "Maybe she didn't enjoy it as much as you did."

"Bullshit," Cooper said. "I know when a woman's pleased, and she was crying out for more."

"It *has* been a long time," Maverick told him.

"I don't care if it's been a long time." He closed his eyes and he could clearly remember that night. "Why didn't I recognize her immediately?"

"It's been six years. People change," Mav said.

"Yeah . . ." He wasn't so sure of that. "Her hair was blonde then, and she wasn't as curvy as she is now, but those eyes and lips . . . they haven't changed a single bit."

"Maybe you didn't want to know," Mav told him.

"I searched for her for a while. It did me no good. She crashed the wedding and then she was gone."

"The all-powerful Cooper couldn't find a woman," Mav said with a laugh.

"Joseph gave me a necklace she'd dropped," he admitted. "I still have it."

"Oohh, this just gets better and better," Mav told him.

"Dammit, Mav, can you be serious for two seconds," Cooper said with a glare.

"Confront her about it."

"And say what? Hey! Remember me? I'm the one who made you scream an entire night until you disappeared on me?" Cooper said with sarcasm.

"Or you could be a little less crude," Mav told him.

"I don't know . . ." Cooper leaned against the wall and thought about it. "Maybe I will just try to figure out what is going on in her brain before I reveal that I know who she is."

"That sounds like a recipe for disaster," Mav warned.

"I always have liked living on the edge of danger," Cooper said, warming up more and more to the idea.

"It's your funeral." Mav glanced over at the clock and sighed with relief. "I have to get to the base. So we'll meet up next week and you can fill me in."

Cooper waved his hand distractedly. His mind was reeling and he wasn't sure what he was going to do next. The only thing he knew for sure was that he had to see Stormy soon. He wasn't going to figure anything out sweating in a gym.

A smile lifted his lips. Let the games begin.

CHAPTER TWENTY

Never happy to wake, Stormy stumbled from her bed and moved to her dresser, trying to decide what she was going to do to fill her day. When nothing came to her, she took a shower, then climbed back into bed and sat there watching the sunrise. When enough time was wasted, she decided hiding out had to end.

She dressed and then slowly opened her bedroom door. There wasn't a sound to be heard. Maybe Cooper was gone. He was a pilot after all. Sherman had told her the owner of the house was gone a lot.

With the lighting of this place and the solitude, she could create jewelry designs all she wanted and no one would be the wiser. It calmed her to draw, to dream, even if she didn't have a lot of faith she'd ever make those dreams come true.

Feeling a bit more confidence, though, she made her way down the stairs and stepped into the kitchen. That's when she realized she hadn't had a chance to go shopping yet. And dang it, she was starving. She'd gone through her bag of protein bars and chips the day before.

Opening the huge Sub-Zero fridge, she was impressed and intimidated. It was filled with items she'd never even heard of, or items she had heard about and never had a desire to try. Caviar, truffles, and coconut water lined the shelves, along with meats and cheeses she didn't recognize.

When she spotted the organic turkey bacon and farm fresh brown eggs, she decided that was as normal as she was going to get. Pulling the items from the fridge, she vowed to replace them as soon as she could find a store that carried the higher-priced items.

Moving over to Cooper's six-burner commercial range that had barbecue vents to the outside, she wondered if she should even try to operate it. There was a distinct possibility she would burn down his house.

Never one to be a quitter, she decided to give it a go. While her bacon cooked, she roamed the kitchen, falling instantly in love with the giant walk-in pantry, again stacked with items she'd never heard of before. She really needed to introduce Cooper to the joys of basic grocery staples. The idea of turning his world upside down with the delight that comes from having a secret stash of Oreos had her smiling.

This kitchen was highly intimidating with its dark granite counters, custom wood cabinets, built-in espresso machine, and appliances that looked far too smart for her to operate. She desperately hoped the cottage was a little more down to earth.

Just as she was sitting down at the breakfast bar, she realized she wasn't alone.

"Make yourself at home."

Cooper moved to the counter facing her, pulled down a coffee cup, and filled it before taking a nice long swig. Then he turned and leaned against the counter and smiled at her.

"I'm sorry. I thought you'd already left. I'm going to replace the food. I just haven't had a chance to shop yet," she told him, hoping he'd leave before her eggs got cold.

"Go ahead and eat. I don't get very many opportunities to cook. My mom likes to keep me stocked full of groceries even though I'm gone so much I don't get to enjoy them half the time. But then she feels like she's doing her job as a mother, she tells me." Hadn't Sherman told her she might need to shop for him? It seemed that wasn't true.

"Well, I'm still going to replace it," she said.

When he stood back and said nothing more as he drank his coffee, she decided not to let her food go to waste. She looked down and slowly finished her plate while he threw a bagel into the toaster. Then he pulled out cream cheese and smoked salmon from the fridge.

"How about we have dinner together tonight?"

His invitation scared her. She took her plate to the sink while she thought about her answer. Confusion filled her at how much this man's presence affected her moods, her body, and her mind. She wanted to plaster herself against him and see if her memory of their one night together was nothing more than her vivid imagination or if it really had been as spectacular as she remembered.

She wanted to run screaming in the opposite direction, too. Because she had a feeling that six years had only improved Green Eyes. He was larger than he'd been back then. Well, at least his shoulders were. She wasn't so sure a woman could handle other parts of his body being larger without him ripping her in two.

Shaking her head, she tried to push away her erratic thinking. Nothing was helping. This man was haunting her and now he was far too close on a daily basis for her to chase her ghosts away.

"Come on, Stormy. It's just dinner." There was something in his eyes that was different today, something she didn't trust and was making her nervous. She shifted on her feet as she stepped away from him.

Say something, anything, she commanded herself. Why in the world was she so damn speechless? Silence had never been something she was known for.

"We're living here together, so if we're both here at the same time, I guess we could have dinner," she finally said.

Cooper looked at her for several moments, his expression utterly unreadable. He didn't seem upset or happy. She couldn't figure out what he was thinking.

"Good, then it's a date," he told her before moving toward the front door.

"Well, it's not a date," she called out after him.

He stopped and turned back toward her, a smile on his lips.

"What is it then?" he asked, a sparkle in his eyes.

"It's just . . . well, it's just . . . um, two people living in the same house, sharing the appliances," she finally said, wanting to kick herself once the words were out.

"Okay, Stormy, we'll share the appliances tonight then," Cooper said before turning back around and moving to the front door.

He walked out and Stormy let out a low growl as she cursed herself all the way up the stairs. She didn't think it possible for this situation to get any more awkward if she put on a tutu and started dancing around topless.

Okay, that might make things just a tad crazier. But then at least she could be committed to a crazy house and not have to face Cooper ever again. The man had kissed her and still didn't know who she was. It was pretty humiliating. Though he had paused and wondered for a moment if he knew her, at least.

She could have told him. But that would make it so much worse for her pride.

None of that mattered. For now, it was time to go to the store, get the paper, and start job searching.

The town of Gig Harbor was small and quaint. She could easily make her way through it walking. That would mean she couldn't carry as much, but that was okay for now. It was just her and Cooper. She'd keep it simple. It'd be a nice contrast to the emotional turmoil her housemate had stirred up inside her.

By the end of the day, there was an extra skip in her step.

The problem with her successes of the day, though, was that now she felt like she might not want to leave Cooper's after all. After only a day, she was becoming accustomed to the wonderful little town that felt oddly like home.

CHAPTER TWENTY-ONE

Stormy was unsure of whether she should come down the stairs that night and have dinner with Cooper or not. But she so wanted to tell him her good news. She wanted to tell someone at least, and he was the nearest person to her. Instead of doing just that, she paced in her room.

She had heard Cooper come home an hour ago, and now she could smell something cooking. And the smell coming up the stairs was making her stomach rumble.

"Stormy, it's time to start sharing appliances."

Cooper calling up the stairs made her jump, though she didn't know why. Now if she didn't go down, she was going to look really bad. She had to join him, didn't she? After all, he was offering her a place to stay for practically nothing.

Okay, she could do this.

She opened her door, crept to the top of the staircase, and slowly descended. Still unsure about the situation, she hesitantly entered the kitchen and found him in an apron stirring something on the stove.

"Can I help?" she asked.

"Nope, sit down and enjoy my talents as a chef."

"A pilot and a chef?" she asked with a laugh. "Any other talents?" Where in the world had that come from?

"Oh, Stormy, I have *many* talents," he said. He paused and looked into her eyes, and she lost her breath. When his lips turned up, she knew exactly what was on his mind.

Her cheeks instantly flushed. She knew of some of the man's talents, and they were definitely noteworthy.

She tried to help again, but he wasn't having any of it, wanting to impress her. He was doing a good job. After he'd poured a glass of wine for her, she sat on the stool as he whipped around the kitchen. The smells continued to make her stomach rumble.

"How's the wine?" he asked as he pressed against her back, making her jump and a tiny bit of wine drip down her chin.

Before she was able to clean it up, he leaned more into her and swept the drops of wine away, his rough finger rubbing against her bottom lip for a moment before he lifted his hand and sucked his finger into his mouth. He held her gaze captive, his lips far too close to the edge of her own.

"*Mmm*, pretty tasty," he told her with a low growl that instantly had her wet and wanting.

"Yeah . . . it's pretty good," she said, her voice husky.

She clenched her thighs together as she finally managed to turn her face forward. His breath heated her neck as he reached for a stick of butter on the counter and then finally walked away.

She didn't breathe for several moments. When he turned and looked at her from the safety of the other side of the kitchen island, the knowing light in his eyes alerted her that he was very aware of what he was doing to her. Stormy's eyes narrowed in frustration.

But she couldn't seem to stop his flirting or the reaction she had to it. He continued moving over to her side of the island, touching her while he finished up, and she was a wreck before she'd had a single bite of his delicious meal.

Cooper brought out the food and placed it on the table, then pulled the chair out for her to sit. Before her was a platter of barbecued steaks, corn on the cob, and mashed potatoes with gravy. Yum. She was so happy he hadn't made something with snails or fish eggs.

Barely having an appetite now, she took her time folding her napkin on her lap as she waited for him to dish his plate up.

"Dig in before it gets cold," he said when she didn't move.

"I thought I'd wait for you," she said.

"There's plenty here. You don't have to worry about me getting enough," he told her with a laugh.

She began serving herself and the smell of the steak was mouthwatering. Grilling wasn't one of her strong suits, so she always enjoyed a perfectly cooked steak. If only her stomach would quit turning, she might enjoy the meal.

"What was your day like?" Cooper asked as he dug in to his meal.

"It's been a good day, very busy," Stormy replied as she took her first bite. Yep. Delicious.

"Really? What did you do?"

Stormy played with the food more than she ate it as she tried to form words on her seemingly swollen tongue. When his foot touched hers beneath the table, she visibly jumped before locking her feet to the floor. She didn't look up at him this time, knowing she would see that same confident smirk on his face. She chose not to react to his blatant touches.

"I got a job today," she said.

"Really? That's great." He didn't seem to be anything less than genuine, which made her continue.

"Yes, at a diner here in town," she told him. "The Devoted Kiss Café."

"I've eaten there a lot. They serve a great *panino*," he told her.

"I will have to try a few of them so I can let the customers know what's good," she said. "I know it's just a waitressing job, but it's a paycheck," she added.

"A job's a job," he said, already halfway through his steak. She'd only had a few bites of hers.

His foot swept across hers again, this time drifting over her ankle. She looked at her steak like she was expecting it to come alive and begin mooing at any moment. She pushed herself back a little bit so it wouldn't be so easy for him to keep touching her.

"Well, there are certainly some better than others. I used to want to design jewelry," she admitted.

He didn't say anything and she was curious enough to glance across the table at him. The interest in his eyes made her glow inside whether she wanted to or not.

"Really? That's fantastic," he said. She was shocked by his reaction.

"Most people I've ever said that to sort of roll their eyes," she said with a laugh, like it didn't really matter.

"Why? You obviously have talent," he told her.

"How would you know that?" She didn't share her designs.

"I've seen your sketches in the garbage can," he said with a wink.

She gasped. "You've dug through the garbage?"

"I've been trying to figure you out. You're very secretive."

"It's just a dream. A silly one."

"I think we all start with a dream. It's those who are brave enough to make their dreams realities who change the world."

She sat there considering his words, and then she smiled. Wouldn't it be amazing for her dreams to actually come true? Suddenly embarrassed to be the center of attention, she decided to change it back to him.

"I'm sure flying jets is pretty exciting."

He paused as if knowing exactly what she was doing. But thankfully, he allowed her to get away with it.

"Yes, I've loved to fly since I was young. I'd go with my uncle Sherman a lot and I got the bug. My brothers and I all did."

"You have brothers who fly, too?" she said. "Dang, you must break quite a few hearts."

"Nah. We don't have a lot of time for women, not more than a night. There's a difference between being in a committed relationship and having a woman for a night. You either choose to fly or you choose a life," he said.

"There are lots of pilots with families," she told him.

"Yeah, and there's a lot of cheating pilots, too," he said. "I wouldn't ever want to live that way."

"You don't have to cheat if you don't want to," she scolded him.

"I wasn't saying I wouldn't *not* be able to cheat," he told her, setting down his fork. "I'm just saying I've seen a lot who do. I've never had a desire to commit myself."

"Sounds like a lot of guys I know," she grumbled.

There was a moment of silence between them and then he laughed, surprising her again.

"How many men have you been with, Stormy?"

The question made her choke on the bite of potatoes. After a moment, she was able to get them down and then took a nice long swallow of wine.

"That's really none of your business," she finally said.

"Why not? I think we would be great together," he said, leaning a little closer to her. "Imagine the two of us on a nice firm bed . . . or a really hot shower . . ."

He trailed off and then went back to eating as if he hadn't just turned her knees to jelly. She looked at her plate as she tried to figure out if he was messing with her. The chances were that no, he wasn't. Showers and beds were obviously his MO. Crap. Staying with this man wasn't going to be an easy thing to do.

"When is the cottage going to be ready?" she asked, her appetite gone.

"Oh, I don't know, a week, a few weeks. You know how repair men are," he told her. "Is the bedroom you're in not comfortable?"

"Oh no, of course not. It's beautiful and more than I could have imagined. I just don't want to be invading your space for too long," she hurriedly said.

"Don't worry about me. I'm enjoying the company."

She wanted to run fast and far away. Before she could excuse herself without seeming rude, though, his gaze zeroed in on her again.

"Why don't you tell me about yourself, Stormy? I know nothing," he said, leaning back, but not letting her escape those fantastic green eyes.

"There's really nothing to tell. I've led an uneventful life," she lied.

His eyes narrowed the tiniest bit for a moment before the expression disappeared.

"I don't believe that. I bet you've had an exciting life, traveled to exotic places, and sought out adventure," he countered.

"Nope. Really, nothing like that," she said, swallowing the lump in her throat. "Why don't you tell me what it's like to be a pilot?"

If she could turn the attention away from herself then she would be much better off here. He stared at her for several heartbeats, and then he must have decided to let her off the hook.

"I flew as a hobby from the time I was young. I never dreamed of making it a career, but when it came time to decide what I was going to do the rest of my life, the only thing I could think about was airplanes. So here I am," he said with a shrug.

"There's got to be more. How does it make you feel knowing you are responsible for so many lives?" she questioned, not realizing that she'd leaned toward him.

"When I first got my stripes and was a copilot on Alaska Airlines I would walk through the airport and kids would stop me, asking for autographs, their eyes filled with wonder. It took me back to the days when I was a young boy so enamored with pilots."

"Yeah, I was pretty in awe of pilots myself when I traveled," she admitted, forgetting she didn't want to share information with him.

"Are you still enamored with them?" he asked with a wink.

Stormy found herself blushing again. It was ridiculous. It was just a comment that shouldn't have mattered at all. She'd been flirted with before. But it wasn't normally by men whom she had slept with or whom she still wanted to have sex with.

Dang it! No, she didn't want to have sex with the man. Once had been enough.

"I think I'm over my fascination," she finally said.

"That's too bad," he said with a pout that made her laugh.

"Let me do the cleanup since you made dinner," she said as she stood. This dinner was getting to be too dang intimate for her.

"I insist on helping you." He stood up, and together they cleared the table and began doing dishes.

When they were finished, the grandfather clock chimed the late hour. Cooper yawned and leaned back against the counter.

"It's getting late," she said as she realized the time. It was unnerving how easily they had slipped into a happy domestic rhythm.

"I guess we should go to bed then," Cooper said, and the look he sent her told Stormy he wouldn't mind it being the same bed.

As much as she didn't want to be tempted by that, she couldn't help that she was.

"Yes, it's time for bed," she said quietly. "Good night, Cooper. Thank you for a perfect dinner and an even better conversation. And thanks for the room."

She turned away, not wanting to add anything else. She was at the bottom of the stairs when he grabbed her arm and stopped her.

Without a word he tugged her toward him, grabbing her hips and pulling her against the hardness in his slacks so she had no doubt he was turned on. Then he kissed her, making her knees shake as his hands tugged on her hair.

She moaned into his mouth, unable to stop her reaction to this man who had been touching her all night, who was on her mind nonstop. When he lifted her leg and pressed even more tightly against her, she felt an ache she hadn't felt for six long years.

This man did this to her, made her into a wanton woman, made her want to forget about anything and everything except for him and the pleasure he could and surely would bring to her.

She was almost ready to beg for more when he released her. His eyes were dark as he gazed at her.

"Anything you feel like telling me?" he asked, his fingers tracing her lower back.

She was stunned into silence for several tense moments.

"No . . . ," she finally answered on a shaky breath.

His eyes narrowed for a moment before he released her. She had to grip the rail and pray she could remain upright.

"Good night, Stormy. Sleep well." His tone of voice told her the opposite.

"Good night," Stormy finally replied, and then she continued walking up the stairs.

Sleep was going to be very difficult if she was able to get any at all.

CHAPTER
TWENTY-TWO

Her breath coming in and out in pants, Stormy pushed herself harder and faster as she ran on the treadmill while watching the sun flash on the waves as they lapped against the shore. The view was perfect in Cooper's state-of-the-art home gym.

Her eyes narrowed as she looked over at the cottage, where no one was working. How was it going to be repaired if the workmen weren't there doing anything? She decided to ask Sherman about it as soon as possible.

A runner she wasn't, but the energy zinging through her body had called for an outlet, so she'd been in the gym for the past hour, and though her muscles were screaming, her mind still wasn't letting go of thoughts of Cooper and that kiss they'd shared two nights before.

Finally she couldn't take it anymore, and she stopped the machine, her knees nearly buckling as she got off. Water! She needed water. Carefully she ascended the basement stairs and walked to the kitchen.

Before she reached the fridge, she noticed a note with her name on it. Her thirst temporarily forgotten, she slowly moved toward it and picked it up as if the paper would give her an electric shock or something.

I think you do have some things to tell me. I'll be gone a few days, but I want you to know that I'm anticipating my return.
        Cooper

Leaning against the counter, she read the note three times through. What did he mean that he was anticipating his return? What did he mean that she had things to tell him? Did he know? He couldn't know. Her heart thudded harder than it had on the damn treadmill as she read the note yet another time.

Finally, she set it down and got her drink, then sat there at the counter with every worst-case scenario filtering through her brain.

She wanted to smack herself as the day progressed.

Just because she'd had a couple of spectacular kisses with Cooper, and he'd left her a note she was obsessing about, didn't necessarily *mean* something.

What Stormy needed to do was focus on herself. After living in this perfect little sea town, and talking to Cooper about dreams she'd forgotten about, she was thinking that maybe she'd give her hopes a chance.

The worst that could happen was she would be terrible at it. But what if she was good? The necklace she'd lost so many years before she'd designed in high school, and her teacher had said she had a real eye for art, a true talent.

Instead of focusing on a man, shouldn't she focus on herself? He was going to be gone for a few days. By the time he got back, maybe she would be more in control of herself.

So for the next two days, Stormy made sure she wiped away any thoughts of Cooper.

With the house all to herself, Stormy couldn't help but smile. The cottage was taking forever, but soon she'd even have her own space. However, after living in Coop's giant mansion, she wondered if she'd feel cramped in the cottage even though it wasn't actually that small.

Of course, she was so used to the constricted confines of apartment living—the sounds of television sitcoms through thin walls, the anger of domestic disputes, and the young couple upstairs making their nightly session as obvious as possible—that the cottage would be paradise in comparison.

But here at Coop's private property, all that could be heard was the sound of the fountain in the front yard, the splash of waves on the beach, the occasional toll of harbor buoys, the wind through the trees, and the periodic cry of gulls sailing above.

Cooper was halfway across the Pacific Ocean, she thought with a smile.

She needed to take advantage of the situation instead of holing herself away in her room when she wasn't working.

Stormy wasn't going to waste any opportunities, so she made the executive decision: sweet white wine and a skinny-dip in the hot tub. Soon she would forget all about the days of freezing in her apartment while huddled beneath her covers. Tonight she would feel like the rich and famous. She would even drink from crystal.

Smiling with selfish delight, she sprinted up the stairs to her room where she quickly slipped into a silk bathrobe, then closed her bedroom door behind her as she headed back downstairs.

She rummaged through the kitchen for a proper glass. "Now we're in business," she said aloud as she pulled a chilled bottle of wine from the cooler. She hoped he wasn't saving the bottle for a special occasion. She couldn't help but giggle guiltily as she dug through the drawer for the bottle opener.

"Ah, there you are," she murmured, pulling it from the drawer and placing it on the cork.

The bottle open, she poured a glass, spilling some on the floor. She'd get that later. Pulling fresh strawberries from the fridge, she quickly moved to the French doors and opened them, the cool air making her breath instantly fog up.

Walking through the doors, Stormy flipped the porch light switch, but nothing happened. Thinking by some chance the first time was a fluke, she flipped the switch on and off once more; still nothing. She didn't let it stop her. The moonlit deck was a more relaxed setting anyway.

Moving quickly to the far side of the deck, she made quick work of pulling off the hot tub cover and setting the temperature to something that seemed just under scalding, then she turned on the jets.

The steam from the hot tub plumed into the cool air as a slight hint of chlorine filled her nostrils. Casting off her robe, then perching her strawberries and champagne on the tub's ledge, she stepped into the bubbling water.

Midway in, she stopped for a moment, her hands across her chest as she glanced around, double-checking that she was truly alone. Electing to sit in the darkness, she left the hot tub's lights off, then slipped completely below the surface, submerging even her head with a handful of strawberries inadvertently following her.

Her stress evaporated as quickly as the steam from the hot water, and Stormy knew the days ahead would only get better.

CHAPTER TWENTY-THREE

Cooper grumbled as he drove down the road. A frustrating woman, cancelled flights, and sick flight crews were making him want to take that time off his uncle Sherman had suggested.

After pulling into the driveway and whipping into his garage, Cooper walked into the house, instantly disappointed by the darkness. Looking at the clock, he realized it was just a quarter past ten. Stormy had to be in her room reading or something because she didn't normally go to sleep so early.

"Stormy, I'm home," he called while loosening his necktie. He was more than ready for their talk. He walked up the stairs while unbuttoning his top. Then he stood in front of her door for a moment. It was closed with no light shining from beneath it.

Frustrated, Cooper walked into his bedroom, slipped off his shoes, he kicked them away, then removed his name bar and pilot wings, and set them on the top of his dresser. If he couldn't talk to the dang woman, then he may as well take a hot shower and get food other than airline garbage.

It didn't take long to shower, and then Cooper wrapped a towel around his hips and made his way back down the stairs, swinging into the kitchen for a beer and crackers.

Before he knew what was happening, his feet slipped out from beneath him and he found himself flailing while trying to stay upright. He failed. His fall was painful and the sound of bare skin smacking against granite tile echoed through the kitchen.

"What the hell . . .?" Cooper groaned as he sat up, noticing the puddle that had caused this wreck.

Eventually he placed his hands beneath himself, pushing up off the floor and back onto his feet, with his pride wounded and his back aching. "This is obviously what I get for allowing a damn housemate," he grumbled.

A shudder passed through him, and that's when he noticed the cool air drifting across his skin. Slowly, he walked around the corner of his large kitchen island, taking care not to slip again on the slick floor, and then he stopped when he saw the French doors slightly ajar.

What the hell? His irritation was growing by the minute. When he stepped up to the door and heard the sound of bubbling water and the hum of the hot tub, he growled low in his throat.

Just as quickly as the irritation had grown, it quickly dissipated. Because if the door was open and the tub running, then that meant she was out there. Maybe his night was looking up after all.

With a smile in place where a scowl had been moments before, Cooper stepped onto the deck, moving with purpose toward the tub he could barely see. It was cold out, but that wasn't a bad thing, considering he wore nothing beneath the towel tucked in at his hips.

Suddenly, though, as he reached the tub and was about to call out to her, the figure in the water shifted, rising from the steam. He was nearly knocked over when she jumped from the hot water and sped past him toward the back door.

What if that hadn't been Stormy? He hadn't gotten a good look at the person.

"Stormy. If it's you, answer now," he called. There was no answer.

Cooper dashed after the person, exploding into the kitchen and quickly glancing across the room.

The person went down hard where Cooper had fallen not that long ago. The body slid across the floor as if diving for home plate.

Cooper moved forward, and then once again lost his footing on the wet floor, not counting on the added water his escape artist had left behind. Falling forward, he tried to catch himself, but it was no use.

Sliding across the floor, he tumbled into the hot tub bandit, both of them now rolling around in wine and chlorine-scented water.

Cooper froze again, but this time it wasn't from his need to fight. This time, it was because he had no doubt whom he'd just captured—and somewhere in their tumble his towel had fallen away.

There was no way he could hide the evidence of how he felt about this woman, not when there wasn't a single stich of clothing between them.

Neither of them spoke for several tense moments as both of them tried to gain back their breath.

"I . . . uh, thought you were in Japan," she finally said.

"Cancelled flights . . . sick people," he mumbled. "Why didn't you answer me?"

"I was panicked being naked," she said in a gasp.

Stormy was still beneath him, but that didn't help. With her hands against his shoulders, her fingers moving slightly, he was about to lose control.

Cooper found himself reaching up, his fingers gliding across her soft cheek as he gazed down into her lovely dark eyes.

A slight moan escaped her mouth, and that was it for Cooper. Her lips were moist and parted and he wasn't resisting for a moment longer. Bending down, he captured her mouth, and together their moans floated around them.

With every rise of Stormy's soft breasts against him, and the rhythm of her tongue mating with his, Cooper became harder and harder. Pushing her thighs apart, he rested his throbbing manhood against her moist opening.

She was clutching at his hair, no sign of regret within her. Gripping her hip tightly with one hand, Cooper leaned back slightly and then pushed forward, sinking himself fully within her heat.

She cried out—and Cooper froze.

"Are you going to keep playing games or are you going to admit that you know who I am?" he asked, suddenly furious.

He'd lost control for a moment, and he was still on the verge of doing it again, but dammit, he'd meant to talk to her first about this before plunging within her sweet folds.

"I . . . uh . . ." She wasn't forming coherent words and he was growing more and more angry.

"Is this a game?" he asked.

With no other choice but to strangle her or let her go, he withdrew from her body, wanting to cry out at how wrong that felt.

"No!" she cried out, quickly sitting up with her arms wrapped protectively around her knees.

"What else am I supposed to think?"

She was quiet for a moment. "You didn't want more than a one-night stand back then and neither did I," she said, her voice still too quiet for him to figure out what she was feeling or thinking.

"Maybe I did want more," he said. He thought of the locket he still had.

"Don't lie, Cooper. It was a great night—but it was only supposed to be one night," she said, irritation in her voice.

"Then what are we doing here now?" he asked.

"We were about to have sex," she grumbled.

He went stock-still for a moment, but Stormy didn't see the warning in his anger. She grumbled something else and Cooper shot to his feet.

"Is it sex you want, Stormy?" he demanded.

Now she was understanding the full extent of his anger. Her eyes rounded.

"Not when you're ticked off," she said, but her breathless excitement belied her words.

"If it's a night of sex you want, *that* I can give you."

Leaning down, he easily lifted her up and then began moving toward the staircase.

"Cooper, what are you doing?" She gasped as she hit his chest. "Put me down!"

"Gladly," he said, anger and passion mixing within him. He made it to his room in record time and unceremoniously dropped her on the bed.

"Caveman," she snapped, her voice still a bit breathless.

"Oh baby, you haven't seen anything yet."

And then the talking stopped as he joined her on the bed.

CHAPTER TWENTY-FOUR

Stormy should have been furious with Cooper but all she felt at this moment was excitement. The need in his eyes was something she'd never seen before in a man, and she wanted him, but hell would freeze over before she would admit it.

"Do you like games, Stormy?" he asked as he straddled her on the bed, holding her arms above her head.

Her breath was coming out in pants and she almost hated him for making her want him so badly.

"I think you're the one who likes to play," she finally replied when he didn't move.

"That's right, baby. I do love games," he said, his lips turning up. "And I win *every single time* I play."

It took a moment for those words to process, and when they did a shiver rushed through her. She wasn't sure if it was excitement or fright. But Stormy knew beyond a doubt that if they didn't have sex very soon, she was going to perish for sure.

Suddenly, he leaned across the bed and reached over to his night-stand. She couldn't see what he was doing, but then she sensed what felt like silk being placed around her wrists, and then she couldn't move her arms. Next, a cloth was being placed over her eyes, and the already dim room went dark.

"What's going on, Cooper?"

"We're playing, Stormy," he replied.

When Cooper moved, leaving her vulnerable on the bed, she twisted to get out of her binds. This was taking a turn she wasn't too sure about.

"Are you too afraid to play now?"

The rush of air was against her ear as he whispered the words. Then his hand began trailing down her throat and over the swell of her breasts, making her core heat to molten levels.

Stormy could lie to him, tell him that she didn't want to do this anymore, but her body would betray her. As his fingers swept across her nipples, they hardened painfully, and her back arched as a low groan ripped from her.

"I think you love this game," he murmured, and then he was atop her body again, and even if she hated the control he had, she couldn't deny how much she wanted this man to take her.

Still, she wouldn't tell him that. Even if she had to continue biting her lip to keep from speaking.

Her erect nipples reached for him as his fingers smoothed down her quivering flesh. And when his tongue suddenly swiped the area he'd been touching, she did cry out, her body nearing an orgasm without him even moving below her waistline.

Then he was lying on top of her, and she felt his thickness pressed against her opening. She pushed her hips up, telling him she was done with foreplay, that she wanted him inside her. But Cooper didn't give her what she wanted.

She was close to begging him for fulfillment when his lips were upon hers, his tongue thrusting inside her mouth the way she wanted his body to. He took ownership of her mouth, possessing her exactly how she wanted to be possessed.

And while he kissed her, his hand trailed down her hip. He leaned over, and then without warning, thrust two fingers deep inside her while his thumb rubbed against her swollen nub.

"Tell me you want more than my fingers, Stormy," he demanded before taking her bottom lip between his teeth and nipping it.

She was silent, shaking her head, refusing to give him what he wanted.

"You either tell me you want me to fuck you or this stops. I don't do forced sex," he growled into her ear as his fingers pumped in and out of her body.

She was so close . . . If she just held out a moment longer she wouldn't have to ask him.

As if knowing the moment she was about to peak, he suddenly pulled his fingers from her swollen folds, and then ran his tongue along the sensitive skin of her neck.

"This is your last chance before I'm finished," he warned.

She was still silent, but then she felt him withdrawing from her. In a panic, Stormy struggled to break free from her binds and reach for him.

"Fine!" she shouted. "I want you, Cooper."

"Good."

He said nothing else, but suddenly his welcomed weight was atop her, and he was grabbing her hip as he fit himself between her legs.

In one solid, hard thrust, he buried himself inside her, and Stormy reached for the peak of pleasure that was so close.

Cooper pumped in and out of her, while he bent down and once more captured her lips. It was rough and hot and taking her breath away. She never wanted it to end, but she wanted to feel the satisfying grip as she fell over the edge of pleasure.

Picking up speed, he plunged even deeper inside her, and Stormy was lost as she shattered around his thickness, her moan captured by his mouth as she shook in his arms.

"That's it, baby," he groaned, his lips ripping from hers as he threw his head back and yelled, his thickness pulsing against her throbbing walls.

And then he collapsed against her, both of them breathing heavily for several seconds. Stormy tried moving her arms again, only to realize they were still bound. She was about to say something when Cooper shifted and untied her.

He then lifted the makeshift blindfold he'd made out of a silky tie.

"What was that?" she finally asked when he pulled her against him and gave her a look she couldn't quite interpret.

"I've wanted you for a while. I figured out a few days ago who you were and I've been pissed you haven't fessed up," he admitted, his anger returning.

"I figured you didn't recognize me so I wasn't going to say anything," she snapped.

"Our first kiss I knew it, and that was the perfect opportunity," he said, moving over and sitting up.

She covered herself as she glared at him.

"Don't put all the blame on me. I don't forget who I sleep with," she countered.

He glared at her, and her after-sex glow was fully over now. She was just as angry as he was. She began getting up and he grabbed her arm.

"This conversation isn't over," he said through clenched teeth.

"I don't want to talk to you anymore."

"I make mistakes, but that shouldn't allow you to make a fool of me," he told her.

"I never set out to make a fool of you," she thundered, yanking her arm until he released her. "I'm not perfect. I make mistakes, too." She rose and stepped farther away, taking his sheet with her.

"Well then, we're a perfectly imperfect pair, aren't we?"

"I guess we are," she told him.

He didn't reply and she began moving toward his door.

"Where are you going?" He began to move off the bed. She held up her hand.

"I'm going to my room where I want to be alone."

Then she rushed out the door, running across the hall and entering her room, locking the door securely behind her. She stood there for a while and listened, but he didn't follow her.

It was what she wanted, she told herself as she stepped into her bathroom. Having sex with him again had been a huge mistake.

She was telling herself that hours later when she wasn't able to sleep.

CHAPTER
TWENTY-FIVE

The music was great, the volume loud, and the liquor flowing freely, but still Cooper couldn't find it in himself to relax and enjoy the night.

"What's your problem?" Nick asked.

"I don't have a problem." Cooper growled. "What's yours?"

"I'm a free-loving spirit. There's nothing wrong with me," Nick told him with a laugh.

"Yeah, yeah, I've heard it all before," Cooper said. Nick was a good guy, inside and out, though he also thought he was a comedian. In reality, he was. Still, Cooper wasn't feeling too loving toward him at the moment.

"Loosen up. I only get to be home for a couple weeks before I'm shipped off again, and I want to have some fun," Nick told him.

"I came out with you tonight, didn't I?" Cooper pointed out.

"Yeah, but you've been a downer all evening. How in the world are you going to play my wingman if you keep acting like a pouting puppet?" Nick asked.

"I didn't plan on playing *any* games with you," Cooper told him.

"Come on, Coop. I need a girlfriend for the night," Nick said with a laugh.

"Yeah, and since you're such an ugly bastard, you need my help," Cooper said, cracking his first real smile of the evening.

"You're the ugly one of the family," Nick quickly replied.

"Okay, enough with the insults," Cooper told him. "Who do you have your eye on?"

The two brothers looked around the upscale bar, scanning the crowd. Yes, there were a lot of gorgeous women surrounding them, sipping on their drinks and giving certain men the look that said he could be next to buy. But none of them were catching Cooper's eyes.

How could they when all he seemed able to think about was his new housemate, who happened to be the best lover he'd ever had? Since their night together the week before, she'd been avoiding the hell out of him. Now that he'd reawakened his body to her, he wasn't too pleased about that.

But it was good he wasn't seeing her, he tried convincing himself. Even though the woman had only lived in his place for a short time, he was beginning to get used to her presence. In fact, he couldn't really imagine the house without her in it now. She'd made herself scarce since their fight, but her touch was in every single room. He couldn't escape it and wasn't sure he wanted to.

Fresh flowers from his garden adorned the table, Stormy making sure they were cleaned up every day. And her perfumed scent lingered in every room, ensuring it was the first thing he noticed the moment he walked in the door.

Each night he passed her shut bedroom door, he felt himself grow hard. And each time it happened, he ended up in the bathroom with the faucet turned to cold. Never had he been that guy who enjoyed relieving himself.

It was too damn good when he had a woman there to do it for him.

Yes, he knew he could get Stormy back into his bed, but he also knew that was a road filled with complications that he just didn't want to deal with. Plus, he was pissed at her and the games she was playing. So what in the hell was he supposed to do?

Apparently suffer. At least that's what he'd been doing.

"The blonde over there is giving you the eye," Nick whispered. "And her friend looks to be just my style."

Cooper followed Nick's gaze and found an attractive, short-haired blonde who was indeed showing interest. Without giving himself a chance to change his mind, he sent a smile her way and crooked his finger.

Like clockwork, the two women slowly made their way across the bar.

"Hi, I'm Julie," the blonde said. "And this is my friend, Debbie."

"Nice to meet you two ladies. Care to join us?" Nick quickly said, standing up, ever the gentleman.

Cooper stood up as well, though almost reluctantly as he held out a chair for the blonde. What had her name been again?

"What are you doing out tonight?" Nick asked as he sent a questioning look his brother's way.

"We work over at the Realtor office across the street. Debbie and I just made a big sale and we're out celebrating," the blonde said.

"Yeah, Julie is a shark when it comes to sales," Debbie told them.

Julie! That was it.

"We will have to help you celebrate, then," Cooper said, finally finding his voice as he gazed into Julie's eyes.

He had his swagger back. *Yes!*

After a few more rounds, Nick was standing up with Debbie and leading her to the dance floor, leaving Cooper behind with Julie.

"You haven't been real talkative tonight," she said with a sympathetic smile. "Rough day?"

"I don't know," he told her honestly.

She laughed. "How do you not know?"

She was pleasant to be around, not overly flirty or needy, not bitchy, a nice girl. Maybe he'd introduce her to Wolf.

That thought made him pause. What the hell was wrong with him? He'd never tried to pass a woman off who was stimulating, pretty, and obviously interested in him.

"It's just been one of those days," he said with a laugh. "Can I get you a refill?"

"No. I think I've had enough for the night. I have an early day tomorrow," she told him.

Dammit. She was his kind of woman. Obviously not an overindulger.

"I was thinking the same," he said as he signaled the waiter to pay the bill.

She stood up, and he quickly jumped to his feet. "Can I give you a lift home?"

She looked him over for a moment and then smiled. "Maybe next time, Cooper," she finally said. "Here's my number. Give me a call."

She turned to see where her friend was, but Nick and Debbie were quickly approaching.

"We're going to get out of here," Nick said with a smile sent Cooper's way.

"Yeah, me too," Coop said as he grabbed his coat.

Nick raised a brow at his brother, and Coop gave a slight shake of his head. Nick gave him a taunting smile.

"All right, Captain, get some rest before you take up one of the big ones in the morning," Nick said.

Coop sent a glare his brother's way. He didn't need Nick to tell the ladies he was a big, bad pilot so he could get some tail. It was a game they'd played for years. At least the ass knew better than to tell them he was the damn CEO. He'd had enough wallet chasers to last him a lifetime.

"A big one?" Julie asked, pausing in her exit.

"Yeah, my big brother here is a pilot," Nick said as the four of them made their way toward the front of the bar.

"Ooh, that's impressive," Debbie said as she gave Cooper a look of interest.

"Not as impressive as Nick being a chopper pilot for the Coast Guard," Coop quickly said, and Debbie's eyes went right back to Nick.

His brother didn't care all that much if she was interested or not. He'd either sleep with the woman or he wouldn't. And then he would disappear in the morning. Nick was even more of a bachelor than Cooper, and that was saying a lot.

They made it out front, said their good-byes, and Cooper eagerly headed home. Maybe he'd see his elusive housemate. It was sad how much that thought perked him up.

CHAPTER TWENTY-SIX

Shooting straight up in bed, Stormy frantically wiped the sleep from her eyes as the pounding of her heart thumped in her chest. It took a moment, but finally she was able to brush the panic away and calm herself.

With surprise, she swiped her fingers against her cheek and found tears. Never before had she had such a vivid nightmare, one that woke her with terror.

Now that she was awake, there would be no use going back to sleep. She'd had a hard time falling asleep the night before, tossing and turning. When she'd heard Cooper walking in the hallway, then pausing at her door, it had made her heart race for an entirely different reason than this nightmare.

Living in this place for the past few weeks hadn't been good for her health, unless she counted it as a cardio workout because her pulse was racing all the time. That could be great for her since she didn't work out nearly as much as she needed to.

Taking her time in the shower, Stormy washed away her worries and fears, and then got ready for the day. She didn't have to work this afternoon, which was great. If it was nice out, she'd take a stroll down by the water and then maybe go and play in Cooper's garden.

She loved all the flowers he'd planted—or to be more realistic, that his gardener had planted. But she'd contributed a lot to the yard's maintenance since her arrival, so maybe that would save him some money eventually. Today would be a good day to mow if she could figure out how to get the blasted machine started. She'd never done it before. She hadn't lived in a place that required mowing.

When she began her descent down the stairs, she heard voices, and it made her pause. Maybe Cooper had company over and wanted privacy. She wasn't sure what to do. After standing there for several moments, ultimately the smell of coffee pushed her forward.

If he had guests, she'd just get her caffeine and then be on her way. When she stepped into the kitchen, Cooper was sitting at the breakfast bar with two of the three men she'd seen in the pictures all over his house.

Damn! Their pictures hadn't done them justice at all.

"Come and join us for breakfast, Stormy," Cooper called, not seeming to mind her interruption. She was shocked by how nice he was being all of a sudden.

They hadn't spoken two decent words to each other since she'd walked from his bedroom. She didn't trust the smile he sent her way.

"It's okay. I'm going to grab coffee and go out back and sit on the deck," she said. He was probably just being polite anyway.

"That sounds like a great idea. The sun is warm already this morning," one of the men said. "I'm Maverick, by the way, or Mav. Cooper told me he had a sexy housemate, but his description hasn't done you proper justice." The man gave her a smile that she was sure had dropped a few women's panties a time or two.

"Um . . . thanks," she said, unsure how else to reply. "I'm Stormy."

"Oooh, beautiful looks and a sexy name," the other brother said as he stood and came right into her personal bubble. He smelled good, too, as if his looks weren't enough to make a woman's heart stutter. "I'm Nick. We're Coop's brothers."

"I've seen your photos on the walls so I sort of figured," she said.

"I'll join you on the patio," Nick said, standing there and waiting for her to pour her coffee.

She was trapped into visiting with the sexy brothers now.

"Can you give my roommate some space?" Cooper grumbled as he pushed Nick aside. "How are you doing this morning?"

She was stopped in her tracks as she got the full power of Cooper's gaze centered right on her.

"I'm . . . uh . . . I'm good," she finally managed to stutter and she pulled her gaze from his.

"You seem upset. Are you sure?" he pushed.

"I'm fine, really," she told him. He didn't budge. "I had a bad dream and it threw me off," she admitted.

"What was it about?" he asked, his voice too intimate, his brothers sort of fading away as she stood there with Cooper.

"I can't even remember," she said, the visions that had terrified her already beginning to fade. "I was trapped . . ."

"I hate those sort of dreams," Cooper said. He didn't seem to be mocking her.

"Yeah, really sucks," she said with an attempt at a chuckle.

Her coffee was ready, so she held her cup as she began walking toward the back door, the three brothers on her heels. It was quite overwhelming.

"Did you make this quiche?" Nick asked as he sat down in the chair next to hers before scooping a big bite in his mouth.

"Yeah. It was just an easy recipe I learned long ago so I wouldn't starve," she told him.

"Well, it's fantastic. You can come to my house and make me some anytime," he said with a wink that had her cheeks flaming.

"Knock it off, Nick. You're embarrassing her," Cooper scolded.

"Just saying that a woman who can cook is always welcome around me," Nick told his brother, not backing down in the least.

"She's not available to cook for you," Cooper snarled.

"Touchy," Mav said with a laugh as he sent a wink over to Stormy.

"I can't really cook—not that many things," she told the men. All this flirting coming her way was really throwing her off her morning routine.

"I might make an exception for you then," Nick said before he stuffed his mouth again.

This time she laughed at the innocent flirting. Now she could see he was just trying to irritate his brother, but she didn't understand why. She and Cooper weren't a couple and neither Nick nor Mav had any idea that she'd slept with Cooper six years ago.

"I'm going to kick you guys out of my house if you don't lay off Stormy," Cooper threatened. Both brothers laughed.

"Do you know why Coop's been in such a bad mood lately?" Mav asked her.

"I, well, I haven't seen him much since . . ." She stopped when her cheeks went scarlet. "I just haven't seen him much," she finished in almost a whisper.

"Have you seen him enough to notice his bad mood?" Mav seemed to be the one who really liked to push buttons.

"No, I can't say that I have," she lied, definitely feeling put on the spot.

"That's it. You're both a-holes," Coop said as he stood. "Let's leave now so I can show my appreciation of you in the ring."

"Ha. Last time we were there, your ass got whooped," Mav pointed out.

"My mind was elsewhere," Coop said with a glare.

"Where was your mind?" Mav asked all too innocently before looking at Stormy and winking.

She began to blush again, though she had no idea why.

"You're embarrassing Stormy," Cooper snapped.

"Ah, she's tougher than that," Nick said. "I can tell."

This time when he winked at her, she smiled, and a small chuckle escaped.

"Yes, I'm pretty tough," she told him.

"See, Coop. You're all worried for nothing," Mav said.

"You're going to be the one to worry," Coop said, giving his brother a preview of what was to come by slugging him hard on the arm.

"Yeah, you're tough when we aren't in the ring," Mav said as he stood up and began dancing around Coop.

"Okay, we don't want to get in a match here and accidently run into the pretty lady," Nick said. She smiled gratefully at him.

"Yeah, yeah, the brother who's always the voice of reason until he's being a smart ass," Mav said before getting in a shot at Nick's arm. He then went dashing back into the house and presumably out the front door.

"See ya soon," Coop said with a look that left Stormy's belly quivering before he dashed off after his brothers.

When she was able to get her legs to quit trembling, she made breakfast and cleaned up. Then Stormy realized she missed the noise. They were full of laughter and taunts and the house seemed more like a home with them in it.

But she had to remind herself this wasn't her home—not for very long. So it would be best not to get too comfortable. That was easier said than done.

CHAPTER TWENTY-SEVEN

Cooper was at the controls of his jet, descending over Seattle. Wolf was busy calling out checklist items as Cooper responded with either *set* or *check*. Cooper, turning the control yoke to the left, began a sweeping turn.

On a clear and picturesque afternoon, the view from the flight deck windows was breathtaking. Below, in full view, Cooper could see the Space Needle and waterfront. As he gazed out the window his thoughts were of Stormy, wondering what she was doing.

After spending time with his brothers the other day, he'd come home and she was nowhere to be found. Then he'd been away for a couple days. But now, he had time off, and he was going to make good use of it.

"Wolf, what's the time?"

"Quarter 'til two. Pre-landing checklist complete."

Cooper was done with his anger. Now he wanted her back in his bed. Since pushing her wasn't doing it, he was dead set on seduction.

If he rushed, he could make it to the café and maybe talk her into going for a ride. Well, at least a car ride, maybe not the ride he wanted to take her on . . . Though that was a definite possibility as well.

Thoughts like that made his uniform far too uncomfortable.

"All right, checklist complete, gear down, and we're cleared to land. Listen, once we pull into the gate, I want to take off as soon as that door opens. You think you can wrap everything up without me?"

"You got it. Hot date?" Wolf smirked, peering over his sunglasses at Cooper.

"Hot date? I'm hoping so," Cooper said with a laugh.

"You hope so? What's that supposed to mean?" Wolf asked. "You never did call my cousin, so I know it's not with her," he accused.

"There's another girl so I didn't want to do that to your cousin. This woman is . . . I don't know how to describe her. She makes me go a little bit crazy," Cooper admitted.

That made Wolf laugh. "Have you actually met a woman who's your match?" Wolf said, uncontrollable laughter making him shake.

"No!" Cooper thundered. "I just really like to . . . uh . . . spend time with her," he said. For some reason he didn't want to dishonor her by talking about how good she was in his bed.

"This is too awesome. CEO of Trans Pacific Airlines and captain of the big, bad Boeing 757 and you have lost your game and are all fluttery over a mere woman. I have to say I worry about you, man," Wolf said between guffaws. "A hella rich and single guy with a giant-ass house and no one to spend your money on."

"I'd rather be single than divorced. And I definitely don't want a woman all over me for what's in my bank account," Cooper said with a glare. "You should also remember that I know your secrets, too, Wolf, and just how much is in your bank account."

"*Shh*. We don't spill each other's secrets," Wolf said, actually looking around, though they were locked up in the flight deck. "And, yeah, divorce sucks. Beth took off, said she couldn't stand me being gone anymore. I don't think she could stand me, period. Last thing she said was that she had met someone new. I guess there's always flight attendants, right?" Wolf murmured a curse under his breath about his soon-to-be ex-wife.

"Sorry, man. That was a low blow," Cooper said.

"It's all good. We did meet in Vegas and got married drunk," Wolf told him with a shrug.

Though Wolf was making a joke of the situation, Cooper wasn't a fool. He knew his friend was hurting. But men didn't talk about that sort of stuff—well, not unless the friend actually said they wanted to talk about it, and then it was just awkward.

"Well, you never know. It might work out for you," Cooper said.

"I don't want it to work out. Not when there's a sea of beauties every single stop I make on this plane," Wolf told him.

Cooper wasn't buying it. But instead of saying something serious, he decided to make a joke. It was what was expected after all. "Flight attendants?" Coop scoffed. "No, bad news, never. Stay away from the sky mattresses, they leave you with more than back problems."

"Not all of them, buddy," Wolf laughed. "Did you see that hot little number, Tori? Dang, I wouldn't mind taking her out on the town."

"Who?" Coop asked, going through his mental checklist.

"She's new here, but damn she has sass," Wolf said with another laugh.

"I'll have to check her out," Coop said.

"As long as you realize she's already taken," Wolf told him.

"Ha. Okay then," Cooper said. "But if she's that good, she won't look twice at you,"

"We'll see . . ."

They left it at that. If only conversations were this easy with the opposite sex, Coop thought.

Maybe tonight was the night he was going to get Stormy back into his bed. He hardened to a rock with just the thought.

It was a good thing Wolf didn't look down or Cooper would never live down the mocking. Trying to concentrate, he flew the plane, wishing he could land it right in Gig Harbor just to get him there faster.

Soon, he thought. Very, very soon . . .

CHAPTER TWENTY-EIGHT

Nearing the end of her shift, Stormy wiped down tables and glanced at the clock every thirty seconds, which made the time drag ever slower. Business was ridiculously lagging today, making her want to cut out. Only a few more minutes left, though.

When the clock finally signaled quitting time, she sighed with relief and told her co-workers good-bye before going to the back and gathering her things. It was only a fifteen-minute walk home, but her feet were aching a bit today and she wasn't looking forward to it.

When she stepped out to the curb, a flashy Porsche pulled up and she hated the anticipation she couldn't help but feel when Cooper stepped from it, looking positively delectable with his captain's hat on and his tie loosened around his neck. Their eyes connected as he moved toward her.

Maybe she wasn't over her fascination of pilots as much as she'd thought. No matter how she tried to fight her attraction to Cooper, her body had other ideas. Just the sight of him caused a stirring in her stomach and made her bones feel like rubber. She was in trouble and there wasn't anything she could do to stop it.

"Hi, Cooper. What are you doing here?" she asked when he was standing before her.

"My schedule changed and I hopped an early flight back from New York. I'm home for three days. I thought I'd give you a ride." He paused and butterflies fluttered in her stomach at the look in his eyes. She was about to respond when he continued. "We could let the top down and enjoy the sun and wind in our hair. We'll pretend we don't want to rip each other's clothes off for a couple of hours."

Heat settled between her thighs and she pressed them together. What she should say was no, and start walking, maybe burn off some of the sexual energy. Those weren't the words that came out of her mouth, though.

"Sounds like fun." She followed him to the car and couldn't help but be charmed when he opened her door.

"How was your day?" he asked while putting the top down.

"It was long and boring. I prefer having lots of customers, not only for the tips but because time flies."

"Yeah, I like keeping busy, too," he told her. "And I like speed," he added with a waggle of his brows. She was a little nervous being in the Porsche after that comment.

"How was New York?" she asked. "I think it would be pretty exciting to go there."

"Trust me, it's not as fancy as people think. I got into JFK from Los Angeles at about six last night and got to the hotel at eight. Then back to Seattle today and here I am, a true miracle of modern science and ingenuity," he responded.

"Well, it would be a thrill to see all the cities. I've traveled a lot, just not from the front seat, and not to anyplace people would choose to vacation."

"I'm not going to downplay the front seat. You have a view from there unlike anything you could imagine. Maybe I'll sneak you up there with me on one of these flights. You can ride shotgun."

Stormy's heart thundered at the statement. The ride in the front seat that immediately came to mind wasn't exactly PG either, dang it.

Cooper hit the freeway and then Stormy's breath was taken away for a whole other reason. The wind whipped through her hair, and she quickly reached into her bag for a rubber band. She tied her hair up and laughed with glee as they shot down the road, going well above the speed limit.

Passing cars on the left and the right, she couldn't help but notice that Cooper handled the car like a race car driver, not slipping across the lines a single bit as they sailed down the highway. When he pulled off at an exit about thirty minutes south of Seattle, she missed the speed as they crawled through a small town.

"This is a small restaurant, but one of my favorites," he told her, pulling up to a building she wouldn't expect someone like him to frequent. "Don't judge it by the looks. This has the best food in all of Washington."

He put the top of the car back up, then told her to wait while he came around and opened her door. She wasn't in a hurry to get out because she wanted to put her hair back into place and add a dash of lipstick.

"Do I look completely windblown?" she asked. She hadn't been expecting to go out in public.

"You look stunning."

The way his eyes darkened as he looked at her made the flutters reappear, and Stormy wondered why she was pushing this man away. She had to be insane.

It was a little early for dinner so the place wasn't crowded, but the older hostess greeted Cooper with a smile and hug before turning her eyes on Stormy, making her feel like she was coming up short.

"Table for two?" the woman said.

"Yes, Sally, out back," he said.

"Ah, looking for some romance are we?" she said with a cackle.

"Of course," Cooper said, then turned to Stormy with a wink.

She, of course, blushed and looked to the floor. What was she doing?

They were led through a small dining hall where the wooden tables were decorated beautifully with cloth and exquisite settings, fresh flowers in the middle, and a lit candle, the atmosphere romantic.

They were taken outside, where patio lights and heaters were strategically placed around the deck, though they didn't need them quite yet.

"We'll have some appetizers and drinks, and then eat dinner while the sun is setting," Cooper told her.

She wasn't even handed a menu. For a moment that offended her, but then she was impressed when he placed an order. Most of what he asked for sounded delicious.

When the Escargot Royal with a toasted bagel came out, though, she passed. Cooper laughed at her as he took a bite. She sipped on her red wine, surprised when she enjoyed the smooth flavor. Normally, she was a white wine sort of girl.

"Sometimes it's important to try new things. I learned that long ago," he told her, offering a bite of the escargot.

"I don't mind stretching the boundaries, but I'm not eating snails," she insisted. Instead she picked up a coconut-encrusted tiger prawn and dipped it in Thai chili sauce. That was much better.

They talked and slowly the wine relaxed Stormy as she gazed out at the stream trickling by and ate her roasted beet and baby spinach salad, the tangy raspberry vinaigrette dressing delicious.

"You must really enjoy living in this area and finding places like this," she said.

"I grew up in Gig Harbor and spent my entire life there. My dad worked in the city, but didn't want to live stacked on top of people, and my mom fell in love with the small harbor early in their marriage."

"Are both your parents still alive?" she asked. She'd only heard him make one comment about his mother.

"My dad passed several years ago, but my mom is still here, thankfully. She's amazing. I can't believe you haven't actually met her yet. She comes to visit quite often," he said with a laugh.

"You enjoy her visits?" she asked.

"Of course I do. It's my mom," he said.

She laughed at that. "You would be surprised how many people forget they have parents who love them. I adored my parents, but I have so many friends who never visit, never call, don't even know what their parents are up to," she said. "I would give anything to have them back for even five minutes."

"I'm so sorry you've lost them, Stormy," he told her while reaching out for her hand. "Family is who we can count on when the rest of the world fades away. There's nothing I wouldn't do for mine," he told her.

Her admiration for the man jumped up a few more notches. She didn't need to keep looking for reasons *not* to fall for this man.

"Yeah, I agree. I wanted to get out on my own and prove I could do it, but there are so many times I want to just run home and cry on my mother's shoulder before I remember she's not here anymore," she admitted.

"I wish there was something I could say to make your pain go away." His fingers continued rubbing her hand, which made her fidget with the silver bracelet she was wearing so she wouldn't reach out for him. "That's beautiful. I see you wear it a lot," he pointed out.

"I love it," she said with a smile. "My mom and I went to a class and made the bracelet then designed a few of the charms. Then every new place we would go, we'd add a new charm to it. It really was the thing that started my love of jewelry design."

"It looks like there's room for another one," he said as he ran his finger over her wrist, making her pulse jump.

"Yep, a few more spots," she answered with a gulp as she tugged on her hand. "It's too bad they aren't here to help me finish it."

He didn't release her right away. The longer he touched her, the more nervous she became. This wasn't supposed to be as romantic as it was turning out to be. It was just supposed to be friends sharing a meal.

"Just remember the good times you had. And you can complete the bracelet in their honor," he pointed out.

"When I think about making the charms, I get scared, like if I do that, then I'm really trying to go for my dream, and failing at it horribly," she said shyly.

"I think you should go for it. Why don't you?"

"Because school isn't cheap and it seems like there's never time to do it," she told him. Yes, it was an excuse, but she didn't believe in herself enough to make a career out of creating art.

"Where there's a will, there's a way. I think you should pursue your dream," he said as he leaned across the small table to be closer.

She was very quiet as she tried to decide if she was going to allow him to kiss her or not. But she pulled back at the last minute. It was just too intense.

Their dinner was served and it was as delicious as he'd promised. She had butternut squash ravioli with wild Maine lobster. He had the New York steak and potatoes. When they finished, both were comfortably full.

"Let's watch the sun set," he said.

He didn't give her a chance to tell him no. Instead, he wrapped an arm around her and pulled her over to a fire pit with benches around it. She was afraid to even breathe as they watched the sunlight dim over the creek.

"I'm glad you picked me up from work," she told him, enjoying the feel of his arm around her. "Thanks, Cooper. The night has been perfect."

"It doesn't have to end now," he said.

Something about the darkness gave her a bit of boldness. Turning to see his silhouette in the soft light from the fire, she struggled with how much she wanted to lean into him, accept the kiss he wanted to give her.

He didn't give her any more of a choice.

He took her mouth without giving her a chance to rethink it and the kiss overwhelmed her with how right it felt, how familiar. She took pleasure in his arms, heat warming her within as his lips caressed hers, growing more and more hungry with each passing of his tongue.

Finally, she pulled back before she got to the point of no return.

"Yes, it does have to end," she finally said.

He looked as if he was about to argue, and then he surprised her instead when he stood and helped her stand.

"Thank you for accompanying me. Now, let's head home."

Cooper paid the bill, hugged the hostess good-bye, and then escorted her back to his car. He played the radio on an oldies country station on the way back, both surprising and delighting her.

When they got back to the house, he walked her to the bottom of the stairs and kissed her cheek. "Thank you again."

He turned and walked away.

She couldn't tell how he was feeling by his tone. She almost wanted to rush back to him. But she knew that wasn't a wise idea. So instead, she made her way up to her bedroom—alone.

When she finally lay down, she wondered why she was fighting this so badly. There wasn't a reason to.

Maybe because she knew if she slept with him again, he was going to own her heart. And she didn't think he would want to keep it for very long. It might just be worth a little pain now in order to avoid a hell of a lot of pain later.

CHAPTER TWENTY-NINE

Three days came and went without Cooper making another move on her. Stormy wondered if that had been his one and only attempt at romance. The thought of it was slightly heartbreaking, even if it was for the best.

Then one night she couldn't stand being in her room any longer and found herself slowly coming down the stairs, unsure if she were intruding on Cooper or not. Before she saw anything, Stormy could hear the crackling of a fire and the smell of something delicious in the air. The darkened house was lit by the flickering glow that emanated from the great room.

The couch was positioned in front of the fire with the coffee table in between. On the table were two plates and two glasses of wine. Cooper sat quietly on one end of the couch, looking incredibly inviting.

Her cheeks flamed. What if he had a date? The thought of that made her eyes prickle with tears, though she felt like a fool to be feeling that way. It would be good if he had a date, she tried convincing herself. But the pressure on her chest assured her she really didn't feel that way at all.

She turned around to scamper away before he could see her humiliation. But that's when he called out to her.

"Come sit, Stormy."

"What is this?" she questioned as she turned back to him.

"You're on my mind constantly. I thought we'd have a nice evening together," he told her.

Stormy's breath caught as she looked at this man telling her that she meant something to him. Was it real? It seemed real. He felt real.

She had two choices. She could accept the invitation or she could run and hide. Stormy was sick of running and hiding. So she moved forward and sat—on the other end of the couch, which made Cooper chuckle.

Handing her a glass of wine, he raised his own in a toast.

"This is to you, Miss Stormy Halifax. You make me . . . I don't know, feel something I haven't felt in a very long time."

Dang, she loved hearing him say this to her. It brought back that moonlit walk, that night when she had felt special. Was her prince back to stay?

"Thank you, Cooper. You've been incredible," she said.

"I should warn you, I'm doing all I can to get you to come back to my bed—willingly," he said with a smile and a wink.

She flushed as the image of the two of them entwined on his bed shot to the forefront of her mind. Oh, how she wanted that more than she wanted breath. But it couldn't happen. She decided it was time to change the subject.

"Now that I've met your brothers, why don't you tell me more about your family?"

"That's a boring topic," he said with a slight choke. Of course it was a lie.

"I've met the Armstrongs, or a good amount of you, and boring is never something I would use to describe your family," Stormy said with a raised eyebrow.

"My dad was a pilot for Pan Am, but died several years ago. My mother was a talented photographer who sold her art in galleries around the country. Just your average family, really—I have three brothers, no sisters."

"That would explain all the photographs of you around the house. You obviously enjoy spending time with your family."

"Yes, my brothers and I are incredibly close."

"Okay, so I know Nick is in the Coast Guard, but what does Maverick do?"

"Are you sure you want to hear about them? I'm much more interesting," he said with a laugh.

She agreed. But to know him she needed to know his family, too.

"Yes, I'm sure I want to hear."

"All right. First there's Nick, who you know is a Coast Guard pilot. Then there's Maverick, who flies an F-18 for the Airforce and is based here at McChord Field. Then there's Ace . . . Ace has been away for a while."

The slight crack in his voice intrigued her, but she could see that wasn't something she could push him to talk about so she didn't.

"It's really cool that you all share a love of flying," she mumbled.

"Yeah, it just sort of happened. Our father and our uncle were pilots, and we all fell in love with flying at a young age, none of us realizing that it would become a career for us," he explained.

"What made each of you choose such different avenues of flying?"

"I don't know, to tell you the truth. When I decided to do it as a profession, I wanted to fly bigger and bigger planes, though I'm telling you it's not as much of a joy as flying my personal aircraft. Mav always wants adventure and speed, and I think Nick likes being a hero," he said.

"You are quite the trio," she said. She desperately wanted to ask about Ace, but he wasn't speaking of his youngest brother so she didn't want to pry.

"Do you want more wine?"

"I think I'm good," she told him, knowing she didn't want to lose her wits.

The darkness of the room, the warm fire, and the wine were quickly sinking her resolve. And the look in Cooper's eyes nearly burned her alive.

"Good, then I'm going to hold you."

He didn't give her a chance to refuse him; he simply stood up, picked her up, and then sat back down, pulling her onto his lap.

"I don't think this is a good idea, Cooper," she said, though she wasn't trying to pull away.

"A lot of things in life aren't a good idea," he replied.

His hand trailed down her back and Stormy leaned into him without even realizing it. This man was affecting her more than she wanted him to.

He said nothing else and she felt her eyes drooping as her head rested against his chest. She struggled with whether to take this to the next level, to make love with him again . . .

Soon the decision was out of her hands. She drifted peacefully to sleep.

Cooper glanced down, realizing Stormy had relaxed enough in his arms to let her guard down. Smiling, he gazed at her peaceful beauty. He leaned in and gave her a kiss on the forehead.

"We're getting closer," he whispered.

He slowly stood, cradling her in his arms. He was falling for this woman in a way he'd told himself he never would. And it was both terrifying and exciting. But even being shaken to his bones, he still couldn't manage to take her to her own room.

He slipped inside his door and laid her on the bed, not even letting her go for a moment as he clasped her in his arms and held on tight.

For the first time in a long while, he fell asleep with his lips tilted up.

CHAPTER THIRTY

The ringing of the doorbell startled Stormy as she was putting the finishing touches on a new bouquet on the kitchen table. She'd never had access to beautiful flowers, and now that she did, she decided it was a luxury she would continue when her time at Cooper's was over. She loved how bright they were and how they left a subtle scent in the air.

She turned toward the door. It was the first time someone had come to the house with just her there. She didn't know why she was concerned.

Obviously whoever was visiting had the code to the gate to get in, so there was nothing to worry about.

When she peeked out the side window and found Sherman standing outside, she immediately unlocked the house and threw the door wide open.

"I've missed you," she said, not hesitating as she threw her arms around him.

"I was going to say the same thing, young lady. I thought you promised to call me when you were free for a visit."

"Oh, Sherman, I'm so sorry. I've been busy with work, and well . . ." She trailed off.

"What are you hiding from me?" He was on instant alert.

"It's nothing. But I did want to ask you what is happening with the cottage. There are guys there, but they don't seem to know what they are doing. And then no one will be there for days at a time. One time I even saw three men sitting out there on the cottage porch drinking beers," she finished in a hushed voice.

His cheeks flushed, and she figured he was probably upset. She didn't want to get anyone fired, but she also thought it fair to let him know what was happening.

"I will have to check in on that," he finally murmured. "Now tell me what it is that you're hiding. I know it's something."

Should she tell this man she was dating his nephew? What if he thought she was using Cooper? That would break her heart. Still, the way he was looking at her made her feel like she had to confess.

"I've sort of been dating Cooper, if you could call it dating, but I probably shouldn't say we're dating. It's more just . . ."

She trailed off. Had she really just been about to tell Cooper's uncle that she and Cooper were friends with benefits? What in the heck was wrong with her?

"Cooper sure talks about you an awful lot," Sherman said with a secret smile she couldn't quite understand.

"Yeah, well, we are living under the same roof," she easily explained.

"Are you happy with him?" Sherman asked as he moved into the kitchen. He grabbed a soda and some chips and then sat down.

"Yes, but it isn't anything serious," she said, not wanting this conversation to get back to Cooper and freak the man out.

"Any time two people are in an intimate relationship, there's nothing casual about it," Sherman assured her, making her squirm in front of him. The only thing holding her in place right now was that she had convinced herself it was nothing serious.

"That's not what I meant exactly," she hedged.

"I wasn't born yesterday, missy, and you know there are many forms of intimacy. Don't mistake what you have with my nephew as casual."

"He holds himself back," she said, feeling as if she were tattling.

"There's been a lot that's happened in his life. There's reasons for that, but he's opened up a lot since meeting you. I've seen him blossom in the past month or so," Sherman assured her.

"He doesn't talk about his past. I don't know a heck of a lot about him, actually," she said with frustration. "Besides the fact that he's a pilot and has pilot brothers and one who is gone."

"The boys had a very difficult time when they lost their father six years ago. It wasn't easy on any of them, and they had to do some growing up," Sherman said with a sigh.

"Six years ago?" she asked.

"Yes. Why?"

He'd immediately clued in to her uncomfortable shuffle on her seat.

"No reason," she said, not making eye contact. Had Cooper's father died before they'd had their night together? If she had the courage to ask him, she just might know. "What's happened with his family?"

"I'm not one to gossip," Sherman said before smiling.

They both knew that was as far from the truth as a polar bear living in Arizona.

"I won't say a word to anyone," she promised, holding her fingers up and sealing her lips.

Sherman smiled as he got a bit more comfortable. This might be a long story.

"The four brothers were once so close, but life has a way of sweeping our feet out from beneath us," he said with sadness.

"Please tell me what happened. I want to understand." Anytime Ace's name was mentioned, Cooper became instantly distant. She wanted to know why.

"I'm warning you it's a long story . . ."

"It's a good thing I have nowhere to go," she replied.

"Well, it begins when Bill and I were just kids," Sherman said.

"I wish I could have met him. He sounds like a smart man, and a great father," Stormy said.

"Yes, he was a great man. And he saw a pattern starting to form with his boys. A pattern that terrified him . . ."

His eyes became distant as he slipped into the past and began speaking. "A long time ago, Cooper's father and I lived a privileged life. We knew only excess, but excess doesn't make for a happy life, at least not when you live under the abusive hand of an alcoholic father and a mother too weak to stand up for herself, let alone us. Of course, in those days, people kept to themselves and the help didn't dare intervene or stop the beatings. All they could do was console us and cover our bruises with fine clothing. As children, we needed an escape, a place to freely wander and explore, to be children, free from the oppression of our drunken father and his plans to shape us into the rulers of his financial empire." He paused, seemingly looking into the past by the glaze in his eyes.

Stormy didn't interrupt.

"Bill was five years older than me, so I was only ten years old when he met Evelyn. It was love at first sight, even though they were so young. Evelyn's family was all farmers, but they were pilots, too, mostly crop dusting and such. Well, in any case, never mind what a looker Evelyn was, Bill could have her—I was instantly in love with the airplanes. It took Bill a little longer to become infatuated, but soon both of us spent our summer days flying. It was an escape from our father. He eventually noticed we weren't home much anymore. He decided to show us what a real man he was when he found out we'd rather hang around a poor farmer than in the luxury of our expensive home."

Stormy wanted to tell Sherman he could stop talking. She could see how much pain this story was causing him. But she didn't say a word and he continued on.

"I know this is about the past, but it influences what happened later with Bill and the boys," Sherman said apologetically.

"I want to know," she told him gently while laying a hand on his arm, hoping to ease the pain but knowing she couldn't.

"We got home from Evelyn's house one day and Father was drunk and pissy. He told us there were union men who were trying to encourage a general strike. Of course, Father wasn't going to allow that, and he wanted us to see exactly what he was going to do about it, how he was going to deal with anyone who openly opposed him."

"Oh, Sherman . . ." Stormy was afraid she knew where this was going.

"It's okay, darling. It was a long time ago. Our father told us that the common men were nothing more than savage beasts, that their role in life was to support those smart enough to make the money. Money was what ruled the world. Without it, people were nothing. Hell, had Bill not met Evelyn, the both of us might have eventually believed that crap," he said, obviously horrified at the idea.

"Bill and I were silent on the drive to the mill. But the driver didn't even fully stop the car before our father jumped out at the main gate, having spotted the union rep. In front of all of his employees, he beat the man bloody, leaving him lying on the ground unconscious."

Stormy gasped. "No one tried to stop it?"

"You don't understand how different times were fifty years ago. Our father controlled the town. He had all the money and provided the jobs. People were afraid. I get that now, though at the time I didn't," Sherman said with a shake of his head.

"I couldn't just stand there," Stormy said, a tear falling.

"If you had children to feed, you might feel differently," he said. It wasn't judgment in his tone, but acceptance.

"Bill and I had never seen anything like that. We'd seen our father in a fit of rage before, and we ourselves had experienced the brutality of his temper, but we'd never seen him nearly kill a man. We were terrified.

Bill grabbed me by the arm and practically dragged me from the car. We went straight to Evelyn's place. She was in the barn with her dad working on their old bi-plane when we stumbled in."

"Did your father chase you down?" asked Stormy.

"No. That was the last time we saw him, actually. Later that night, Father was shot and killed by the very man he had beaten. He went to the mill that night and he never came home."

"Oh, Sherman. I'm so sorry," she said.

"Yes, it was tragic, but it wasn't hard to say good-bye. He'd grown worse the older he got, and we were afraid of him. Our mother was afraid. Suddenly we were free. And I think it's because he left us that we turned out to be half-decent human beings," Sherman said.

"Did you give up your inheritance?" she asked him. Never had she seen Sherman flashing his wealth, and he was always at that dilapidated café. It made sense.

Sherman laughed as he patted her knee. "I'm a very wealthy man, Stormy."

She looked at him with confusion. "I don't understand."

"We knew we didn't want to be like our father. But we screwed up. We screwed up big time. No, we were never as cruel as that man, but we spoiled our family, we partied hard, and played harder. We lived a lavish lifestyle for a lot of years. And then, Bill got cancer. It was one of those really nasty types that eats at a man slowly. He was dying, but he wanted to change things before it was too late," Sherman said with a sigh.

"What things did you want to change?"

"We agreed right then and there that the money would be pulled from the boys until they figured out how to live their lives in the right way. Bill's last words to his sons were of disappointment and Ace took it the hardest. He was the most spoiled. Bill and I spoke about it, seeing too much of his grandfather in him. We were hoping to stop that cycle. We tried explaining it, but they were too upset to listen."

"Why would he be so angry about that? It doesn't seem as if the others are."

"Oh, they were all angry, but not about the money. The boys had already amassed quite the bank accounts by then. They were angry that their father thought of them as failures when he died," Sherman told her.

"But the three I've met are anything but failures," she defended.

"They've grown up, become fine men, and taken responsibility for their lives. But no matter how much they've grown, each still feels he is a disappointment to the man they all idolize. They have to work through that, and part of the process is having a woman by their side who sees them for who they truly are," Sherman said as he looked Stormy in the eyes, making her nervous.

"Cooper and I are just friends . . . really," she said somewhat hesitantly.

"If you think that, then you have some more growing up to do of your own," Sherman told her, not unkindly.

She wanted to change the subject fast.

"What about Ace? Why is he angry at his brothers?" she questioned.

"He felt betrayed by his brothers when they did exactly as their father had wanted, getting jobs, changing into the men we always knew they could be," Sherman said with a shake of his head. "He's been on a mission to do the opposite of what his father insisted on since the reading of the will, but I know he'll come around. He loves his family too much to stay too far away. I see him once in a while and it fills me with joy when I do. He can't stay away from his brothers even if he tries to."

"Why don't they just make him talk to them?" She couldn't imagine anyone refusing the Armstrong brothers when they were determined to do something.

"They most likely will do that eventually. They have to find *themselves* first, though, before they can save their brother."

"I feel like I've invaded Cooper's life by hearing this," she admitted.

"Honey, I have a feeling you're going to be the one saving Cooper."

Stormy was silenced by his words. Long after Sherman left, she sat in the loveseat in the living room watching the fireplace flicker as the weight of his words rested on her shoulders.

She wasn't even sure if she could save herself, let alone someone else . . .

CHAPTER THIRTY-ONE

Was there really a way to measure time? People make comments such as *I'm running late*, or *There's no time to do this or that*, or *Time is running out* . . . But really, time keeps on turning no matter how you try to measure it. There are the same amount of hours in each day, and the same amount of days in each year. Time doesn't stop. It's steady. It's reliable.

And time kept on passing as Stormy remained in Cooper's house. The cottage had been long fixed, but he'd insisted there was a mold problem in it now from the water damage. She didn't see any mold, but she didn't want to argue because she wanted to enjoy each moment of time she had left with Cooper.

Time. It truly was a curse, she thought. If she could have one superpower, it would be to freeze time, or at least to slow it down. Because she didn't want her time with Cooper to end—not anytime soon.

On this beautiful summer morning, Stormy sat in the lighted bedroom with her legs curled beneath her, notepad in hand, while she sketched a pattern on paper. Pulling away, she smiled as she looked at the intricate bracelet she'd created—swirls of metal came up around a circled compass.

She'd spent days perfecting the design, originally wanting to create something for Cooper, but now knowing it was far too feminine for a man. Maybe she could use the compass to create a pin for his suit, though. It was something she'd have to think about.

Glancing up, she noticed the faint outline of the red alarm clock and the blurry numbers. She blinked to clear her vision. Once the world came into focus, Stormy realized that she'd been sitting in the same spot for hours.

She had a whole day off and the entire house all to herself so it didn't really matter, but the cramps in her legs insisted she had to get up and move around.

The peaceful silence of her perfect morning was interrupted when her cell phone began vibrating. She smiled when she saw that it was Lindsey.

"Hey, Lindsey," she croaked, before laughing. "Sorry, I've been drawing all morning. I'm just coming back to the real world."

"Hey, darling. I need girl time. Are you free later?"

"I have the day off, so yes I am."

"Yay. I came down last night for a medical conference, and I don't have to be back to Bellingham until tomorrow morning."

"What time is your conference over?"

"I'll be finished up by noon, or should be. I'll text when I'm done and we can meet up?"

"Okay, sounds good. Talk with you soon."

Hanging up the phone, Stormy leapt up and decided it was time to get ready for their lunch. She could sit in the perfect light and draw all day, but she missed Lindsey so she headed into the bathroom.

She saw a bright blue envelope taped to the mirror and slowly approached it, a smile on her lips.

Before Cooper, she'd never received notes before. She liked it.

Her name was beautifully written out in calligraphy on the back of it, so she carefully took it down and ran her fingers along the seal before opening it.

Inside was a card and a pressed rose. She pulled both out and gently set the rose on the counter before reading the note.

My Dear Stormy,
Meet me at Trans Pacific's hangar number 7 at eight tonight.
Wear a dress—and nothing else.
    Cooper

Instant heat surged through her at the words. She had wasted too much time not being in Cooper's bed, and now that she'd had him again, she couldn't get enough of the man.

"It seems I have a date to get ready for," she whispered as she glanced at herself in the mirror. Then to her surprise a giggle escaped.

A new dress was certainly in order. Though time kept on ticking, Stormy ignored it. Because as long as they were together, she wanted to make sure he never forgot her again.

That meant she was going to knock his socks off—and his pants, too.

Rushing to get dressed and ready so she could run out the door the minute Lindsey called, Stormy found herself restless as she sat on the back deck checking her phone every two minutes.

The day was progressing beautifully, bright blue skies with not a cloud in sight. Like a blanket, the warm sun beat down on the landscape of Gig Harbor, reinforcing how much she loved her new home.

I'm here.

Stormy jumped up at her friend's text message. It was about time. Rushing around front, she smiled as Lindsey stepped from her car.

"Stormy!"

"Lindsey!" Stormy rushed forward and the two embraced. "It's so great to see you. I can't believe it's been months already. I hate how time flies," Stormy complained.

"I know. It's been too long. But, from the look of things, your life has sure changed. I couldn't believe it when you gave me this address," Lindsey said with a wicked grin. "Did you meet a bank president or something?"

"Let's go shopping for a fantastic dress and I'll explain everything on the way," Stormy offered.

"Okay, how about coffee first, then shopping. My tank is running low," Lindsey said.

"Agreed."

They got into the car, drove down the long driveway, waited for the gate, and then sped off.

Lindsey lived in Bellingham, Washington, and the two had been friends since working in a café together back in Seattle when Stormy had first arrived. They'd bonded instantly.

"I want info, woman," Lindsey insisted as they drove toward the mall in Bellevue.

"My old neighbor, an incredible man, heard I needed a place to live, so he told me his nephew had an extra room. I was wary, of course, but I didn't have a lot of options," Stormy began.

"Wait! You were about to be homeless and you didn't once think of calling me?" Lindsey demanded with outrage.

"You're in a relationship, living in that tiny place, and I wouldn't even think about bothering you with my troubles," Stormy told her.

"Well, if we talked more often, you would know that my relationship ended and I would now love the company. Matter of fact, if you ever want to leave paradise, I have a room open for you," Lindsey said.

"Oh, Lins, I'm so sorry," Stormy said, reaching for her friend's hand.

"I'm not. He hit me and I gave him a black eye and very enlarged testicles," Lindsey said with a smile.

"Why didn't you call me when that happened?" Stormy demanded.

"I was embarrassed and, I don't know, being independent," Lins told her.

"I wish I were as strong as you, Lins. Dang, I would have paid money to see that man rolling on the ground gripping his balls," she finally said, a chuckle coming out.

"I can't believe he thought he would get away with it. I grew up with four brothers."

"Did you tell them?" Stormy gasped, imagining what they would do.

"No. I saved the pathetic man's life. If I had told them, he wouldn't have walked again. I did warn him that I would tell them if he ever came near me again," Lindsey said. "Not that I'm not perfectly capable of taking care of myself, but just to ensure I never have to see his face again. He went all white and scampered away."

"You were with him over a year. I'm sure it's difficult," Stormy told her.

"Not really. I'm used to being alone. I've yet to find a man who isn't afraid of my brothers. I lose respect for them when they are," Lindsey said.

"Yeah, I kind of like tough men, too, but relationships are complicated," Stormy said with a sigh.

"I'm far more interested in hearing about your man," Lindsey insisted.

"He's not really my man. I'm living in his house. We had sex at the Anderson wedding six years ago, and I was so embarrassed about it that I didn't even tell you, and then we've been having steaming hot sex now for a while. We're just . . . I don't know, we're just friends with benefits, I guess you would call it," Stormy told her.

"Yeah, we will see how that turns out," Lindsey told her with a laugh. "We're going to find a dress that is bound to drop this guy to his knees."

The two women spent the remainder of their afternoon going from store to store, trying on countless outfits. Just as they were giving up hope of finding the right outfit, Stormy walked from the changing room feeling like a million dollars.

Stormy wasn't a dress-up sort of girl, not normally. She wasn't down on herself, but she had never looked in the mirror and thought she was stunning. This dress changed that. It was like it was made for her. A black cocktail dress that, while modestly cut at the top, showed off just enough cleavage to tease. The hem fell just above the knees and somehow managed to make her legs look like they went on for miles. Her favorite part, though, was the plunging back. It was elegant and sexy and she felt more glamorous than she ever had in her life.

"Hot damn! That man's pants are going to be down before you take two steps," Lindsey said as they walked to the front register.

"That's the goal," she said with a wink.

When the day was over, they were both sorry to see it end, even if Stormy was anticipating her night with Cooper.

"Promise me we won't let so much time pass before we see each other again," Lindsey pled as they sat in the driveway.

"I guarantee you'll hear from me so much that you'll be sick of my voice," Stormy replied, her eyes filling.

"I'll hold you to that," Lindsey threatened.

Stormy reached across the small space and gave her friend a hug. Then she opened her door and climbed out. She stood in the driveway with the dress draped over her arm, waving as Lindsey sped away.

Now it was time to transform.

CHAPTER
THIRTY-TWO

It was exactly three minutes until eight, right on time . . . or a little early.

Stormy laughed quietly to herself as she realized she'd actually managed to make it somewhere on time. A slight squeal from the brakes of the yellow cab she'd hired to bring her to the hangar could be heard across the entire place as it came to rest outside the vast rusted building.

Being careful not to snag her new dress, Stormy stepped onto the uneven asphalt, wobbling a bit due to her choice in footwear. It had been a while since she'd worn heels. Stormy leaned against the cab with one hand while trying to maintain her balance. With a quick "Thank you," the quiet cab driver took the money, nodded his head, and barely gave her a chance to step away before he drove off.

A shadow of worry surrounded Stormy when she found herself standing alone, wearing a short dress in a vacant lot. When she looked upward, the rusty, faded blue hangar loomed over her like an unsightly set in a horror flick. It was not helping her current state of mind.

Nevertheless with some glimmer of hope, she scanned the hangar's surroundings, looking for Cooper's car. Why hadn't she reminded him she didn't have a car and asked him to pick her up?

Because she was independent, that was why.

Scanning the wide expanse of asphalt, she let out a relieved sigh when she spotted the trunk of Cooper's Porsche. She stepped toward the huge hangar door, her eyes still uneasily drawn to the rusty exterior of the building.

Well, it was an adventure, at least. Stormy pulled the metal door open, and hoped she wasn't stepping onto the set of the next crime scene in the papers.

"Hello?" she shouted. "Cooper, are you here?" The room was far too dark, giving her the shivers. Yep, she was definitely in a horror flick.

There was no response. She was growing irritated. Deciding to go back outside and return the way she came, she reeled when two arms wrapped around her. The shriek she let out vibrated off the metal walls. Her heart thudded, until she inhaled deeply and the sweet smell of his familiar cologne filled her nose. Her panic ebbed but not her irritation.

"I was getting frustrated," she said.

"I'm trying to surprise you, woman. Now be silent," he said with laughter in his voice.

She was about to reply when his hands slid across her stomach and down her thighs before coming back up and lightly tracing her breasts. Her breath panted out. The darkness of the room, his hands, the husky sound of his breath right below her ear—all played a part in making her knees shake.

His hands suddenly stopped their movement and she began to protest when his fingers brushed back her hair. Then she felt the familiar touch of cool silk against her cheeks as he covered her eyes.

"No peeking," he whispered, his hot breath sliding along her ear a second before his teeth gently nipped the spot.

Passion erupted inside her as he pushed against her back and she felt his arousal. He stroked the flame as he softly began kissing her exposed shoulder, moving across the sensitive skin as his tongue darted out.

Moaning, she tilted her head to the side, exposing her neck for easier access. Cooper quickly took the cue and moved around in front of her, where his lips then dipped into the V of her dress.

Although she'd been hungry when she'd arrived, thoughts of food were completely forgotten as he continued to work his magic. But then just as quickly as he'd begun, he pulled away.

"Come with me."

"If we have to," she replied breathlessly, not even caring if she sounded like a pouting child.

Cooper carefully guided her through the dark, then stopped. She heard a muddled clicking noise, and then the once quiet room was filled with a loud buzzing sound as the massive hangar door opened.

Still holding her arm, Cooper guided her outside, onto the pavement of the tarmac.

Goose bumps covered her skin as the crisp evening air flowed over her.

"You look absolutely exquisite, Stormy. The things I want to do to you . . ." he trailed off.

"I wish I could say the same about you, but I can't see," she said with a nervous laugh.

"I like keeping you blindfolded," he said as he kissed her neck again.

"Well, you're going to have to let me in on the surprise," she told him. "Where exactly are we going?" She heard the rumble of large jets filling the otherwise quiet night, and the pungent smell of exhaust slightly tickled her nose.

"Be patient," Cooper said, as he took her hand and began walking once again. "We're almost there."

Patience was one thing that Stormy didn't have. But for some reason, when Cooper spoke, she wanted to give him anything he asked for. That could be a problem—a big, fat problem.

"You know, Stormy, the only thing that can even come close to getting me to stop thinking about you is flying. But even then, it's a struggle not to let myself get caught up in thoughts of you naked and underneath me so I can do my job," he said, making her body throb.

"I'm all for finding a bed," she said, satisfied when he took in a sharp breath of air.

"I'm going to ignore that for now," he said through what sounded like clenched teeth. "We're here. I've been wanting to share something with you for a while."

He took off the blindfold and Stormy gazed at the plane before her.

"I'm going to take you up in my baby," he said, excitement beaming off him.

"Oh . . .my," she gasped.

Stormy looked at Cooper's large, twin-engine Cessna airplane. Oddly shaped, the aircraft had an elongated nose and a large tail section. The body was lined with round porthole windows. Immaculate white paint covered the metal skin with small sky-blue accents adorning the wingtips, nose, and tail. A bold navy-blue stripe lay against the lines of the aircraft. The combination of metal, plastic, and fabric came together to create a true testament of modern aviation.

Stormy's stomach sank. Soaring heights had always made her nervous. The peaks of tall trees, cliff edges, the crests of waterfalls, and the view from small airplanes all made her terribly uneasy.

"I'm not the biggest fan of small planes," she told him."

Cooper looked at her with worry. She could see it was unfathomable to him that anyone would be afraid of taking the beautiful piece of machinery out for a spin. She didn't want to disappoint him, but she didn't know if she could do it.

"She isn't exactly what I'd call small. A glider plane is small," he told her with a smile.

"It's a lot smaller than a 747," she pointed out.

"A lot of people fear personal aircrafts, but once you're up, they aren't scary anymore."

"I'm having a hard time believing you on this one," she told him.

"How about this? We'll get inside and sit down. If you panic, I won't even start the engine. If you feel comfortable after a few minutes, then we'll rev it up. At any point, you can tell me you're done and I'll stop, no hurt feelings, and no pushing you. I promise not to do anything you can't handle," Cooper said, while nodding his head toward the craft.

"You promise we can stop if I ask?"

"Absolutely," he said as he looked at her with encouragement.

"I guess . . ." she said, and he didn't give her a chance to back out of the first step—getting on the actual plane. He gripped her hand and moved forward.

With reluctance, she followed him behind the wing.

A quick flip of the handle and a slight tug was all it took for the entry to swing open. Folding outward, the stairs and door, all in one, came down. Cooper placed his foot on the bottom step, ensuring it was locked in place.

"Ladies first," Cooper said as he leaned forward and motioned for her to climb inside.

She took a few steps back. "I'm trying here," she said.

"All you have to do is look inside, remember. I won't start the engines unless you tell me it's okay. You'll see that it's actually just like a car, only with wings. There's nothing to it. We'll be perfectly safe."

Still unsure, she peered around the corner, poking her head into the opening but not stepping inside. Looking up and down the cabin, she could see tan leather seats, plush carpet, and a small set of blinds over the circular windows.

Cooper bounded up the steps ahead of her, and with a grin, he stretched out his hand. "Do you trust me?"

Reflecting on the topic of trust, she soon realized she had no reason to doubt him. A strange confidence overtook her fear as she again looked deeply into Cooper's sapphire eyes.

"Yes, I do," she said, a little surprised at the calm settling inside her. She removed her heels, grabbed his hand, and climbed aboard.

As they began to get situated in the flight deck, Stormy's dress snagged on the seat. Baffled as to why he'd requested she wear a dress, she couldn't resist questioning him.

"Tell me again why I wore a dress for a plane ride?"

"Because, beautiful woman, I'm taking you out for a nice dinner when we land," he replied.

"Dinner? Where?"

"It's a surprise."

Knowing Cooper was busy with prepping the plane for flight, Stormy sat quietly and watched him work. He held a checklist with one hand, mumbling a few audible words with the primary ones being *checked* and *set*.

As if conducting a symphony he moved or adjusted what seemed like every knob, button, and switch in the plane's flight deck. Entranced by the show, Stormy continued to sit patiently, letting her imagination run wild. It flip-flopped from dirty to clean and back to dirty again with ease.

"I'm going to start her up," he said, giving her a minute to tell him no if she wanted.

"Okay."

She really was a lot more comfortable. It did boil down to her trusting him. And she did.

Cooper finished by tuning the radio to talk with air traffic control and informed them he was ready to start. Opening the small side window, Cooper placed his face close to the opening and yelled, "Clear prop." With one single motion he engaged the starter and pushed up the throttles to feed fuel to the starving engines.

The plane vibrated with harmonious rhythm as both engines began to stabilize. These vibrations only fueled Stormy's confused emotions, not knowing if it was anticipation or anxiety of the upcoming flight.

Nonetheless, her heart was beating rapidly and strong enough to be felt at her fingertips. Her right hand clamped tightly around the armrest perched on the outer door and her left was hanging onto Cooper's inner thigh.

"Whoa, not quite so tight, there."

Stormy realized her nails were probably drawing blood and released her grip with a faint "Sorry."

Cooper smiled as he started to taxi the airplane across the tarmac and toward the runway. "It'll be all right," he assured her, placing a hand on her exposed leg.

Stormy soon realized that she wasn't the only one enjoying the moment as she moved her hand a bit farther up his thigh. It seemed her previous assumption about making him bleed might prove impossible, as all his blood seemed to be flowing elsewhere.

The glare of the setting sun over the end of the runway reflected on the slightly dull windshield as Cooper maneuvered the plane in perfect alignment with the runway centerline.

The brakes moaned as Cooper stopped to perform the final checks before takeoff. Once he was sure they were ready, he took Stormy's hand and placed it on the throttle. With her hands cupped within his, in a single smooth motion he gingerly guided her arm forward, advancing the throttle to takeoff power.

The twin engines responded almost simultaneously to the rush of fuel, bringing them to a deafening roar. Stormy's heart raced with anxiety over the task she was performing. Unlike the previous vibrations, the plane now shuddered and surged like a creature trying to break free from its bonds.

As if to free it from captivity, Cooper released the brakes. Responding with a leap forward, the rapid acceleration of the Cessna immediately pinned Stormy back into her seat. Trying to calm her nerves, she moved her gaze out the side window, where she watched the hypnotic pattern of the lights that lined the runway as they passed faster and faster under the wing and out of sight.

"All right, here we go," Cooper said as he gently pulled back on the plane's yoke.

Like an eagle flying high into the sky, the plane's nose rose effortlessly above the horizon. The loud spinning of tires on pavement turned into the steady buzz of electric motors as the wheels retracted into their bay. Stormy likened the deafening sound of rushing air to the roar of water over a rocky edge.

Feeling her heart pounding in her throat, Stormy concentrated on the ever-dwindling landscape below. The rooftops that lined the runway became smaller and smaller, then faded from view.

"See? Not so bad," Cooper shouted over the engine's noise, while smiling a bit. Pulling back even farther, Cooper banked the plane to head out over the waters of Puget Sound.

Stormy's fears began to melt away as Cooper flew the plane effortlessly over the shimmering water below them and they seemed to dance on the wispy clouds.

The flight deck was lit only by the subtle green glow of the instrument panel and the occasional bright surge of light from the wingtip strobes. Below her was a vast expanse of twinkling lights.

The tall office buildings, still lit up as people hadn't yet gone home for the day, and the layout of surrounding suburbs created fantastic designs of light. Highways, side streets, and city roads were filled with white and red flowing lights of traveling cars like blood flowing through the city's concrete veins.

Cooper made a large sweeping turn to the left and continued flying through the sky. The view below faded in and out of darkened countryside and small lit communities.

Stormy turned from the window, looking at Cooper, his tanned skin glowing with the dim flight deck lights. She watched as his muscles flexed with every correction he made to the yoke. She could do anything, face the scariest of her fears, with him beside her. That was a sobering thought. Maybe she was now forever lost to Cooper Armstrong. It might just be too late for her to ever let him go.

CHAPTER THIRTY-THREE

Stormy could no longer resist touching Cooper, so she placed her hand on his thigh, rubbing it lightly. Without saying a word, he grabbed her hand and placed it against his growing hardness, stroking her hand lightly against the bulge.

Hunger poured through her. Maybe she could make this flight a heck of a lot more fun, she thought, deciding she was going to be someone she normally wasn't—for at least the next hour.

Using one hand, she unzipped his pants, releasing his impressive manhood. Frustrated by not being able to get close enough, she reached down to unbuckle her seatbelt. Finally, she had free rein on his body, and she wasted no time plunging her hand into his pants. Wrapping her fingers around his solid steel caused a soft groan to escape him, filling her with confidence to push forward. The plane suddenly dipped to the left, throwing her slightly back.

Stormy paused what she was doing. "What was that?"

"A bit of turbulence. It looks like a storm is headed in," Cooper responded, moving her hand back with what looked like reluctance. "You should probably put your seat belt back—"

The plane suddenly dropped and rocked about like a boat on a choppy lake.

"Probably a good idea," Stormy said as she sat back and instantly tightened her seat belt.

"Just a bit of turbulence, nothing to worry about," Cooper said with complete calm.

The stars began to fade away as water droplets hit the windscreen and streaked down the side windows. Cooper showed amazing resolve as he gripped the yoke and concentrated on flying as the plane bounced up and down.

As they approached Portland, Cooper let her know they were arriving during the last push of flights for the evening. Like rush hour in Los Angeles, the sky above the airport was bustling with inbound jets from all over the country, and the chatter over the radio with air traffic control was uninterrupted. Stormy relaxed in her seat while she watched Cooper perform the magic act of talking to air traffic control, setting the instruments, and controlling the plane.

Flashing lights could be seen as they descended out of the clouds. The view below began to get closer as Cooper guided the plane in for landing. The runway was clearly in view, and to Stormy, it looked like a large freeway outlined by white, yellow, and red lights.

Like a field of sapphires twinkling beside this freeway of colors, the taxi edge lights glowed ever so brightly. After crossing the threshold, Cooper pulled the throttles back to idle as both engines sputtered to a slow rumble.

Though comfortable with her plane ride, Stormy was *still* ready to be on solid ground. She gripped her seat again as the plane bumped abruptly, the landing gear making contact with the asphalt below.

Cooper pulled off the runway onto the directed taxiway. With only the single nose wheel light to illuminate the center white line, Cooper had to rely on the bright blue lights that lined the taxiways for navigation to the local jet center. The rain was now a full-fledged downpour and visibility was reduced. Relying on orange guide wands, Cooper maneuvered the plane into parking.

With a slight squeal of the brakes, the large twin-engine aircraft came to a graceful stop amid large business jets, making the Cessna look like a model airplane. Cooper shut down each engine, one at a time. Each sputtered to a stop that shook the plane like an out-of-balance washing machine.

With the plane stopped, Stormy made quick work unbuckling her seat belt.

"Should we have dinner?" Cooper asked, a wicked look in his eyes. "Or skip straight to dessert?"

"Dessert," she whispered, more turned on than she had ever been in her life. "Always dessert."

"Come here, Stormy."

He didn't need to say anything more. With a quick motion, she pulled her dress up to her thighs and straddled Cooper's lap. Her behind pressed against the yoke as she pushed forward, running her hands to the top of his shirt. She felt heat building ever higher as she pressed her core against his rock-solid arousal, only a tiny piece of silk separating them.

Cooper leaned forward and captured her lips in a scorching kiss that would eventually have all the windows fogging up. She undid the top button on his shirt. She wanted to rip them away, but instead, with trembling fingers, she undid the rest one by one.

Stormy could barely breathe when Cooper slid his hands inside her dress and pulled it up higher. Unadulterated desire shimmered in his eyes, making her feel beautiful and wanted.

As his arousal pressed against her core, she began to push against him. The contact was driving both of them crazy. Her breasts were swollen with desire, her peaked nipples pressing roughly against her bra. His hands slowly started moving from her hips, up the curve of her back, stroking her skin the entire way. She knew he appreciated the plunging back of her dress as well. His hands slid down to her lower back and found the zipper. With one smooth motion, he pulled it down over the curve of her ass.

Next, he grabbed the straps of her dress and began pulling them off her shoulders, his warm fingers sliding down her arms.

Suddenly she heard voices and her entire body tensed. "I think I hear someone," she whispered.

Cooper seemed to have no worries about the milling people outside, because he didn't even hesitate as he continued removing her dress, revealing her pink lace bra.

As his eyes greedily ate up the view of her nipples straining against the fabric, she forgot about the people, too. She tugged against his head, needing him to take them into his mouth. Cooper hesitated too long, though, so she wrapped her hands around his forearms and pinned them to the back of the seat as she deepened the kiss between them. As their tongues entwined, he freed his arms, then made quick work of unhooking her bra, finally releasing her breasts.

As they pressed together, flesh against flesh, she could feel her swollen nipples pushing against his chest, finally giving them a hint of relief. He broke away from her mouth as he began to lick his way down her neck.

With every kiss against her skin, he gave her a gentle bite, making her cry out over and over again. He worked his fingers around to her chest, finally taking the weight of her full breasts into his hands, his thumbs skimming across her taut nipples.

Finally, his mouth reached the upper curve of her heaving chest, his tongue caressing the flesh. Then, his tongue traced one budding nipple. He gently sucked her deep into his mouth before retreating and scraping his teeth across the edge.

Her body shuddered as her insides burst into a raging fire. She pulled his head in closer, guiding him against her skin, not wanting him to stop. When he pulled away, she let out a groan of protest until he softly blew his warm breath on the wet skin, sending goose bumps across her body and making her cry out in pleasure.

His hands continued their journey, making their way to her thighs, slightly grazing the inside with his short fingernails. She tried opening herself to him, but the confined space was constricting. His hand skimmed up her leg until she could feel him touching the sheer fabric of her panties.

He moved his fingers over the lace encircling her leg. She moaned with acceptance, begging him to continue. In one quick movement, his strong fingers ripped her panties away and tossed them to the floor.

His intensity made her feel like she was his, and only his. Before she could even cry out, he plunged his large fingers deep inside her wet heat, making her body quiver with pleasure.

Almost delirious in her desire for him, she wanted nothing more than to have his fingers replaced with his erection. As his skillful fingers rhythmically pumped within her core, she gasped with approval, surging into his thrusting hand.

Her heart beat louder than the pounding rain outside the plane, her mind racing with anticipation of the moment he would plunge inside her.

Ready to continue what she'd started in the sky, she grabbed his thick shaft in her hand and began to stroke it up and down, loving the feel of his velvet-covered steel. He groaned his approval as he thrust into her hand, guiding her in pleasuring him.

Stormy's moaning became rhythmic as she desired the real thing with every thrust. More than ready, Stormy gave him one last lingering kiss before whispering in his ear, "Follow me."

She climbed off his lap, then grabbed his hand and led him to the back of the plane. She pushed her dress the rest of the way off, standing before him naked. Cooper's eyes rounded, giving her total confidence in her exposed body.

He looked so unbelievable, standing before her, shirtless, his gorgeous manhood standing proud against his stomach, while his lower half was still confined by clothes.

As if just realizing the fact that he had too many clothes on, he quickly stripped his lower half.

Stormy's eyes widened at the sight of him, completely bare to her; his sexy body and pulsing erection were too far away. Finally, he closed the gap between them and gently laid her on the floor.

She felt his warm breath sliding across her skin as he began kissing the inside of her sensitive ankle before he slowly moved upward. His lips glided up her calves, straight to her inner thighs.

Then, he was where she needed him most. His lips made contact with her dripping sweetness. The growl, escaping his throat as he began nipping her skin, sent a flood of fire through her. Needing him to continue, she grabbed his head, pulling his face into her heat as she thrust her hips upward.

The windows surrounding them were completely fogged. The cold air outside couldn't penetrate the warm cocoon they'd created. The sounds of the busy airport and other people made it clear that they weren't alone, but neither of them even noticed.

Stormy felt the pressure building as his tongue circled her sensitive womanhood, lifting her closer and closer to completion.

"Please . . ." she begged, knowing exactly what she was begging for.

With a new intensity, Cooper's fingers plunged in and out of her heat, while his tongue continued stroking her, leading her over the edge.

"Cooper," she cried out as his tongue slid around her a few more times. She shook as pleasure washed through her, and she fell over and over again into the most beautiful orgasm ever. He swiped his tongue across her a few more times, making her body jump.

"I could taste you all night," he softly growled as his head lifted and he looked up her body, their eyes connecting for one charged moment. The sight of his barely leashed passion had her body quickly heating up again in anticipation of what was to come.

Cooper looked away as he began kissing a trail up her skin, encircling her navel with his tongue. Continuing up, he made one more pass across her rounded breasts, gently licking each nipple before continuing on. Then, his lips were against hers again in a passion-filled kiss.

She heard the foil packet crinkle and then finally, he pressed against her and there was nothing to stop them. With a strong thrust, he plunged deep inside her, filling her so full, she cried out as relief washed through her. Quickly, he found a fast rhythm that satisfied them both, her body lifting up, matching him thrust for thrust.

Stormy lost all sense of time, all sense of anything except for the exquisite pleasure he was bringing her. He continued kissing her, his tongue thrusting into her mouth at the same time her body accepted him deep inside her. Their bodies slid together as passion consumed them on a never-ending ride of ecstasy.

He was hers—and she was his.

"Come for me, Stormy. Give yourself to me," he demanded.

The sound of his lust-filled voice, the feel of his thick staff filling her over and over again, the taste of him on her lips—all of it sent her over the edge, and she exploded, her body gripping him, pulling him even deeper.

"Yes," he called as he slammed his body against hers one final time and he released deep inside her folds.

Cooper collapsed on top of her, his breathing taking some time to settle, before he managed to turn them both, and then he held her close to his side. She felt sated and cherished at the same time.

And she wanted to do it over and over again.

CHAPTER THIRTY-FOUR

Cooper opened the door of his plane to a flash of lightning and the rumble of thunder. The rain was blowing sideways as the wind increased speed.

"We better hurry if we want to stay dry." Cooper grabbed Stormy's hand and helped her down the steps, straight into the pouring rain.

"Something tells me we're not going to stay dry," Stormy commented as she stepped into a puddle.

Having no coat, umbrella, or hoodie, anything to cover themselves—Cooper knew they'd have to run for it. Not letting go of Stormy's hand, he bolted across the tarmac.

Stormy tugged on Cooper's hand, dragging him to a stop. "I can't run in these heels. I'm going to kill myself."

"Well, take them off—let's go," he said loudly to be heard over the sound of the rain and wind.

"No way. My feet will get wet."

Cooper looked at Stormy, now drenched with water running down her cheeks. He burst into laughter. "You're soaked already," he said, not able to curb his amusement.

Stormy had a look of disgust on her beautiful face, making him laugh all that much harder. This woman was so honest with her emotions—an open book for the world to read if only they took the time to look.

He shifted, realizing that's why he was able to trust her whereas he'd never trusted another woman. She was brutally honest and he felt his guard chipping away more and more each time he was in her presence.

"I don't see how this is—" she stopped mid-sentence, realizing that standing in the pouring rain to have a discussion was only making matters worse. But how could it be worse? They were absolutely soaked to the bone, and she was concerned about getting her feet wet. She cracked a smile—a smile that turned into full-blown laughter as she joined him. "You're not so dry either," she made sure to tell him.

"Well, if you don't want to get your feet wet, then I'm going to carry you."

Before Stormy could respond, Cooper swooped her into his arms and flung her over his shoulder before sprinting toward the terminal door.

Cooper nudged it open with his foot; the wind caught it and it burst open as he ran through. They knew they made an amusing sight: Stormy in his arms and the two of them still roaring with laughter.

He stopped in his tracks, his smile starting to deflate as he noticed the room was silent and all the patrons were staring at them. There he stood, dripping water on the pristine floor, holding a woman over his shoulder, while laughing almost hysterically.

Cooper gently slid Stormy down his body, making sure she was steady on her feet before he let go. She turned to see all eyes trained on them. Her laughter soon slowed to complete silence and he watched her as she nervously brushed the wet hair from her eyes. They began walking, slowly; the only sound that could be heard was the squishing of water from Cooper's wet shoes.

"Ahem . . . evening, gentlemen," Cooper said while clearing his throat and nodding his head.

Cooper and Stormy approached the front desk, where a spunky and attractive secretary couldn't wait to greet them.

"Well, good evening, Captain Armstrong," she paused slightly as she focused on their watered-down state.

"Good evening, Andrea. Could you have the guys top off the plane, and tow it back to the hangar for the night?"

"Absolutely, Captain Armstrong," Andrea responded, grabbing the radio to relay the order. ". . . and your limo is waiting out front."

He saw the surprised delight on Stormy's face, and felt a moment of triumph at getting their date right.

With a smile to Andrea, Cooper then locked arms with Stormy and escorted her to the door. A jet-black limo sat parked in front of them with glistening chrome wheels and soft yellow courtesy lights.

"I thought we could ride to our destination in style." Cooper opened the back door and motioned with his hand, "After you." Stormy climbed inside the limo with Cooper shutting the door behind them.

"Where are we going?" Stormy questioned as they got situated.

"That's a surprise."

Stormy looked nervously at her appearance in a compact mirror she pulled from her purse. "I can't go anywhere nice looking like this," she replied, her words tripping over themselves.

"You told me you trusted me, so keep doing that." Cooper smiled as the car began moving.

The hour-long ride seemed to end far too quickly as Stormy desperately finger-combed her hair and tried repairing her makeup. It was no use. She was a drowned rat.

When the door opened, swinging outward, the driver standing beside it, she thought about refusing to exit. But she'd promised to trust Cooper.

Stepping out, she smiled as she looked at the front doors to what had to be a hotel.

"Welcome to Allison Inn and Spa," a uniformed man said, taking her hand.

"Thank you," she told him, feeling terrible in her wet clothing.

"You are gorgeous," Cooper assured her. "Let's get you inside."

"Do you have bags, sir?" the man asked.

"They've already been delivered," he told him.

When Cooper gave his name, the man seemed to stand a bit more at attention and immediately took them inside, bypassing the normal check-in. Stormy didn't know what to think about that.

The man boasted of the hotel's spa and told them to call if they needed anything at all, but that according to Cooper's instructions, they wouldn't be disturbed at any time during their stay.

He quickly slipped away as soon as Cooper and Stormy stepped into the penthouse suite that had her gasping in delight. Before she was able to look at all the space, Cooper grabbed her, pulling her tightly against him.

"Now that I have you alone . . ." he said, his eyes going instantly dark.

"What shall we do?" she said, instantly hungry for him all over again.

"First we will change," he said, though he looked as if he'd much rather just rip their clothes off. "Then you will get a night of romance," he added with a huge smile. "Then I will devour you."

"Or we could go straight to the devouring," she huskily said, which made his eyes go even darker.

"Don't tempt me, woman. I've put a lot of time into this," he said as he spun her toward a room and gently swatted her on the butt.

She got even wetter as she moved away.

Stepping into the luxurious bedroom, Stormy felt as if she were on another planet. Cooper had literally whisked her away in his private plane, brought her to a penthouse suite in the wine country of Oregon, and then on top of that there were a couple presents sitting on the bed.

Slowly walking over to them, she ran her fingers through the ribbons and sighed. She wanted to dive right in and open them, but she needed to take a shower first.

Rushing through the shower, she couldn't wait to go back out to the gifts. Wrapping a towel around herself, she approached the bed and began opening the boxes carefully. Her cheeks flamed a little as she pulled out a delicate lingerie set and matching silk robe.

But she wanted to please Cooper, wanted to wear the sexy outfit. So she slipped into it before looking at the smaller package. Her fingers trembling, she undid the ribbon, and then fell back on the bed when her knees went weak.

Fighting desperately not to let the tears fall, she gently touched the locket that sat on a bed of velvet next to a stunning pair of what appeared to be diamond earrings. They were beautiful, but the locket was priceless.

It was the very first piece of jewelry she'd designed and created. And Cooper had obviously found it and kept it. Her heart swelled and her knees were weak. One tear escaped as she slipped it around her neck.

He'd gone and done it. He'd made her fall in love with him.

It took several minutes for her to compose herself, and then she couldn't wait to be in his arms. What a cherished gift he'd given back to her.

When she stepped from the room to find candlelight and soft music along with champagne, chocolate-covered strawberries, and an assortment of appetizers, her senses were overwhelmed.

"Cooper . . ." Her husky voice made him turn his head and the glow that instantly entered his eyes gave her confidence. "I'm ready for more dessert," she said.

He didn't hesitate. His clothes went flying as he rushed across the room to her. He lifted her and turned right back toward the bedroom she'd just exited.

"Romance will come after we've appeased this hunger," he growled.

"I don't think it's ever going to be appeased, but you've given me more romance with this than anything else you could have ever given me," she told him as her fingers ran over the locket she wore.

"I never stopped thinking about you through the years. I needed you to know this. I'm giving up my lucky charm," he said with a gentle smile.

"You use it as a lucky charm?"

"No. You've been my lucky charm all along," he said.

She couldn't speak. But then she didn't have to because all talking stopped as his lips captured hers.

CHAPTER THIRTY-FIVE

Cooper and Nick moved in sync around the hangar where they were working on the P-51 D plane they'd been ecstatic to get their hands on. It was going to take them months, if not over a year, to complete the project, but when she was restored to her former glory, they'd be fighting over who got to fly her the most.

Turning too fast, Cooper knocked over a bottle of oil, the slimy black liquid running through his fingers. He quickly cleaned it up, then got back to his brother who was beneath the plane hard at work.

"Are you going to take all night?" Nick hollered.

"I'm coming," Cooper yelled back with a roll of the eyes.

"Cooper Armstrong! Is that really you?"

Cooper turned around and found Keri Jensen running up to him from across the hangar bay.

"Hi, Keri. What are you doing here?"

"I'm here with my brother. He's taking me up in a few minutes."

"Well, I don't want to keep you," he said.

"I've missed you," she cried.

Keri had been one of his favorite flight attendants to flirt with back in the day, a tall blonde with all the right curves in exactly the right places. Plus, she was perky, fun, and always out for a good time. He'd decided after one night of hanging out with her that he thanked God she was one of the few women he hadn't slept with. They were much better off as friends.

Before he even finished his thoughts, she was launching herself into his arms, her legs wrapping around his waist as she grabbed his cheeks and kissed him with a loud smacking noise.

"Keri, I'm in a relationship. I can't have you crawling on me anymore," he said with a laugh as he tried to untangle her.

"Oh, heck, if you're in a relationship, she'll be the type of girl who will appreciate me," she told him, not moving.

"She's great, but I don't think any girl likes to see her man wrapped around a pretty blonde," he said with a laugh.

"But I've missed you so much," she said with a pout.

"I've missed you, too." And Cooper did love his friends.

"Work has called," he told her with another laugh.

"It's not always about being a mile high in the sky, love. Friends are important, too," she reminded him.

"Yes, I tend to forget that at times," he admitted.

"Okay, my brother is gonna kill me. Love you, darling." She leaned in, gave him another smacking kiss, then jumped down.

"Just think, you actually thought about marrying that girl so you could get your inheritance," Nick said with a laugh.

"For all of two seconds. Then I realized the money just wasn't worth it," Cooper replied with a laugh. "I adore her, but she's just too high maintenance. It took me seconds to decide friendship was the only thing we could sustain."

"Well, looks like you might be getting that money after all," Nick added with a wink.

"Yeah," Cooper said. Though he didn't give a damn about the rest of his inheritance. He had more than enough money of his own. He didn't need any more. But he did want to marry Stormy. It was a wonder to him. "I am going to ask her to marry me," he finished.

"Not bad. A hot wife, more cash in your bottomless pockets, and all the sex you can ask for."

"You're such an ass, Nick," Cooper replied with another laugh. "But yes, married life doesn't seem so bad anymore."

"Are you kidding me?" Stormy was standing in the doorway, her face washed of color.

"Stormy," Cooper called, a smile lifting his lips until he saw her face. Crap! How much of that conversation had she heard? He played it back in his mind. It couldn't have sounded right.

"I thought . . . I don't know what I was thinking," she said, her eyes filling.

"Let's talk. It's not what you think," he said as he held a hand out to her like she was a frightened puppy.

"It sounds like you need to find a wife to get a bunch of money," she said.

Tightness constricted his chest. He'd been so worried about not allowing a woman to use him for his money and here she was infuriated that he'd kept the inheritance a secret from her. How wrong could he have been? Apparently, he was a fool.

But there was a light inside him in the midst of all of this because she was unlike any woman he'd ever been around. She was fresh and pure, and there was nothing even remotely conniving or greedy about her.

"Well, yes and no. I get my inheritance if I marry, but that's not why I was thinking of proposing," he told her. He was fumbling this badly. He wasn't doing well being put on the spot.

"You aren't who I thought you were, Cooper," she said, her tears drying as she glared at him.

"I've never pretended to be anyone other than who I am with you, Stormy," he told her. It was so true.

"Find another bride to get your inheritance."

She turned and ran from the hangar.

"Ouch. You screwed that one up," Nick said.

"You screwed it up. Hell!" Cooper thundered. "I'll go talk to her." He took a step forward to catch her and fell flat on his face.

"What the hell?" Sharp pain shot through his ankle as he looked down to the jack he'd tripped over.

"Ouch," Nick said with another laugh.

"Dammit, Nick. I don't have time for this. I really must go talk to her," Cooper said as he slowly stood and tried to put weight on the ankle. Pain clouded his vision.

"Ha. I don't think you're going anywhere but the doctor to get that foot looked at," Nick told him.

"When in the hell are you going to learn to put your things away," Cooper growled, knowing his brother was right.

"Hey, don't try to change me, man," Nick said. "Let's get out of here. You can grovel with your woman later."

Cooper reluctantly agreed as he limped behind his brother toward his old, filthy truck. "Why in the world are you still driving this piece of shit?" Cooper grumbled.

"Because I love old Bitsy. She's been good to me," Nick said before his grin widened. "Besides, when the big EMP strike hits, your and Mav's fancy electronic cars won't be nothing but pretty lawn ornaments, while this beast will be hauling your asses around."

"It's okay. If it hits, I'll most likely be up in the air, falling to the ground."

"Well, that's a positive way to look at things," Nick said with a roll of his eyes.

The truck roared to life, and they headed from the parking lot in the direction of the urgent care center, where the staff knew the

Armstrong brothers by name. Injuries tended to happen when you were adrenaline junkies.

When his brother stopped talking, Cooper reached into his pocket and pulled out the velvet box he'd been holding on to for three days.

Unexpectedly, he had fallen in love with Stormy. And though she was upset with him right now, when she was calm and the two of them were talking in a reasonable manner, they could get on with their lives.

That improved his mood. Why wouldn't it work out?

CHAPTER THIRTY-SIX

What was she going to do? Stormy was so flustered she couldn't even think. Instead of even trying, she hurried back to the house and called a cab. She had a few items to grab; the rest she didn't care about. She needed time to come to terms with the situation and she needed to do it away from Cooper.

They were going to talk again, but she couldn't even imagine looking at his face right now. Had this all been his way of getting money? Didn't he have enough? How much did one person need?

She walked into the house, then rushed to her room and packed what she would need for the next couple weeks. She'd send a friend for the rest later.

Stepping into the kitchen, she pulled out a pen and paper and jotted down a quick note. She then took the picture of the ultrasound out of her purse. He had a right to know, even if she didn't want to share this joy with him.

Just as she stood up, she heard the front door slam, and her heart lodged in her throat. No! This wasn't happening.

"Stormy!"

A sigh of relief washed through her. Though she didn't want to face any of the Armstrong brothers right now, she'd rather deal with Nick than Cooper.

She stayed quiet, hoping he wouldn't think she was there. When she thought she heard him go up the stairs, she left the note and picture and then rushed to the front door.

"Stormy? What's up with the bag?" Nick asked, blocking her escape.

"Hey, Nick. I . . . um . . . I've got to go," she said, trying to decide if she could rush him to get past.

"Go where?" He wasn't budging.

"I just have to go," she told him.

"Stormy . . ." He seemed at a loss for words.

"Please . . ." Her voice choked. "No!" She pushed past him, and in his surprise he let her go.

She rushed out to the waiting cab, nearly weeping again, she was so grateful it was there. Getting into the backseat, she told the driver to just go. He was confused a moment, but then he pulled out onto the street, not asking any questions.

She told him the address of where they were going after he was a couple blocks away from the house. She leaned back, grateful to have gotten away in one piece.

"What the hell?" The cab driver suddenly swerved, making Stormy's stomach heave. "I'm sorry ma'am. There's a problem."

She looked out the window and was horrified to see Nick's truck blocking them. Had he chased the cab down?

"Stormy, come with me!"

He'd thrown open her door and was standing there looking fierce.

"Nick, what in the world are you doing?"

"I'm keeping you from making one hell of a mistake," he said, reaching in and taking her arm.

"Ma'am, do I need to call the police?" the cabbie asked, only looking half interested in what was going on.

"No, you don't need to call the flipping police," Nick snapped. "Do I look like a maniac?"

The cab driver's brows rose up as if telling Nick that yes, indeed he did.

"No. You don't need to call the police," Stormy said before things got too out of control.

Nick tossed some money at the cabbie, then grabbed her bag and her arm and led her from the cab and to his truck. She reluctantly allowed him to drag her behind him.

She climbed into his dirty truck. "Are you kidnapping me?" she asked, getting some of her bite back.

"Yes," he said, not worried about her temper.

"Well, since you got rid of my ride, then you can take me where I'm going," she told him. Even though she wasn't sure she wanted any of the Armstrong men to know where she was going, she wasn't left with much choice now. She could go to the train station. Then he wouldn't have a clue.

"Take me downtown to the train station," she finally said. She would accept his ride, but not listen to him.

"Cooper's at the doctor's office," he said, his voice sounding solemn.

She didn't want to bite, but she couldn't help it. "What's wrong?"

"It's bad . . ." he began.

"Nick, what happened?" she demanded.

"Okay, it's not too bad, but he sent me in case you were doing exactly what you're doing, and trying to run away."

"Ugh!" She threw her head back and sighed in disgust.

"Why are you running, Stormy?"

She was silent for a while, but he just waited, glancing at her now and then with an anxious expression. She knew she wasn't getting out of this.

"Look, I thought we had something together, your brother and I. Now, I see he's just greedy, that I could have been any woman. I just so happened to be the one around when he got the urge to add to his bank account."

"You do have something," Nick insisted. "What you heard . . ." he began when she stopped him.

"I heard you loud and clear, Nick. Does he or does he not get a large sum of money if he marries?" she demanded.

Nick squirmed in the seat next to her and she had her answer, though she wasn't getting out of the truck until he said it out loud. She needed this. She needed to let go. She gave him a hard look until his shoulders sagged and he let out a sigh.

"Yes. We all get the second part of our inheritance when we marry. But, I guarantee you that Cooper cares about you. Him dating you has nothing to do with that stupid clause in the will."

"I don't believe you," she said with a sigh. Her anger was draining, and she just felt empty inside. Her fingers gently skittered across her flat stomach. What was she going to do now?

"He loves you, Stormy. I know my brother and I know how he feels," Nick insisted.

This was why she hadn't wanted to wait around. She'd known that glimmer of hope would be sitting in her heart at the first explanation that was given to her. Because she wanted it to be real between her and Cooper.

"I need time, Nick. I can't think right now. I just need time, please," she said, her eyes burning, her muscles trembling.

He gave her a look that said he wanted to argue more, but then he hung his head.

"My brother is going to kill me," he mumbled. "But if time is what you need, then I will give that to you. But I refuse to drop you at a train station." His words were firm.

"Okay, you can take me to my friend's house, but you have to promise not to tell Cooper. I want time alone to figure out how I feel without mixed emotions being involved."

"I'll keep your secret."

They rode silently to Bellingham and Nick gave her a hug before leaving her behind. Stormy would get it all figured out, she promised herself. Her fingers rubbing over her belly, she knew she had no other choice other than to figure it out.

CHAPTER THIRTY-SEVEN

The setting sun lay peacefully below the horizon as the vast sea of stars filled the purple sky, mirroring the ocean's surface as if the two were one. The Trans Pacific airliner climbed through the smooth air feeling motionless, uninterrupted except by occasional white puffs of clouds. The interior of the cabin was mostly dark, with only a few reading lights illuminating the beige-colored walls and blue cloth seats.

It would be a long flight and most of the passengers were getting comfortable, preparing to sleep. The flight attendants were occupied in the front galley, chatting about the current company gossip and the newest romance novels by Ruth Cardello, J. S. Scott, and Sandra Marton.

One of the reading lights was softly illuminating a children's book as a mother quietly read to her toddler, who was holding a teddy bear.

An elderly couple seated a few rows back, not able to sleep, continued with their nightly routine. The gentleman sat with reading glasses on his nose, trying to answer the next crossword question. His wife sat in silence, her eyes fixed on her favorite Nora Roberts story. A pair of newlyweds was getting comfortable not far behind them, just having begun their journey on a two-week-long honeymoon.

Cooper and Wolf were busy making radio calls and setting their instruments for the continuation of the flight.

As both captain and first officer settled into their seats, having completed all checklists and entries into the flight computer, the aircraft cruised on autopilot. Cooper agreed to take the first watch, as Wolf began to play a movie on his iPad.

Periodically glancing at the flight instruments, Cooper mostly gazed out the window at the stars above and the purple sunset below. His thoughts, as always, were on Stormy. It had been two days since they'd spoken. Two days since he'd learned he was going to be a father.

Nick had assured him that Stormy only needed a couple days of peace, and then she would listen to him. Well, a couple of days were up and she wasn't answering her phone.

What he needed to do was get this damn plane to Hawaii so he could get turned around and back to the woman who would become his wife—if he could convince her of it. He was a sucker for even taking the flight. One of his guys had a kid in the hospital getting her tonsils removed so here Cooper was.

Filled with impatience, he looked down at his watch, knowing there were still at least ten hours of flying to get there and back again.

About an hour into the flight, the sunset seemed to have progressed little as the aircraft flew westbound for Hawaii, the light of day still present in brilliant purples, shades of peach and pink.

Cooper continued to ponder Stormy, still impatiently stressing about the amount of time it would take before he could speak with her. Soon. He'd waited two days, so a few more hours weren't going to kill him.

With his mind frazzled, he was quickly pulled from his thoughts when the plane shuddered. Good. He'd rather have to pay attention to flying than think about things he could do nothing about at the moment.

"Must be some rough skies," Cooper told Wolf, who immediately put away his iPad. Reaching up, Cooper turned on the fasten seat belt sign as a precaution for those in back.

Seconds later, the instrument panel lit up with yellow caution lights. As the flight deck panels began to blink, an audible *bing* sounded a warning. The two seasoned pilots examined the instrument cluster for the source of the anomalous caution light.

"Looks like low hydraulic pressure, left side," Cooper said. "Wolf, check your circuit breakers to see if that doesn't solve—"

Before Cooper could finish his sentence, a violent explosion rocked the aircraft. The controls now flashed with red and yellow warning lights, the audible warnings from the computer urgent: *bing-bing-bing.*

"What the hell?" Wolf shouted as the master warning on the panel chimed wildly.

"It must've been an internal failure," Cooper yelled. "Begin the restart procedure."

As Cooper reached for the restart checklist, the flight computer and instrument panel again wildly warned of danger: *bing-bing-bing.* "Engine fire—One! Engine fire—One!" The audible male voice of the computer barked at the pilots, warning them of fire in the engines.

"Engine fire! Shut her down and discharge the extinguisher!" Cooper forcefully commanded as the noise of the audible warnings now chimed without end.

The passengers, many shaken from sleep, were startled and now fully awake at the sound of shattering metal and extreme vibrations. A soft orange glow began illuminating the dark cabin through the windows.

As the passengers peered out, they could see that the left-hand engine was mangled and glowing orange with fire, the wing around it torn to shreds. The sound of the remaining good engine spooled up to a high-pitched whine as the plane pitched violently downward, then left as it began to roll into a spiral.

"Everyone, stay calm," the lead flight attendant tried to reassure and calm the anxious passengers, only to be interrupted by the emergency oxygen masks dropping from the ceiling.

The scene quickly became more desperate as fear overcame both crew and passengers alike. Men and women were shakily grabbing for the flimsy orange masks that would provide them with emergency oxygen.

On the flight deck, the captain and first officer struggled to control the passenger jet with its two hundred plus souls on board. The computer continued to bark at the two men: "Bank angle! Bank angle! *Whoop, whoop.* Pull up! *Whoop, whoop.* Pull up!"

"We're losing altitude fast, Coop," Wolf shouted as the gauges spiraled down, like a stopwatch ticking to its inevitable end. The plane was still locked in a spiraling dive.

"I know, I know," Cooper responded with slight terror in his voice as he gripped the shaking yoke, trying to turn the plane back toward the airport.

"Seattle Center, this is Trans Pacific 422, declaring an emergency," Cooper announced. The radio only responded with feedback. "Seattle Center, Seattle, Trans Pacific 422, we're burning up, we're not going to make it . . ." he said, now with an eerie calm in his voice.

Wolf, seeing there was no response from air traffic control, attempted the call with his radio. "Mayday, mayday, Seattle Center. Trans Pacific 422. Emergency, we are going down! Do you copy?"

"Trans Pacific 422, acknowledged. We have all runways open for you, fire crash rescue is standing by."

"No. We're not going to make it. We're going down now!"

The cabin tumbled like a washing machine; luggage and other personal effects were thrashing about as the plane rotated out of control.

The flight attendants were strapped into their seats, one holding the seat belt across her chest, sobbing with fear.

The reading mother now held her child tightly as the child's once captive teddy bear floated weightlessly up and down as the aircraft rolled wing over wing, spiraling downward into the deep blue abyss.

The old couple a few rows back gently gripped each other's hands and looked into one another's eyes, figuring it was their last moment together and wanting to remember their years of happiness. The newlyweds sat in a tight embrace, bitter about the life they'd never get to experience.

"Wolf, let's put her in the Pacific," Cooper exclaimed as he muscled the yoke to pitch the plane's nose up.

"I don't think she's giving us much of a choice!"

For Cooper the world went silent, as if time were standing still. He was responsible for so many lives that were about to end, and though he was doing everything he could to prevent that, a picture of Stormy flashed through his mind. He should have told her he loved her, should have fought to see her.

"I've still got things to say to people," Cooper told Wolf. "We have to stop the aircraft from rolling over on itself if we're to have any chance of making it out of this alive."

The two pilots moved the control yoke with great effort to the right in an attempt to counteract the aircraft from spiraling upside down.

"Wolf, when I tell you to, I need you to add full flaps to try and stabilize and counter the roll," Cooper shouted as he placed his hands on the throttles.

Wolf looked over at Cooper with a nod of his head, approving the plan. He placed his steady fingers on the flap lever.

"Now!"

As the flaps began to cycle down, a shudder could be felt throughout the spinning aircraft. Cooper advanced the throttles, straining every ounce of power from one remaining engine, as the flight computer continued to alarm: "*Whoop, whoop*. Pull up! Altitude! Too low! *Whoop, whoop*. Pull up!*"

The two pilots continued battling the dying aircraft, their muscles pushed to the limit, groaning under the pressure of the g-force and strain of the controls. Their view quickly became dominated by the ocean waiting below.

"Come on, baby . . . come on," Cooper pleaded with the plane.

"We've lost number two!" Wolf called out, as the gauges indicated that the one remaining engine had begun to spool down—the red lights and caution alarms confirmed its untimely death.

Meanwhile, Cooper gave no further heed to the alarms, his aim only to level the aircraft in time to guide it into the water as gently as possible.

The flight computer cried out their altitude, pleading desperately with the pilots to save the plummeting plane: "Five hundred! Pull up!"

The jet continued to spiral, falling below five hundred feet. "*Whoop, whoop*. Pull up! Too low! Terrain! Pull up!*"

In an instant, all people on board Trans Pacific 422 experienced the same jarring flash of brilliant light and deafening noise as the commercial flight disappeared off the air traffic control's radar and into the sea.

CHAPTER THIRTY-EIGHT

Nick lay in his bed listening to the radio. It was a calm night—no storms, no waves, and the chances of a call coming in were slim to none. He wished he could turn off his mind and drift to sleep, but he was used to being on alert when at the station.

Soon, though, his lids grew heavy, and he found his body relaxing as he tuned out the men playing a card game in the other room. Normally, he'd be out there with them, but he was worried about his brother.

It was stupid, really. He shouldn't be worrying about Cooper or Stormy. They were grown adults, for goodness' sake. They would work through their issues. There was something between them, something he'd never expected to see from his hardened brother.

"Hey Dad, looks like you might get your way after all," he whispered.

He could almost swear he heard the heartfelt laughter of the man who'd been gone for over six years now. He missed the old man, even if his father had devastated him on his dying day.

"Time to go, Nick. Gear up!"

Nick shot up in bed as he looked toward the empty door. His crew knew he wouldn't need to be told twice. If they said it was time to go, then he was alert.

"What's going on?" he asked, all grogginess instantly gone.

"A 757 crashed about three hundred miles out. We don't have much more information than that. Don't know if there are survivors. All we know is the tower lost communication after they called in a mayday."

"Shit!" Nick exclaimed. His gut always clenched when he heard the words *plane crash*. He had too many pilots in the family for it not to.

"Say what you're not saying," Nick demanded through clenched teeth.

"It's Trans Pacific," the man finally mumbled.

Nick tried not to panic. He tried telling himself there were thousands of flights a day across the US alone. The chance of this being his brother was slim. Of course, Nick didn't believe in odds. Hell, the chances of him working tonight had been slim to none and look how that was turning out!

Still, he tried to keep a cool head.

"If you need to sit this one out, we can call Tony in," the man said.

"Not a chance, Sean. I'm going to make a phone call first, though. Suit up."

Nick marched into the other room and picked up his phone, horrified when he felt his fingers tremble. He was the chief pilot for the base. He couldn't lose control now. They wouldn't let him fly.

He couldn't get through to his brother, and he couldn't get through to Trans Pacific. He slammed the phone down, cracking its base, and then rushed back out to the room where the men were gathered around the television.

The news announcer was solemn: "No details yet on the crash that's been reported. All we know at this moment is that a flight called in a distress signal, and then the tower lost them. We're sending our crews out to Sea-Tac as we speak to get you more information."

"Let's go. We don't have time to sit around here," Nick commanded.

His crew jumped up, and he hated them all in that moment for the looks they were shooting his way.

"Stop now. It's not my brother," he snapped.

The men said nothing. They worked hard every time they were together, risking their lives for complete strangers in the stormiest and deadliest of seas. No one was going to say a word to Nick. In order to work most efficiently, he had to ignore his fears.

The men fell out, the boat crew already gone, the helicopter crew falling in. Nick made one small detour before he jumped into the captain's seat of the helicopter.

Stopping in the bathroom, he let go of the dinner he'd had two hours prior. When he was finished, he rinsed his mouth, then ran to the chopper.

If his brother was out there, he wasn't coming home without him.

CHAPTER THIRTY-NINE

The night air was brisk, the wind blowing ever so slightly. Stormy stood on the back patio of Lindsey's place, her face raised upward as she watched the stars begin to appear in the darkening sky.

Through the opened door, she could hear the local news in the background, but she didn't care what was happening in the world. All she cared about right now was trying to figure out what she was going to do next.

Suddenly, her peaceful evening was interrupted when the local news began a special report: "Breaking news out of Sea-Tac Airport. Tragedy strikes in the skies again, this time with Trans Pacific Airlines. We've just received word that a mayday was called in."

Stormy's heart instantly accelerated, and she rushed into the house and stood before the television as she watched the brunette on the screen look down at her notes.

"The Trans Pacific Airlines flight was heading for Honolulu and apparently suffered engine trouble. We're hearing reports that it lost contact with the tower exactly five minutes ago. It's not confirmed yet, but they are saying the plane crashed into the Pacific about two hundred miles out. No other details, including flight number, are being disclosed at this time . . ."

Stormy knew that when planes crashed, the airport set up a central place for family members and friends to go for information. It took her exactly one hour to get from her friend's place to the airport, thanks to Lindsey rushing in and out of traffic.

If Cooper had been the captain of that flight and she'd lost him forever, she wasn't sure how she would deal with that. Her fingers glided across her stomach as it cramped.

In a full sprint, Stormy came whirling through the rotating doors into the TPA lobby, where news crews were busy setting up their cameras and giving live reports on the crash.

As she approached the ticket counter, she was desperate to talk to anyone who knew who had captained the flight, but to her horror, all of the Trans Pacific ticket counters were vacant, as if the airline had shut down and abandoned anyone seeking answers.

Panic was taking over, though she tried to fight it. A mewling cry escaped her throat as she collapsed to the ground, her vision going in and out of focus.

She immediately caught the attention of camera crews and reporters, as they zoomed in on her, putting a human face on the late-breaking news of an air disaster at sea.

In the midst of her panic attack, a door opened from behind the ticket counter and an agent rushed to assist Stormy.

The lobby went wild with the sound of camera shutters and electronic flash units firing in frenzy, as newspaper reporters and TV crews sought to capture the image of an airline employee helping the next of kin of the ill-fated flight.

As the airline customer service agent bent over to console Stormy, she put her arm around her, rubbing her back in a circular motion. It was Meredith.

Seeing it was Stormy, Meredith's eyes, already bloodshot with emotion, began to well up as she gave Stormy a mournful glance of pity. As tears came rolling down Meredith's face, Stormy knew, without her saying a word, that it was indeed Cooper who'd been flying.

"I'm so sorry, Stormy," she said. Stormy went limp in Meredith's arms, losing consciousness.

"I need help over here!" Meredith called out.

Within seconds, two airport police officers were on the scene, one officer lifting Stormy into his arms and taking her into the airline office behind the ticket counter.

Stormy awoke in a large room to the sound of several voices, some shouting while others were quietly sobbing. She was lying on her back on a cot when she opened her eyes and saw Sherman looking down at her. He'd been sitting by her side.

"There you go, sweetie. Time to wake up," he said with a concerned expression.

The sight of Sherman peering down at her was a comforting sight to wake up to, but as if a thousand nightmares came to mind all at once, she was reminded all too soon of what had happened and whom she'd lost.

Stormy clutched her stomach, cradling Cooper's unborn child. The agony of loss still overwhelming, she could only sob and shake her head from side to side, as if by saying *no* she could change the situation. Stormy clung to Sherman.

"I'm so glad you're here," she finally said.

"I'm glad you're here, too, sweetie," he assured her.

"I don't know if I can get through this alone," she told him, her eyes spilling all over again.

"You'd be amazed at what a person can survive," he told her. "I was there when Coop took his first flight, and I'm here now, with you. You're not alone, sweetheart."

Sherman took Stormy's hand and held it tightly as they both said a whole lot of silent prayers.

"I don't know if I can take the silence anymore," Stormy said after a while. She had no more tears left to cry.

Sherman looked at Stormy, his eyes bright and wide. "Stormy, he's alive. That boy is alive. I know it. I can feel it in my bones, so don't you lose heart, you'll see."

She looked at him with hope. "Do you really believe that?"

"I do, darling. I really do. And you know what?" he said with a smile.

"What?"

"I bet it will be his brother out there saving his ass," he said with a chuckle.

"I hope so," she said, finding that she did have some tears left after all.

CHAPTER FORTY

Water lapping against his legs, Cooper slowly opened his eyes as a groan rumbled from his throat. His eyesight was blurry and he blinked trying to get his bearings. As his thinking cleared, he reached his hand up to his throbbing head.

Feeling a warm sensation, he pulled his fingers away, blood dripping down his hand. He had a substantial gash on his forehead from hitting the side window upon impact, and boy could he feel it.

Cooper began to look around to assess his situation. The flight deck was a mess of broken glass and crumpled metal. Water flowed in through the windshield and streamed down the instrument panel with each pulse of the waves.

The sound of groaning and creaking metal filled his ears as the body of the plane shifted in the gentle sea. Cooper reached down and undid his five-point harness as thoughts moved away from his well-being to that of his passengers and fellow crew members. He glanced over at Wolf, who was still unconscious in his seat.

"Wolf, wake up." Cooper shook Wolf's shoulders, saying his name over and over.

At that moment, the creaking became louder as the plane's nose pitched drastically downward. The damage she'd sustained was substantial and it was nothing short of a miracle that she was still floating at all. But the forward portion of the cargo bay was filled with water and accelerating her burial at sea. Water rushed in through the windshield, filling the flight deck at a faster rate.

With the water now chest level on Wolf and rising, Cooper's attempt to wake him became more frantic. "Wolf! Come on, buddy, wake up." Cooper was now shaking Wolf violently with both hands. Wolf's eyes began to crack open as the water level rapidly approached his neck.

"Cooper, what in the hell is going on?" Wolf's eyes were now open with panic showing as the freezing water registered.

"The plane is sinking fast and we have to get out of here now," Cooper commanded.

"I can't seem to get this seat belt undone." Wolf was straining, now terrified and spitting water out as it surged up to his face.

"Hold on. Let me try," Cooper said as he took a deep breath and dove under the frigid Pacific water.

Cooper ripped and pulled on the seat belt mechanism with all his strength, but to no avail. He resurfaced and spoke as calmly as possible. "Wolf, hold on, buddy. I'm going to find something to cut it."

Cooper's gaze now looked all around as he tried to spot something that was sharp enough to cut the tough belts.

The water was getting dangerously high and every second wasted meant Wolf was closer to death. Cooper took another deep breath and dove under, still trying to free his distressed coworker from his seat.

The water was dimly lit by the slight glow of the instrument panel lights, but they were fading fast as water found its way into the electrical system. Cooper surfaced for air, still unsuccessful in his attempts.

"I'm sorry, buddy. I can't get this damn thing undone," Cooper said somberly as he grabbed Wolf's hand.

"Can you do something for me?" Wolf asked while pulling Cooper's shirt toward him. Wolf's face suddenly became peaceful as the water continued rising.

"Anything."

"Tell that sexy flight attendant that it wasn't just a one-night stand. I liked her enough that it scared the crap out of me." Wolf gripped tighter to Cooper's shirt as the water covered his face. Cooper was fully prepared to go down with his copilot, not willing to leave a man behind.

Just before he turned away, he saw something glisten underneath the water, illuminated by the flickering light. It was a large shard of glass that had broken from the windshield. Adrenaline flooded his body as Cooper dove beneath the water, grabbed the glass, and began cutting the seat belts.

One by one, the straps snapped. Wolf's body, now seemingly lifeless, was free. With one arm around his friend, Cooper pushed his way through the flight deck door and out into the flooding cabin.

The plane pitched violently forward, causing a large influx of water through the open exits. Cooper glanced at Wolf's face and noticed he was becoming paler. He knew Wolf had no chance of survival without CPR, and soon. He could hear the sounds of passengers and the faint voices of flight attendants calling out instructions from outside the craft. It appeared they'd gotten everyone off in time.

The aisle was full of floating personal effects that he had to navigate around to get to the open exit row door. As Cooper emerged from the opening, a bright light shone on him. He looked up, hearing the pulsing blades of a helicopter as it flew past and out of sight.

The bright orange and white paint could be seen on the side of the helicopter, telling Cooper the Coast Guard was here. A small sense of relief came over him as he pulled Wolf over to the wing and held on, Wolf on his back with Cooper holding his chin above the waves. The helicopter disappeared from the wreckage, presumably to summon assistance.

"Captain! Captain, over here," one of the flight attendants shouted as they paddled a raft closer.

The sea lay silent as the water lapped the edges of the plane's fuselage. The surroundings were dimly lit by fuel burning here and there on the water's surface. Cooper could see yellow life rafts filled with passengers. The once piercing screams that had filled the air were now a quiet rumble as people sobbed their relief.

The flight attendants' training had paid off for everyone on board, it seemed, as they'd quickly and safely ushered the passengers out of the submerging cabin and onto the bobbing rafts.

For what had seemed like an improbable task, Cooper and his first officer had done their job. The plane was intact and all souls accounted for, but further efforts were needed to ensure everyone's continued survival.

"Is everyone off the plane?" he shouted.

"Every single passenger is accounted for," she gladly told him.

Cooper had to fight tears as he glanced at his crew, all of them doing their job, going above and beyond, and not allowing a single soul to lose his or her life. This was the airline he owned; these were the people he employed. He'd chosen well.

He could abandon ship now.

Cooper reached out and grabbed the rope that encircled the yellow raft. "I need help over here. Wolf needs CPR."

With the help of some passengers, Cooper lifted Wolf and placed him on the floor of the raft and then climbed in himself. He pushed the boat clear of the airplane and began CPR on his friend, giving him one good breath and watching his chest rise and fall. He then began chest compressions.

"Come on, Wolf, breathe." Cooper continued the cycle of one breath and fifteen chest compressions, each time checking for signs of life. Passengers from their raft and others turned to watch, their minds no longer focused on their own woes.

"Wolf, come on, man. Don't make me face Tori. The girl terrifies me." Cooper got more desperate as the chest compressions became more violent.

At that moment a slight gurgling could be heard as Wolf cracked open his eyes. "That's it, spit it out, buddy." Cooper sat Wolf up, patting him on the back. An explosive spray of water came out of his mouth as his lungs took in a deep breath of fresh air.

Applause could be heard from the bobbing rafts as the passengers showed their appreciation to the pilots for saving their lives. Exhausted from this traumatic event, Wolf laid his head on the side of the raft. He grabbed Cooper's hand and with a raspy voice said, "Thanks, man. I owe you one."

Cooper cracked a smile.

"We'll discuss terms later."

Now it was time to find out how many people had been hurt.

"What is the status on injuries?"

"As far as I know, Captain, lots of bumps, bruises, cuts, scrapes, and some broken bones. However, nothing life-threatening."

"That's good to hear. Let's make sure we attend to the wounded the best we can and try to pass out as many blankets as you managed to snag."

"How about we get you bandaged up first?" the flight attendant asked.

Cooper reached up and wiped blood from his gash. He'd completely forgotten, during all the commotion, that he'd been wounded.

The flight attendants began doing what they could to bandage the wounds and keep the passengers warm. Although the water was calm, the slow-pulling currents moved the rafts farther away from the sinking plane.

As the rafts drifted, the plane went down quickly. The sea water bubbled and sprayed into the air as the creaking metal frame dipped below the water's surface.

Everyone turned to watch as the last portion of the jet, its tail, was claimed by the sea. It seemed surreal to Cooper as he watched the Trans Pacific logo disappear from sight with a swirl of sea water marking the grave of the only casualty of this horrific event.

The night became colder and the passengers fought to stay warm while adrift in the middle of the sea. Only a few random spots of burning jet fuel remained unextinguished by the lapping water. A few hours seemed like days as the hope of a rescue started to fade. Why wasn't the helicopter back?

"I thought they'd be here by now," a passenger said from an adjacent raft.

Everyone's attention seemed to be on Cooper, as he was their leader. "What should we do, Captain?"

Cooper turned and looked out over the survivors as they gazed back at him, hoping for some modicum of reassurance. This was what his father had always wanted out of him, to be able to lead, to assure, and to make a difference. His head was spinning with how much had changed in the past six years. His heart ached that his father wasn't there to see the man he'd become.

"They've already spotted us and we have our locator beacon activated. It shouldn't be too much longer." These words seemed to satisfy them as there wasn't much of a response. Not thirty minutes from the last spoken word, a low rumble accompanied by a consistent splashing sound could be heard.

"Look over there," a passenger shouted as they pointed into the darkness.

"It's a ship!"

Out of the darkness came the sharp white and orange bow of a Coast Guard cutter. The large ship was accompanied by three smaller boats with bright lights that pierced through the now approaching fog bank. The deep whine of the smaller boats brought a sense of relief for the passengers and Cooper.

Not long after the boats arrived, helicopters started circling above. He didn't see the Coast Guard orange on their sides. As he looked closer, he caught a glimpse of the side of one of them labeled NEWS 19. Fury filled him as he glared up at the vultures hoping to get the first pictures of dead bodies floating in the water. Well, they were out of luck.

Cooper turned to Wolf. "They're here to get us, bud. We're going home."

Wolf nodded his head, still out of it from the crash, but he managed to crack a smile.

The Coast Guard began to pull passengers on board, immediately giving them dry clothes and warm blankets. Cooper waved to one of the boats to come in his direction. It approached alongside his raft, its wake causing the light boat to move up and down in the water. A Coast Guard lieutenant leaned over the side.

"I have one that's injured and needs immediate medical attention," Cooper told him.

Wolf was pulled into the boat.

Cooper sat back against the raft's side, refusing to board the ship until every last passenger was picked up out of the water.

Cooper now sat alone in his raft, floating on the cold waters of the Pacific, tuning out the sound of people talking. The water in the raft sloshed from side to side with every rock of the sea. He sat with his life vest over him and a blanket wrapped around his body as he fought the cold.

With his shaking hand, he reached into his soaked pants pocket and retrieved a little black box. The once cardboard box was now more mush than cardboard. He opened it and peeled away the soaked parts, revealing the stunning diamond ring, sparkling in the lights from the Coast Guard vessel.

"Everyone is on board, Captain, but we've had a request that you get flown home," the man said.

Cooper smiled, knowing exactly where that request had come from. As the ship backed away, he could hear the distinct sound of the humming rotor of a Coast Guard helicopter.

The light became more intense as it neared his position. The light's rays were interrupted temporarily by a man in a basket being lowered down. The man grabbed Cooper's hand as he pulled him into the basket alongside him. The cable swayed back and forth as the helicopter crew began to reel the basket up.

"Brother, it's so damn good to see you!" Cooper exclaimed.

"Not as good as it is to see you. You scared the shit out of me this time, Coop," Nick admitted. "I couldn't even fly this bird."

"Yeah, it would be the same for me if the situation were reversed," Cooper told him.

"Where are we landing?"

"We're taking all passengers to the Red Cross crash assistance center."

"You gotta pull some strings and give me a reroute, Nick."

"Sorry, brother, no can do. Orders are to take any survivors to the center to get checked out."

"Don't make me pull the older brother card. I need to get to Stormy, and if the fates are with me, she'll be at the airport," Cooper said, getting frustrated.

"You're going to get my ass chewed, Coop," Nick said.

"Just take me to Sea-Tac," Coop repeated, before admitting to his brother, "I love her, Nick. I have to tell her I love her."

"All right man, but this is only because I'm a sappy romantic," Nick replied as he ordered the helicopter to turn toward the Seattle airport.

It was just past midnight when Nick touched the helicopter down on a taxiway across from the TPA passenger terminal, where all flights had been cancelled for the remainder of the night.

At the exact moment the helicopter touched down, Cooper slammed open the sliding passenger door on the right side of the rescue helicopter.

Through a gale of rotor wash and the deafening noise of the helicopter's engines, Cooper dashed from the rescue helicopter in a full sprint to the terminal.

"Hey—what the hell are you doing?" one of the guys cried, reaching out in a vain attempt to pull Cooper back in.

"Let him go. He knows what he's doing," Nick radioed back through the mic on his flight helmet. "If we get busted for letting him off here, I'll let him take the heat, but I somehow doubt anyone will say anything to the captain that pulled off an ocean landing at sunset in a Boeing 757 with zero casualties."

Cooper ran into the terminal, his uniform still damp with seawater, his body aching from the crash. He pushed past the concourse and kept on going. Cooper was now suffering from fatigue as his body shook and his damp uniform clung to his body.

It seemed to take forever, but finally he made it to the ticket counter and was thrilled to see familiar fingernails clicking on a keyboard.

"My heavens! Cooper, what are you doing here? You should be at a hospital!" Meredith chastised.

"Stormy?" Cooper began as he leaned against the counter.

"Stormy?"

"Yes, is she here? I need to see her . . ."

"No, she's been taken to the hospital."

Panic flooded him more than when he'd been crash landing in an ocean that wanted to swallow him and his crew whole. What had happened? "Which one?"

Meredith told him, and then he stopped listening. He ran through the terminal. He had to find her.

CHAPTER FORTY-ONE

Her eyes opened and Stormy was startled by the monitor on her finger and the machine echoing her heartbeat.

"What's happening?" she croaked.

"You're being monitored in the hospital," Sherman said. She turned to see his ashen face by her side.

"Sherman?" She didn't have to finish the sentence.

"Coop's okay," he told her. "He's on his way here now."

"I can't sit here!" She yanked at the device on her finger and began sitting up, the monitors instantly screaming. A nurse ran in.

"You have to stop," the nurse ordered.

"No!" Stormy surged from the bed, her head a little light as she stood up. The nurse tried to keep her back, but Stormy needed to find Cooper. She couldn't do that lying in a bed.

She leapt for the door, nearly knocking over Nick, who was just coming inside to tell Sherman that Cooper would be there any minute.

Rushing to the stairs, she made it to the overhang that looked out at the lobby, her gaze scanning the crowd of people reuniting. She couldn't find Cooper anywhere. At the bottom of the stairs, she was swallowed up in the crowd before she finally saw him.

Her heart racing, she pushed past the people in her way and flew across the room, grabbing his arm.

"I've been so scared. I really thought I lost you," she whispered. "I need to tell you that I . . . I love you." Tears were streaming down her face and she didn't care.

The man turned around and to Stormy's horror, it wasn't Cooper.

"Why, thank you. It's not every day a beautiful woman throws herself at me. In fact, it's usually every other. So . . . do you come here often?" The man smiled and she couldn't tell if he was serious or not, but she was mortified.

"I'm . . . I'm sorry. I thought you were . . . I thought you were someone else."

The man really did look like Cooper, though. His height, skin tone, and hair were nearly if not completely identical, but now that she was closer, it was obvious that they had different builds. And the guy was wearing a very expensive designer suit. Through all of this, though, Stormy was struck most by his eyes.

Unlike the piercing green of Cooper's, this man had gray slanted eyes, which captured Stormy's gaze in a seemingly endless moment. She felt as if she were crossing paths with a lone wolf in a frozen wasteland.

"Have we met before?" Stormy finally asked.

The man, appearing a bit worried, suddenly straightened his tie and cleared his throat.

"Yeah. I meant to call you back, but I lost your number. It's so great to see you again."

"Again? Have we met?"

He seemed to hear her this time, and the man let out a relieved breath while unsuccessfully trying to pass off his previous comment as misplaced humor. "I would certainly remember you, darling. Why *haven't* we met before now?"

She gasped. "Oh my gosh, you're Ace, Cooper's brother." How had she not figured that out instantly?

"Yep, the old man's my brother," Ace finally admitted.

"I'm your brother's . . . friend." Stormy stopped short of declaring herself his girlfriend, considering what had taken place the last time she'd seen him. But did any of that really matter now? She corrected herself. "Girlfriend, I'm his girlfriend."

"Well, which is it? Do I have a shot or not?"

"No, not a chance," she said. Her heart belonged to only one Armstrong. "I *am* Cooper's girlfriend. Or at least I hope I still am."

"Where is my brother dearest? I hear he narrowly escaped death."

Damn, this man was hardened. But Stormy wasn't one to judge someone at first glance. And there was something in his eyes that had her wondering if Sherman was right, if he did want to come back home. She didn't know if she'd get the chance to ask him or not.

"I haven't found him yet." Stormy began looking around the lobby again for Cooper, who was perhaps sitting down somewhere. He had to be exhausted.

"Well, we can take different directions and see what we come up with," Ace said, and he slipped away.

Stormy decided to retrace her steps and go back upstairs to her hospital room. Maybe he was searching for her, too.

And then he was there.

The room full of people fell away as her eyes locked with his. And right then, in that moment, she knew everything would be okay. He broke away from his uncle and Nick, and though he had to be exhausted, he ran to her.

No words were spoken as he lifted her, his lips connecting with hers as she sobbed against him, so grateful to be in his arms again.

It was too soon when he pulled back, but Stormy knew words had to be said. Tears slid down her cheeks as she touched his face. The past hours had been miserable thinking she might never get to do so again. It put things into perspective.

"I'm sorry, Cooper. I should have trusted you. It all seems so petty now," she cried.

He held his hand up and cupped her cheek.

"No. I was the one who should have told you everything. I understand why you reacted like you did."

"It doesn't matter. I promise you it doesn't matter. All that I care about right now is the fact that you're okay," she said.

"I haven't been honest with you, Stormy. I've withheld a lot of information," he began.

"I don't care," she told him.

"I don't just fly for Trans Pacific Airlines. I own it," he told her in a hushed tone.

That made her stop for a minute. "Wow."

"I love flying and I could never settle for working for someone else. I have a lot of money, Stormy, and I'm sorry if I've hidden things from you. It's taken me a long time to earn my trust back in all people, but you, I trust with my entire heart," he told her.

"Oh, Cooper. I don't care what you have. I just want to be a part of your life," she said with tears streaming down her face.

"I love you, Stormy. I was planning on telling you this sooner, but things got messed up," he said, a sparkle in his eyes. "By the grace of God, the sea refused to bury me in its depths; instead, it brought me back to you."

"I love you so much," she replied. "I'm sorry I left—that I ran away. I won't run again."

"It doesn't matter," he said, repeating her words.

Suddenly, he let her go as he dropped to one knee, pulling from his coat pocket a very mushy black ring box. There before her, a brightly polished gold ring was shining like the sun, set with three diamonds, the center stone larger than the surrounding accents.

"Stormy, marry me and I'll cherish you for as long as I have left on this earth. I'll give the entire inheritance to whatever charity you want. I'll do whatever it takes to prove to you that I want you, only you."

With her left hand still in his, Stormy placed her right on his cheek, gently caressing his jaw. Never breaking eye contact, she knelt down on both knees, lightly kissed him on his lips, and nodded her head.

"Yes, Cooper, yes. I want to be yours for the rest of my life. And I do trust you. Even if I forgot that for a few days." Tears of tender joy streamed down her face as she smiled and kissed the corners of his mouth. Cooper removed the diamond ring from the crumpled velvet box and slipped it on her finger.

As Cooper and Stormy embraced, the lobby erupted into applause and the sound of cameras clicking as the crowd of passengers, friends, and family all hugged and congratulated each other and the new couple. Something that could have been a great tragedy was ending so beautifully.

Sherman looked down from his vantage point, and he caught a glimpse of someone he hadn't seen for too long. When the man looked up, their eyes connected.

As the two locked gazes, for a fleeting moment Ace smiled, perhaps out of gladness for seeing his uncle, Sherman hoped. But quickly, his nephew regained his composure, his eyes again became ice, and the lone wolf walked out the doors, to wander and lust after the desires of his soul.

And Sherman's heart broke.

CHAPTER
FORTY-TWO

Cooper stood face-to-face with his reflection, smartly dressed in his uniform. Over the harbor, the frosty January morning had left the world blanketed in a white lace of frozen dew. Cooper's mother lightly knocked at his door and entered the bedroom.

"Today is your big day. Your bride looks splendid, absolutely angelic. Your father would be . . . *is*. Your father *is* very proud of you. I *am* proud of you, too, and I love you." Resting her face against his shoulder while lightly rubbing the small of his back, Evelyn embraced her son.

"I know. I know he's proud of me. It's a funny thing, but I understand now why he chose to do things as he did. I have so much peace inside me, and it's all because I fell in love."

"Yes, love keeps us sane," his mother said with a sad smile.

"I'm sorry you've been without him for so long," Cooper told her.

"Thank you, son. That means more than you could ever imagine."

Peering back out the window as he reined his emotions in, he decided he liked the cold and ice. It was clean, crisp, and beautiful.

"We better go. I don't want to keep my bride waiting."

"Yes, let's not keep my new daughter waiting." Evelyn smiled at her son as she took his hand and led him from the room and downstairs to a waiting limousine, where Sherman and his brothers were already sitting.

"Are you ready to be tied down for time and all eternity?" Nick asked with a punch to his arm.

"Yeah, I am," Cooper said, not even embarrassed.

"What in the world has happened to you?" Maverick asked with a laugh.

"I fell in love. You should try it sometime," he told his brother.

"No thank you. I prefer to hold on to my balls," Mav said with a wink.

"Yeah, without a wife, I'm sure you're doing that a lot," Cooper told him.

"Hey!" Mav scowled. "I have no problem finding women to warm my bed."

"Yeah, but at the end of it all, you're still left with an empty bed," Cooper said.

"This is a conversation a mother shouldn't be hearing," Evelyn told her sons, reminding them she was there.

"Sorry, Mom," Mav quickly muttered.

"Let's just focus on your brother since this is his day," Evelyn suggested.

"I think that sounds like a plan," Nick said, happy for once not to be the one getting in trouble. "Besides, you're a national hero who's marrying a beautiful girl. Plus, I'm going to be an uncle. And since I helped so much in the relationship, I think you should name my nephew after me."

"Stormy and I were thinking of naming him William Sherman . . . or Will." Scanning their faces for reactions to the name of the little boy that would be coming in the spring, Cooper fondly smiled at his mother.

"That's a wonderful name, son. Baby Will is a wonderful name and this grandma can't wait to meet him."

CHAPTER FORTY-THREE

"Lindsey, my hair is beautiful." Stormy gazed in the mirror at her best friend, who'd been fussing with the do all morning.

"I know, but I'm so nervous," Lindsey replied.

"Isn't that supposed to be my line?" Stormy questioned with a laugh. Though, she didn't feel nervous at all. She just felt excitement.

"Yes, it is. How are you feeling?"

"I was sort of afraid that Cooper would snap out of the shock of the crash and run away when he realized he was engaged, but I know he loves me," Stormy said with a secret smile.

Placing both hands on Stormy's arms, Lindsey replied, "Of course he does. I've seen the way he looks at you . . . and it's true love. There's no mistaking it."

Stormy smiled at her best friend as she thanked her for always being there. But soon they were interrupted as a knock sounded at the door.

The door creaked open and a soft voice broke the silence.

"Hello, dear. I wanted to see my beautiful daughter-in-law before the big moment."

"Please, come in." Stormy gave her a smile. Evelyn had been so kind to her from the moment they'd first met.

"You are absolutely stunning, darling," Evelyn said.

"Thank you," Stormy replied quietly.

She turned and gazed at her image in the mirror. She'd chosen simple and comfortable, but the dress was indeed stunning. It was white, but unique in style. The bodice of the dress was adorned with lacy designs of silky, white, gilded ivy and jasmine flowers. The waist flowed into a billowing gown with ornate accents surrounded by small gems that made it look as if she were walking through a field of flowers.

At the waist, pure silk encircled the front, ending in a diamond-studded pendant of her own making that was affixed to the dress. Evelyn had been so impressed with Stormy's designs that she was backing her in a jewelry shop where she could create custom jewelry and finally pursue her dream. Her world kept getting better and bigger each and every day.

"It's time." Sherman stood in the doorway now, tears in his eyes.

"Oh, Sherman." She moved to him and kissed his cheek. "Meeting you has changed my entire life. There aren't words to express how much you mean to me. Thank you for walking me down the aisle. I miss my dad so much, but I know he sent me you. He brought you into my life when I was at my most vulnerable and you've lifted me back up when all I wanted to do was lie on the ground and cry."

Sherman's eyes shone as he gazed at her, and that made her cry all the more.

"I've only known a beautiful, strong, confident woman from the moment I met you," he said. "Yes, you might have thought you were broken, but you never have been. I'm the one who is so grateful our paths crossed, and I do believe it was your father. He gave us to each other when we both needed someone so desperately."

"Thank you." His words meant more to her than she could ever explain.

And then it was time. Now her stomach tensed just the littlest bit. The ceremony she could do without. But knowing at the end of it that she and Cooper would belong to each other, well, that made her having to be in the spotlight worth it.

She'd finally found what she wanted from life. It was funny how everything could go from so chaotic to nearly perfect in such a short amount of time. All she'd had to do was stop fretting about the small and big stuff, and then life had managed to come around.

Now she was walking to the man she loved. And they were going to have a very happy ever after.

Their family and friends gathered together in a quaint chapel that early January afternoon. Both sides of the aisle were bathed in color from the light that shown through the stained glass windows lining both sides of the sanctuary.

The room was adorned in sheer white fabric, draped from the ceiling and woven down the pillars that lined the sanctuary. The swaths of fabric swept around large porcelain vases containing brilliant yellow and red roses.

Stormy, dressed in her wedding gown, appearing like a queen fit for coronation, stealthily peered through a cracked side door at the sanctuary altar. It was all so dreamlike, all too perfect, and yet it was also all for her. A tan and calloused hand reached for hers.

"It's time," Sherman said. "But if you're having second thoughts, you know I'll sneak you out of here right now."

"Oh, Sherman, that's why I want to marry Cooper. Because I know I don't have to." Stormy smiled as she took her place next to Sherman, who looked so suave in his black tuxedo.

Cooper stood silent at the altar. That was all she needed to know.

In unison, a quartet of violinists and cellists placed their bows on their strings to play the first prolonged note of Pachelbel's Canon. As the tempo of the soothing rhythm picked up, the wedding procession began their stoic march down the aisle.

Sherman escorted Stormy in perfect step to the music, preceded by the groomsmen and bridesmaids. The petal-covered aisle glowed in the afternoon sun still beaming brightly through the windows. Each row of guests turned to admire the bride as she passed by.

As the bridesmaids and groomsmen took their places at the altar, the string quartet ended their piece. Cooper and Stormy exchanged their vows before family and friends. The wedding went without incident, the scene both tender and elegant.

Upon their final *I dos* and the ceremonial kissing of the bride, the string quartet once again struck their chords to the tune of the wedding march. Those gathered in witness amongst the pews stood and clapped in praise of the union between two souls destined for each other as the happy couple made their way down the aisle, hand in hand—man and wife. Cinderella had found her prince.

CHAPTER FORTY-FOUR

The wedding reception was well underway in one of the downtown Seattle Crown Plaza's large ballrooms. The hotel staff was busy catering and tending to the needs of the guests as the jubilant wedding party celebrated with laughter and good spirits.

Meanwhile, a whole different sort of excitement was taking place in a neighboring janitor's closet where Ace had taken his latest prize.

The woman moaned, her legs spread and resting on the shelves holding various cleaning supplies. Ace, almost in boredom, thrust himself to completion inside her. Barely even a hint of sweat showed on him, he'd been so uninvolved with the woman. He gave the unnamed girl one last kiss before pulling out, tossing the condom, and gathering his pants.

Staggering a bit when he stepped from the closet, he stopped to get his bearings. His head was spinning from the amount of alcohol he'd consumed.

Stumbling around the corner from the hallway to the entrance of the adjacent ballroom, Ace entered the party with a crash and a calamity of broken dishes and spilled champagne. The music ground to a halt as the partygoers turned in his direction.

"Ace?" Nick was the first one to recognize the brother he hadn't spoken to in seven years.

"What are you doing here?" Maverick asked as he came to stand beside Nick.

"I invited him," Cooper said. "I didn't think he'd show. I wish he wouldn't have now," he added, as the three looked at their brother still sprawled on the floor.

"Hey, the black sheep has returned home for the matrimonial bliss of his eldest brother. I thought that entitled me to some celebrating," Ace said, not caring if his brothers were looking down on him—literally and figuratively. What was new?

"Maybe you shouldn't have returned if you still haven't grown up," Nick coldly told him.

"Come on, help me up," Ace said.

With a sigh Nick reached down, and then Ace didn't look so drunk anymore. He planted a right hook against Nick's jaw, sending Nick sprawling to the floor, knocked out.

"Ace!" Cooper shouted, outraged by the unwarranted hit.

Stepping forward, Cooper grabbed Ace by the collar of his shirt and threw him through the doors and out into the lobby.

"What the hell is going on? You disappear for years only to show up at my wedding—my freaking wedding, Ace," Cooper thundered. "I invited you because I've missed you. But if you're going to act like a fool then I can't do this," he finished.

"Sorry, bro. Just wanted to say congrats! Way to go on your sexy bride. Didn't mean to knock out your butler, but come on, the guy's a real bummer, man, a killjoy." The room still spinning, Ace staggered and slurred, turning toward the hotel door to make an exit.

"Butler? That butler is your brother, Ace. You knocked out Nick, you idiot!"

"I don't have any brothers. Piss off." Ace walked out of the hotel and flipped Cooper the bird as he hailed a taxi.

"Let him go, brother. He'll come around someday," Maverick said, suddenly by Cooper's side, his hand on his shoulder. "For now you have to forget about him. There's still a party in there. Plus, if I were you, I might be a little concerned. Uncle Sherm has been dancing with Stormy for quite a while now."

"What about Nick?"

"Nick's fine. He's sitting upright and eating solid food already," Maverick said with a laugh. "All kidding aside, really, Nick's fine, maybe a little embarrassed, but he's fine."

Reassuringly, Maverick put his arm around Cooper's shoulder, ushering him back inside. He ached for his brother, but Ace would eventually come around. He had to—he was family.

EPILOGUE

Stormy rubbed her rounded belly as she attempted to plant some spring flowers. This was her favorite time of year, but the larger she got, the harder it was for her to garden. She was going to have to do something about that.

When she heard the back door open, she sat back and turned, smiling. Cooper was home early. But it wasn't Cooper moving toward her, it was Uncle Sherman.

"Are you checking up on me again, Sherman?"

"Not at all," he lied.

"It's okay. I haven't been alone for more than thirty minutes at a time since I hit my thirtieth week of pregnancy. Cooper has all these worries of me falling down or going into early labor. He's cut back on so much time at work, pretty soon there's going to be a hostile takeover," she said.

"Okay, you might have busted me. And yes, Cooper has called nonstop this morning wondering if I've arrived yet, but I have missed you," he said as he stopped next to her.

"It's only been three days since I saw you last," she told him.

"That's three days too long," he said with a laugh.

"Well, since you're here, you can help me stand. It's either that or I roll around like a baby seal until I find just the right position to push myself up."

She was only partially kidding.

Sherman reached for both her hands and gave a tug, helping her to her feet.

"I don't think there's much more room in there for my great nephew," he said as he gently patted her stomach.

"Yes, I'm hoping he decides to make an early arrival. I don't think I can last another two weeks. I can barely walk," she said as she slowly made her way to the house. "Let me get us both a drink and you can visit with me in the shade. The sun is warming up pretty dang quickly."

"Why don't you sit down and I'll get the drinks. I know where everything is," he said.

"Nope. You're a guest here, and I'm pregnant, not injured."

She left him spluttering on the back porch while she went inside and got a tray with iced tea, glasses, and some of her favorite oatmeal cookies.

They sat and munched on their snacks as Stormy tried to ignore the pains in her stomach. She knew they were nothing more than Braxton-Hicks contractions.

But when the next one hit, searing pain shot through her stomach, and the ground became wet. Wide-eyed, she looked up.

"Oh, I think it's time . . ."

◆　◆　◆

The hospital waiting room was crowded with friends and family pacing back and forth. Time seemed to drag on and on as Nick impatiently watched the clock hand tick down. With his mind working in overdrive he had to break the silence.

"What could be taking so long? Is there something wrong with the baby? Did something happen to Stormy?"

Evelyn chuckled as she rubbed her son's back. "Not to worry, my son. It just takes time . . . trust me."

"That's true but . . ."

Nick was interrupted by the large double doors swinging open and Cooper walking into the room. He removed his mask to reveal a grin that spread from ear to ear, but he was speechless.

Nick piped up, "So . . ."

Clasping his hands together, Cooper said, "It's a healthy baby boy."

The family wasted no time rushing down the hall, led by the new father, straight into the hospital room. Stormy sat on the bed with her little bundle of joy enveloped in his powder-blue blanket.

Cooper sat on the edge of the bed holding Stormy's hand as the family members fought over who got to hold the baby next. He couldn't keep the smile from his lips. What a fool he'd been such a short time ago to think this wasn't the life he wanted to live.

And what a difference he was seeing in his brothers, who were grumbling at each other, both fighting to hold the baby first. But then they were so gentle as they gazed at their nephew in adoration.

Mav won the argument and with gentle hands picked up the bundle. He grinned as he looked at the bright eyes before him, and using a soft voice, said, "I'll definitely be your favorite, little guy."

Finally, Mav passed the baby boy to Nick before he had a heart attack. Nick was the most eager of all to be involved. That was something Cooper had never thought he'd see.

Nick cradled William to his chest as he began speaking. "You really turned out much cuter than I thought you would after having my older brother as your dad," he said, making several people in the room chuckle.

Cooper wasn't one of them.

"Now, I have a lot of stories to tell you about him. I'll start with the time your dad was helping me climb a tree and . . ."

The story continued as Cooper leaned down and kissed his wife.

"I love you, Mrs. Armstrong," he whispered.

"I love you, Green Eyes," she replied.

"How about we kick all of these people out and get working on baby number two," he said with a waggle of his brows.

Stormy laughed deeply at her husband's sense of humor. It very much needed to be improved. "You're a brave man to say that to a woman who's just given birth. Now kiss me and shut up."

He gladly did.

ACKNOWLEDGMENTS

Wow, I can't believe how much I have enjoyed writing this book—this entire series, actually. Since my daughter took an interest in flying and got her private pilot's license, I have become just as fascinated with planes. I still don't like flying on the little ones, but I have to admit, they are a thrill. It's even somewhat enjoyable once I've had a glass (or five) of wine.

I worked for the airlines as a customer service rep for years, and while doing that made some lifelong friends as well, so I've been around these confident pilots for quite some time. There truly is something about them that gives them a little extra swagger because they know they can do something most people can't. I model my heroes after these sexy men in my life.

I have met a new family at Montlake and I'm so glad I've joined them. I adore my editors, Maria and Lauren, who have pushed me to be a better writer. They have been instrumental in truly making this story the best it can be. Their encouragement and tough love have made this a fun story! As always, I want to thank my family and all my dear friends. I am nothing without them, and their continued support means the world to me. I had help from those sexy pilots with different things in this book, as well. So thank you, Drew, Pat, and Chris.

A special thank you as well to Adam and Eddie, who I worked with at the airlines, and who are still great friends, who don't fly anymore, but still love planes as much as the rest and have a vast knowledge of the industry.

Finally, thank you to my fans. Your excitement, love of the books, and encouragement make me want to write day and night. Thank you for bringing me into your homes and for the love you give me. Words will never be able to express what you mean to me.

ABOUT THE AUTHOR

Photo © 2014 Edward Hart

Melody Anne is the *New York Times* and *USA Today* bestselling author of the popular Billionaire Bachelors, Surrender, and Baby for the Billionaire series, as well as the young adult Midnight series. She collaborated with J. S. Scott and Ruth Cardello for the anthology *Taken by a Trillionaire*.

Melody holds a bachelor's degree in business but found her true calling when she was first published in 2011. When she isn't writing, she cultivates strong bonds with her family and enjoys time spent with them, as well as with her friends and beloved pets. A country girl at heart, she loves her small town and is involved in many community projects.

Melody has earned a spot on multiple bestseller lists and is a three-time Amazon Top 100 bestselling author. Best of all, she gets to do what makes her happiest—live in a fantasy world 95 percent of the time. Learn more about her at www.melodyanne.com and follow her blog at www.authormelodyanne.blogspot.com.